CAMPUS
of
SHADOWS

A Psychic Battle for the Soul in a Supernatural Thriller

JO
LOVEDAY

PRAISE FOR CAMPUS OF SHADOWS

"*Campus of Shadows* is a superbly written dark thriller that follows the story of Dave Everest, a student at the University of Mann. His educational experience goes way beyond the usual academics when he befriends a student, Zane Maddox, who offers a darker path of education, one that bears the potential to lose one's soul. Dave meets another student, Maria Vasquez, who is aware there are evil threads on this dark campus and warns Dave not to become involved with them. Will his attraction to Maria save him from those alluring forces that threaten his very soul, or will he lose his will and tread down a dark, evil path that assures the loss of his very soul?"
—Patrick Kendrick, award-winning suspense author
of *Extended Family*, *Witness Protection*,
and true crime *American Ripper*

"*Campus of Shadows* is a gripping story that held me captive from the first page to the last. College freshman David Everest has an unusual learning disability that pales in comparison to the sinister forces that threaten to derail his plans for a bright future. This vivid portrayal of the dark side of campus life kept me turning pages late into the night—a must-read for all college students and their parents."
—S.L. Menear, award-winning author of
the *Samantha Starr Thrillers*
and the *Jettine Jorgensen Mysteries*

"Loveday delves into the slippery slope of addiction, masterfully capturing the emotions and terror one feels along the way."
—Texas Stready, author of
Deep in the Heart of Texas–a story of addiction

"A well-written story with great twists and turns. Loveday's well-developed, complex, and flawed characters offer an interesting view of the nuances of college life—the good and the bad. A worthy read."

—Jeff Shaw, author of the
Lieutenant Trufant thriller series
and *Echo Six* Si-Fi-series

"Wonderful to see a book for adults where dyscalculia plays a role. Jo Loveday knows what she is talking about, and I applaud the awareness for dyscalculia that this book will generate."

—Dr. A.M. Schreuder, author of
Dyscalculia: The Forgotten Math Learning Disability

"Jo Loveday's excellent book, *Campus of Shadows*, describes an earth-bound person's (a person who died, but remained here as a spirit) "possession" of the body of a living student. This may be an unfamiliar concept to readers, but I worked with hundreds of patients with that condition. The book has well-developed characters, an interesting plot, and great dialogue. I highly recommend."

—Edith Fiore, Ph. D.(retired),
author of *The Unquiet Dead*

"From the first haunting sentence, *Campus of Shadows* grips you with the quiet unraveling of a college freshman's mind, and it doesn't let go until the last unforgettable line. I loved this book. It belongs on everyone's bookshelf."

—Jeffrey Phillips, author of
The Past That Kills and the
Jesse Stoker Mystery Series

PRAISE FOR TERMINAL LUCIDITY

"I really enjoyed the thriller element I wanted in this genre. The characters had an overall feel that worked in this universe. It was suspenseful and worked well with what I was hoping for. Jo Loveday does a great job in writing this."

—Kathryn McLeer, *Kathryn's Book Reviews*

"A prescription for suspense: where medicine meets malevolence."

—Deborah Shlian, MD, award-winning author of *Silent Survivor* & the *Sammy Green* thriller series

"Author Jo Loveday brings to life her real-world hospital experience in crafting this realistic medical thriller… Fans of Robin Cook's blockbuster, *Coma*, have a new heroine to route for."

—Victor Acquista, MD, award-winning *Venom and Flame* thriller series author

"This book certainly kept me on the edge of my seat! The accuracy of the medical nature was a total bonus—it made me really "feel" for the characters in the book. A little romance to boot and it made for a very enjoyable read! This is the first book I've read by this author, and I definitely plan to read more! Her style and pacing (are) great! I love a good thriller—my favorite genre and I'm adding her to my favorite authors list to catch more!"

—Becky Rogowski, book reviewer

A LETTER FROM THE AUTHOR

Dyscalculia, sometimes called 'math dyslexia', gives me challenges. After struggling with math for years, I learned I had dyscalculia when a tutor suggested I get tested. I have to check numbers because my brain sometimes flips them.

Geometry helped my math grades in high school, as well as a very patient and kind math teacher. Geometry is about shapes. It made sense to me—a common trait among those with dyscalculia. So, if you ever need help packing, I'm on it!

Phone numbers can be tough, too. I have to keep repeating them constantly until I can write the numbers down. If not, in a minute they are gone or swapped around.

After being late frequently or writing down appointments on the wrong day or time, I had to become very organized on paper to keep order in my life. I have calendars—on my phone, desk, and in my purse—to check during the day. That doesn't mean I'll be on time for your next party, though.

I have given the main character in this story dyscalculia to raise awareness of this lesser-known learning disability. In the research for this novel, I found traits I had no idea were associated with dyscalculia—like being terrible with commas. Thank goodness for my editors!

This story takes a look at addiction. If you have a problem with alcohol or drugs, please seek the advice of a professional. The Alcoholics Anonymous hotline is 800-934-9518. Information on AA can be found at *sober.com* and for Narcotics Anonymous: *na.org*. I have the utmost respect for these organizations and others who work diligently to help people.

I hope you enjoy *Campus of Shadows*!

—Jo Loveday

Chapter 1

Blood splatters across my windshield when a two-inch piece of flesh drops from the sky. I climb out of my car, and into the Florida heat. A constant *chkk-chkk-chkk* draws my attention to a vulture in a gnarled oak, its branches twisted so low they could trip someone.

"Thanks, buddy." I clean the windshield with a fast-food napkin from the long drive up here.

My new apartment complex is painted white with black trim and has a scrawny hedge bordering the single-story structure. Music filters over from the courtyard. I can't wait to get in there.

How hard will my college classes be? Will I be able to take it all in stride?

A lanky priest with windblown salt-and-pepper hair is walking toward me from the courtyard. The long, black vestments are distorted by waves of heat coming off the asphalt, but his gait and his toothy smile are familiar.

"Father Tim."

"David Everest. How are you?"

"I didn't expect you to be the first person I saw when I got to college." I laugh, extending my hand.

"It's been a long time." His outstretched hand and mine connect. "Oh." He tugs his hand away. "I got a shock."

"Sorry, I must have created static electricity when I slid out of the car. Didn't you get transferred to Miami, Father?"

"I did. I was here for a… meeting. A soul-freeing of sorts." A muscle in his jaw tics. "Anyway, I have a friend whose daughter is a student here, and she left something at home in Miami last week. I dropped it off for her."

"That was nice of you."

A gust of wind swirls through the courtyard entrance, blasting me in the face and tearing at his vestments.

He shivers and backs away. "I need to go. Bless you, my son."

Odd that he shivered. It's ninety degrees out here. I am glad he didn't ask too many questions since I've hardly been to church in recent years.

I watch his back while he walks away.

The *chkk-chkk-chkk* sound starts again, and I return my attention to the tree.

The vulture doesn't move. It balances on the branch, staring at me with a weird look, waiting for something. Its beak is black-tipped, as if something dead is stuck in there.

"Get out of here, you dumb scavenger," I say and wave my arms.

The vulture flaps its giant black wings but doesn't go anywhere. It just stares at me.

"You're not going to bother me," I say.

The tune "Bad Guy" blasts from the apartment's inner courtyard. I can't wait to check it out.

A line of hot, bikinied bodies rims the edge of a giant, kidney-shaped pool. More girls stretch out on loungers, with dudes ogling the girls soaking up the sun. *Sweet.*

I stop and take in the pulse of the music and the scent of coconut oil, wondering if these girls are out of my league. No, I tell myself. Freshman year is going to be awesome.

I swing to the right, past a couple of palm trees, with girls sitting tableside in the shade, then head to Apartment

Six. The door is locked. I wish Zane would answer his phone. I called twice on my way here.

Though I search through the crowd for a guy who looks like the dude's U of Mann Eaglechat picture, I don't see him. I'd sure like to unload my stuff and get settled before tomorrow, at my last-minute change of school.

After dodging a string of lounge chairs chock-full of gorgeous women, I smooth the unruly cowlick at the edge of my forehead, which always makes me look like my mother tousled my hair. Good thing I wore my best shorts and a decent V-neck tee.

I spot him. He looks just like the Eaglechat photo: yellow-blond hair, fit, and tan. He's hitting on a girl floating in the pool.

"David Everest?"

I've never heard my name pronounced in such a musical way. A slim, tan girl with long, dark brown hair is grinning at me. She looks familiar, but I can't recall her name.

"It's Maria Vasquez. You saved me in third grade from the fifth-grade bullies."

A scene flashes by, with them pushing and shoving… A big stick covered with blood…

"That was a long time ago. How'd you know it was me?" I drag over a lounge chair, remembering how we shared a classroom and similar interests in elementary school.

The white bikini highlights her curves. My little Latina buddy sure grew up.

"You mean, aside from the same jet-black hair and blue eyes?" A gold cross around her neck swings when she angles toward me. "The scar from where they smashed your arm."

I rub the twinge of pain shooting through the jagged mark on my wrist.

"My parents sold our house and moved, but I'll never forget what you did for me. Are you just getting here?"

"I'm looking for my roommate, Zane Maddox. I think that's him." I nod to the guy tossing out a pick-up line and working it hard.

"It is. Good luck with that." Maria's brown eyes twinkle.

Zane climbs from the pool and strides over. "Hey there! You David?" He reaches his fist out for a bump.

I nod with caution and connect, expecting Maria to burst into laughter.

None comes.

She sinks back in her chair. "You'll like him most of the time, but I'd watch out."

Zane's face clouds. He turns his back on her. "Don't believe that shit. Come on. I'll buy you a beer." He motions across the courtyard. Looks like he's had a few, but he isn't flopping drunk.

I don't know that I'm into drinking the night before school starts. Maybe they have something else.

I scramble out of the lounger, with a wave to Maria.

"You dropped something, David." She hands me a card from underneath the chair.

It's a get-out-of-jail-free card from Monopoly, which someone has drawn a ghost on.

I open my mouth to tell her it's not mine, then notice Zane nodding or winking at almost every girl he passes. They smile, giggle, and reach out to touch him like he's some type of god. I need that skill.

I slip the card into my pocket and hurry to catch up.

"Stay away from that girl. She. Is. Nuts." He leads me around the corner, where three kegs are iced down in the shade.

I'm about to ask him why, but "Wow! Is it like this every weekend?" comes out instead.

"No, sometimes, we have eight or ten of 'em. Then it's a real rager. Go ahead. Tap into it."

"I'm really thirsty. Is there a bottle of water around?"

"This is all we've got." He grabs a cup and pulls on the tap.

I open my mouth to say something but think, *I'm the new guy. Better to roll with it.*

The tap almost fills the red Solo cup before trickling off. He shoves it at me. "Welcome to college."

"Thanks." This will fix the dryness in my throat, at least.

"I'm not kidding about Maria. She's next-level messed up," Zane says.

"I know her from grade school. She was all right then."

"Forget her. There are hundreds of decent bitches here, and they're all fair game."

I check out the landscape of hot co-eds in the courtyard, hoping they'll talk to me. "The eye candy is sweet. I'm in Heaven."

Zane pumps on the keg, but the tap belches out a mass of empty bubbles. "Guess it's time to switch things up. There's a liquor store close by that sells crazy-strong European energy drinks you can't find anywhere else. I'm dying for one. You mind driving?" He lets out a feral laugh.

I'd like to unpack, but I guess I need to get to know him anyway. "No problem."

While Zane tugs on his flip-flops, I catch a whiff of rotting meat and hear the *chkk-chkk-chkk* again. The vulture is watching us from a gutter on the roof over the keg.

Odd that it's here, around a crowd.

"What's that thing doing? Waiting for a dead body?" I nod to the vulture and laugh.

"Who cares? Let's go. I want to keep this party going." Zane whacks the side of the empty keg. The hollow sound reverberates through the courtyard, and the vulture takes off.

My temples pound while I gulp down the beer, and the cold seizes my brain.

The crowd in the courtyard is thick with people not only

lying on lounge chairs, but perched on the sides of them. We pick our way, single file, to the parking lot.

"I can't believe how many people are here."

We pass a group wild dancing to the music.

"That beat's possessed," I say.

"You got it." Zane laughs. "One of the guys is big on social media. He spreads the word and gathers money for a DJ and kegs."

I hit the unlock button.

Zane slides into the passenger seat and strokes the leather with his fingertips. "Nice ride. Daddy buy it for you?"

"Nope." I crank the engine and watch Zane sit up. A smile creases my face.

"What's in it?" He eyes the dashboard in front of me.

"It's a stock engine, but I pumped up the exhaust and put in a new chip that raises the turbo boost." I start backing out.

"Let me hear what this thing sounds like," he grunts.

He'll like this. I push the clutch in and rev the engine.

"Sounds pretty chill." Zane opens the sunroof.

Light hits my keys and makes them glisten.

"Oh yeah. Here's your apartment key. We're in Unit Six." He digs it from his pocket and hands it to me.

The key to my own place. Awesome. I shove it into my pocket, feel a pack of Eclipse gum, pop a piece into my mouth, then hand him the rest. "Want some?"

"Sweet. Show me what ya got." He takes a piece and leans forward, like he's trying to see into the engine.

I dump the clutch. The car shoves Zane back in his seat like an oversized bully.

"Pretty solid, bro. I'm calling you Dave, by the way."

"That's what my friends call me."

The guy seems decent enough to make friends with, even if I *am* at the fraternity all the time.

He hits a button and changes the radio station to some old head-banging crap. Not my favorite, but I'll roll with it.

"Something wrong with your A/C?" Zane asks.

"Shutting the air off for a few seconds got me a couple of extra horses." I close the sunroof, then turn the A/C back on.

"Why are you getting here so late?"

"I was accepted to Elon for football but got injured. I got in here too, but not for football. There's a good med school here I'd like to get into."

He turns to look at me. "Ohh, you wanna be a doc?"

"Yeah, my mom's pretty sick."

He grunts.

"I know it sounds weird," I say, "but maybe I can help."

"Not weird. I get it. Make a right." Zane points. "Last Buck Liquor is about a quarter mile down."

I follow his directions and make the turn. "The girls by the pool couldn't keep their eyes or hands off you. How'd you do that?"

"It's the way you project yourself. I'll teach you how, bro. Stop right there by the front door." He stumbles out of the car.

I contemplate how to tell him about my dyscalculia and get it out in the open. But he probably doesn't care that I suck at math. As fast-moving thunderheads gather above, I dial Mom. When it goes to voicemail, uneasiness grips me. I hope she's all right.

I tell her I'm here, then call Dad.

"Hey, Dad. I made it. Mom didn't answer. Is she okay?"

"She's in the shower. Did you go by the fraternity?"

I spin down the radio dial. "Not yet."

"Oh." He pauses. "What's the apartment like?"

"I only got here a little while ago. There's a party going on at the pool. I haven't been in the apartment yet."

Dad exhales real slow. He's thinking I'm irresponsible for not unpacking the car and going straight to the MGD fraternity house. I grip the steering wheel.

"But I met my roommate."

"What's he like?"

Maria's warning runs through my mind. "Seems fine."

"You should be in the dorms."

"Dad, the dorms were full."

Zane gets back into the car, points his finger forward, and yells, "*Go!*"

I stare, wondering where the drama came from.

"What was that?" Dad's voice jumps louder.

"I'll call you later." I hang up and put the car in gear.

Zane has a red and black can in one hand and two Tequila bottles in the other. He puts the Tequila in the footwell behind him and pops the can open. "Let me hear that engine again." He spreads his feet apart, bracing them against the floorboard.

I hit the accelerator. When I'm about to shift into third, a blue light flashes in my rearview mirror. "Shit." I check the speedometer. "I wasn't speeding."

Zane turns to me real slow. He has a strange look on his face. "There's something I have to tell you."

A white sedan with a flashing blue bar on top is racing toward us. The cop blinks his headlights when he pulls behind me.

My heart hammers against my chest. It's me he wants to pull over.

"You don't have to tell me. We're both underage, and there's two bottles in my back seat. Hurry up and fold the seat down. Toss those things into the trunk so they can't see them."

"Not exactly." Zane keeps his head low, pulls the catch, and lowers the back seat enough to lob the bottles into the trunk. "I hope these don't break."

"That's the least of my worries."

The squad car pulls closer.

While Zane chugs the energy drink, I notice the stuff is called Hell. Great.

He clears his throat, and squirms in his seat, wiping his palms on his board shorts. "I lifted that booze."

Air disappears from my lungs. The blue strobe makes his skin look smoky, ethereal.

"You did *what*?"

"The old guy in the liquor store carded me. I didn't have my fake ID 'cause some tool took it away from me at the bar last week. The old guy went to put something under the counter, so I snagged the Tequila. I didn't think he saw me."

"Are you effing kidding me?" I slam my foot on the brake and throw my hands in the air.

Both vehicles stop.

"I never thought we'd get caught." His face is blank.

Two bulked-up sheriffs with short-sleeved green uniforms run toward us with guns drawn.

People on the sidewalk scurry away. Sweat trickles down my spine. I want to lean back and blot it with my shirt, but I don't dare move.

"This wasn't supposed to happen." Zane's voice is shaky and weak.

"No kidding."

The cop is at my car window. His face is wood-chiseled, carved in controlled stillness. His red hair lies gelled and unmoving. He has a gun pointed at my head. "Get out of the car. Keep your hands in the air."

My heartbeat throbs in my ears while I climb out of my seat real slow, both hands up high. All I can think is that my dad's going to kill me.

"Walk backward toward the sound of my voice. Lean

over the hood of the car and put your hands behind your back," the cop barks.

The sharp edge of the handcuffs digs into my wrists. They lock in with a dull snap.

"We just got a call that you robbed a liquor store. Is that true?"

My gut spasms. "No, sir."

"It appears to me this is a silver Honda Civic with license number R2M 0T1."

The heat coming off the car hood is dizzying. I can't think, can't breathe.

"I didn't rob the liquor store."

"Maybe your friend did it for you." The cop kicks my legs out wider. His fingers probe my pockets. "What's this?" He tugs at the card poking out of the side of my wallet. "Get out of jail free." He bursts out laughing. "That won't work."

I look around for Zane. He's leaned over the trunk, being searched. What an A-hole.

"You reek of alcohol. You boys been drinking?" the other cop says to Zane.

Not a DUI…

My hands get cold. I don't want to lie, but I have to get out of this mess. I dart my eyes to his name badge. I chew my gum fast. "No, Officer Harris, I wasn't. That's why I drove, 'cause I haven't been drinking. I just got to Greenville half an hour ago."

"Save it, kid. We'll check at the lock-up."

A shadow blips across the sun. A vulture is circling overhead.

There seems to be a lot of vultures around here.

"Have a seat." He motions for me to sit on the curb.

The vulture swoops down and lands on a nearby rooftop, staring at me past its black-tipped beak.

The hair on the back of my neck prickles. It's the same damn bird.

Zane plops down beside me at the direction of the other cop.

"This one's got no wallet."

"You didn't even bring your wallet?" I glare at Zane.

The corners of his mouth straighten, and he looks away.

The beer slams against my stomach walls. I should have run the other way when he asked me to drive.

Harris is scouring my car. I cross my fingers, willing him not to search the trunk.

My insides turn to water when he walks to the back of the car. He pops the trunk and grins.

"Evidence," he hollers.

The air closes in around me.

"Get in the squad car," says the bulkier of the two.

When he opens the door, I glance at the name badge: Gallow. The place where people used to be hung. I go limp while he guides me into the squad car.

Welcome to college.

Chapter 2

I'm behind bars. In *jail*. Unbelievable.

I pace the ten-by-sixteen-foot holding cell, back and forth the length of benches bolted to the concrete block walls, trying to ignore the stench of piss and sweat. And the roommate who got me into this damned mess.

An hour ago, I was driving into Greenville, eager to start my new life as a college student. How could I have been so stupid? How could *he* be such an ass?

I steal a glance at Zane. He's so nonchalant about the situation I could punch him.

The sheriff's deputies took us to the department's office at the county jail, out of town near the airport. I guess it's to keep us far from the civic-minded public. We drove in silence past barbed wire fences and protective pilings erected so some pissed-off person can't crash a car through the doors into the building. Then, before I knew it, I was in the cell.

"Aren't you worried about this?" My path in the tiny cell ends, and I trudge past him again.

"Look, I'm sorry the clerk went mad savage and called the cops. It wasn't supposed to happen this way."

"I'll be lucky if my parents don't pull me out of school and stop my life in its tracks before it gets started."

"You need to chill, bro."

I head in the other direction, toward the only other

person in the cell—an old man stooped over his leg. "Are you all right? Your ankle is covered in blood."

"It got scraped," he rasps, not looking up.

"Hey!" I bang on the impenetrable glass door. "This guy is bleeding."

A cop with a blond buzz cut screeches the door open. "David Everest, come with me."

"Wait. The old guy hurt his leg. His sock is filled with blood."

Buzz eyes the old man. "I'll send the nurse."

Another cop fills the entryway behind me. "John Doe, a.k.a. Zane Maddox."

I wrench my head over to Zane. "John Doe? What kind of a freak are you?"

"They only said that 'cause I have no ID." His eyes are filled with apology, like a puppy that's misbehaved.

"Cut the crap. Let's go." The cop takes Zane out the entrance of the building, and I start to follow.

"No." Buzz grabs my arm. "This way."

"Where are they going?"

"Your friend is going to juvy. He can't stay here. He's only seventeen."

The words filter through me in slow motion. The jerkoff's a minor, and I'll be blamed for this *whole* thing. Just. Effing. Great.

"The breathalyzer in the car was broken. Step over here." Buzz takes me to a big gray box with a keypad and the words "Intoxilyzer" above a digital screen.

An icy chill grips me. Did I drink enough to go over?

He hands me a long black tube. "Take a deep breath and blow into this."

I follow his directions. A rush of blood pounds in my ears while my lungs empty. The seconds tick by.

"Point zero six. It's your lucky day."

"Yeah, lucky…"

"Officer Smythe will check you in." Buzz leads me to a desk in a wide-open area. He takes up a stance close behind me in case I bolt.

Smythe lifts his head from his computer screen. There's a bite-shaped scar on his ear. My skin bristles. Did that happen here? Can it happen to me? Or worse?

"David Everest, you're charged with petty theft and possession of alcohol under the legal age."

I ball my hands into fists. My first roommate ever is such an effing jerk.

"The officer will take you to check your belongings." Smythe beams at me.

A zip-lock bag with my wallet, phone, and keys jingles when Buzz picks it up.

There's another rush of blood to my head. My phone. What if my mom calls? I picture her pacing, worrying.

"You have any health problems? Take any medications?" Buzz asks.

My car, my wheels… I worked so hard for that car. What if they mess it up?

"No, none. But I might need some medication after this."

Buzz doesn't laugh. He leads me to a small room with a windowed pass-through. It looks like a ticket booth at a movie theater. The concrete walls of this space are embedded with an icy chill. There's a strange scent in the air, but I can't place it.

"We lock your valuables up 'til you leave." Buzz shoves the plastic bag under the window. "Take your clothes off. Put them through the slot and put these on." He hands me a black bin with green-striped, doctor-type scrubs, yellow ankle socks, plastic slippers, a blanket, a pillow, and toiletries. "Keep your underwear on."

My breath catches in my throat. A horrible feeling travels outward along my arms. My hands start to shake.

The smell hanging in the air is the sweat of raw fear.

"I'll wait right here." He saunters outside the doorless entry.

The felon's suit I have to put on glares back at me. Who has worn these pants before me—a rapist, a murderer? My stomach churns.

I'm shaking so hard that I need to lean against the wall to get my Volcoms off. My favorite shorts. I wore them today for good luck. How did I get myself into this?

Unfolding the large striped shirt reveals "ALACOSTA JAIL" stamped across the back in five-inch letters. I hold it away from me, unable to put it over my head. My heart pounds while alarming scenarios run through my mind. Will I get kicked out of school?

Buzz pokes his head around the corner. "Aren't you done yet?"

I don't want to touch this shirt, never mind wear it. "Almost." My trembling hands find one armhole and then the other. The smell permeates everything: the shirt, the pants, the walls. It makes me want to vomit. I inhale deeply, as if I'm diving to the bottom of the ocean.

You need to do this; there's no other choice.

I close my eyes and shove the branded shirt over my head. It saddles my shoulders with a *thump*. My stomach spasms.

"Bring the bin with you. Walk through the metal detector and step over there by Smythe."

I'm lightheaded and disoriented, holding the bin out front like a shield. I follow, feet sliding around in oversized plastic sandals. We head back to the booking area.

Smythe beams like a concierge. "Have a seat, Mr. Everest. I'm going to do your fingerprints."

The concrete block wall blurs. How do I tell my parents about this? Dad's image appears, holding his phone. What am I going to say?

Hi, Dad. I got in a little trouble. Can you lend me ten grand?

Yeah, right.

Dad, you know how you always say experience is the best teacher…?

A cold shiver shakes me to my core.

"Stand here, Mr. Everest. Face front. Keep your eyes open. Look this way."

A flash illuminates my stark reality. I'm now a criminal. My heart sags, limp in my chest. Will I be branded for life? Will I have to put this on job applications? Grad school applications? Anything I do?

"Turn to your left."

Another flash.

"What happens to those pictures when I prove I'm innocent?" I ask Smythe.

"They stay on file." He punches in more information.

"No way. You mean, you don't get rid of them?"

"A lot of our guests decide they want to come back to visit. This way, we're already familiar with their preferences." He grins at his humor.

Not funny. "Even if I'm innocent?"

"Yup."

My thoughts bounce off the insides of my brain. It's hard to keep them together. "What do I need to do to get out of here?"

Smythe sits down at his computer and starts typing. "You have to go for a first appearance before the judge, post bond… Then you're done."

"How much is the bond?" I pull on a cracked cuticle. The skin tears up into my finger.

"First offense… probably a thousand."

I suck in a breath, telling myself to be grateful it's not ten. "How soon can I do that?"

Smythe keeps on typing. "Nine o'clock tomorrow morning."

The air in my lungs disappears. The shred of cuticle drops to the floor. "I have to stay here overnight?"

He nods. "Have a wonderful stay, Mr. Everest."

"This way, Everest," Buzz calls.

My feet are stuck to the floor. I stare at Smythe, hoping he'll laugh and say this is all a joke for a TV show.

"Let's go, kid."

My reflection flashes at me from the computer next to Smythe. I'm still me. Still the same on the inside, same on the outside. I'll be able to clear my name. It'll be all right.

Buzz takes me back to the holding cell. It's vacant except for a slight metallic smell and a remnant of dried blood on the bench where the old man sat.

"Is the old guy all right?"

"He's fine. You can use this phone. You'll have to call collect," Buzz says.

"Great." I pick up the phone. The mouthpiece smells like rotten eggs. I gag, hang up, then bang my head against the concrete wall. The last two hours replay like a movie inside in my head.

How do I explain this mess to Mom and Dad? I steel myself before returning to the pay phone. The only thing I want is to get into med school to help Mom. Have I ruined that forever?

My hands quiver while I dial my mom's number. The gray cell walls close in, contracting the space and my throat.

I try to clear the wad of tangled words wedged in the back of it.

"Mom?"

The operator interrupts. "I have a collect call from the Alacosta County Jail. Do you accept the charges?"

My legs are weak. I try not to hyperventilate. Should I ask if she's sitting down?

"Jail?" Mom gasps. "The jail? Yes, I'll accept the charges. David, what are you doing in jail?"

My mouth dries up, words coming out as a squeak. I chase my tongue around to find some spit. "I… got arrested."

It's as far as I get because my eyes well up at the sound of her voice. I wish I'd never come here. I wish I were home. My breath comes in spurts.

Mom's voice comes through the earpiece. "I'm going to put the phone on speaker for your dad. David, it's okay. Tell us what happened."

I draw in a new breath. "My roommate asked me to drive him to the liquor store. I was sitting in the car, talking to you, Dad. Remember?"

Dad grunts.

Do they record the conversations here? How much should I say? I look around for a camera or a mic in the cell, then continue. "A few blocks down the road, when blue lights are flashing in my mirror, the guy tells me he stole some Tequila."

"This is the guy you're living with?" Dad's anger has a way of extending tendrils through the telephone, seizing me, shaking me.

"He lost his fake ID, so the guy wouldn't sell it to him. That's why he stole it." My words spill out fast.

"And you think that's okay?" Dad's tone grows louder.

My head throbs. "No, it's not. I didn't know. He just

walked over to the car and got in. He wasn't running or yelling or anything. He just pointed and said, 'Go.' You heard it. You were on the phone."

"You're telling me you had nothing to do with it?" It sounds like an accusation.

"No, I was sitting in the car. On the phone. With you." My hand sweats on the receiver.

Dad breathes long and low into the phone. "You're going to need a lawyer."

"There's a thing called First Appearance tomorrow morning at nine. I have to go before a judge, and they said he'll ask if I want to have my own lawyer or a public defender."

"I'll find you a lawyer." Mom's using her squeaky voice, meaning she's upset.

"After that, I can get out when I post bond." A chip of paint protruding from the wall catches my attention, making me wish I could climb behind it and out of here.

"How are you planning to do that?" asks Dad.

I suck in a breath. My sweaty hand slips. I readjust the receiver. "I was hoping… you would help me. They said probably a thousand dollars since it's a first offense."

"A thousand dollars? This is unbelievable. You've only been in Greenville a few hours, and look at all the trouble you're in."

My stomach tightens, contents churning.

"We'll leave at five o'clock and should be there by nine 'cause there won't be any traffic that early," Mom says in a steady tone.

"Please don't make me stay here another hour."

"I should leave you in there," Dad growls into the phone.

"There may be a whole bunch of people who have to see the judge. You might not be the first one." Mom's voice is stronger. "Where are you?"

"The official name is 'Sheriff's Department of the Jail.' It's by the airport."

"Where's your car?" asks Dad.

I tighten my grip on the phone and brace for the next onslaught. "They impounded it."

"That means a towing charge. Geez, David. What else?"

A bead of sweat trickles down my wrist.

"We'll take care of it." Mom's voice is soothing.

Dad grunts. "At least we've got another son who's got a brain in his head."

"Frank, stop it. You don't have a learning disability," Mom says.

A rough-looking guy with a tattoo of a spider extending across his neck and cheek is brought to the cell. He snarls at me and says, "Hurry up."

"I've got to go. Someone else needs the phone." I bite my lip and sink down on the vacant bench, eyes burning. Why do I always screw things up? I return the phone to its cradle.

The deputy nods for me to follow him.

Dazed, I walk in silence.

Twenty men now fill the holding cell. The space is cold and dull, the occupants guarded, blocking all feeling. I'm the youngest one. Twenty others had been brought in, then taken elsewhere.

The door clicks when a guy with a mullet and a scowl is brought in. His eyes are weird, like a man possessed.

He stares at me and then at the stainless steel toilet.

Is it some kind of threat? Visions of him trying to smack my head on the edge of it or drown me inside race through my mind. I drop my gaze to the floor and picture punching and kicking Zane until he runs crying.

It's getting harder to stay awake. The thought of Mom fills my mind—her struggles, her hopes for me. I've let her down.

A loud voice barks, "Line up for First Appearance."

My eyes fly open to a uniformed sheriff. I'm in jail. I must have fallen asleep. That's kind of good, I guess. At least I didn't have to talk to any of these other guys.

I bolt to the door.

"Single file, boys," a new cop tells us.

The old man goes first. He spots me, smiles, and points to a large bandage below his pant leg. I grin and give him a thumbs-up. Mullet follows, then me.

The cop leads us across the booking room and down a concrete hall to a makeshift courtroom. The people in here are vile. A sorry group with scraggly hair and missing teeth. I'm the only one in the room who looks like a student.

The officer points to a row of benches. "In the front row, boys. Once it's full, start on the second."

When the old man starts down the aisle, Mullet trips him. The old man falls.

I bend down to help him up, and Mullet knees me in the chest. While I gasp for air, Smythe and Buzz pull Mullet away.

"Damn these addicts," Buzz mumbles.

Smyth holds Mullet tighter. "The old guy is learning disabled. He's been in here a bunch."

"A lot of the addicts are LD too," says Buzz.

A flash of me being bullied by guys and spurned by girls goes by. I feel for the guy, so I shoot him a smile.

The old guy starts down the row. I file in behind him, wondering if I'm literally following in his footsteps.

At the front of the room, there's a sheriff's deputy on the right, a technician on the left, and a big TV in the middle. The TV picture is divided between the judge's bench and the courtroom at the downtown courthouse. Families are in the courtroom, eyes filled with disappointment and despair.

Was I supposed to tell my parents to go there? My stomach contracts. Who do I ask?

"All rise for the Honorable Judge Marc Reeder," the TV bailiff calls.

The group does as directed.

When everyone settles back into their seats, I wave at the officers on the side of the room and give them a pleading glance. They ignore me.

Mullet doesn't, though. He's seated at the back, far away from everyone else, with Smythe and Buzz on either side. The man grunts and scowls at me.

I snap my gaze away, fighting off a shiver.

"David Everest, please approach the bench."

All eyes turn to me when I stand. I flatten my lips to avoid a grimace or smile and pray this goes well. With a quick step, I make my way to the front of the room.

"Mr. Everest, you are charged with being an accessory to a crime of petty theft and possession of alcohol under the legal age."

The words bounce around the inside of my skull and make my stomach knot up.

"Are you a student, Mr. Everest?"

"Yes, Your Honor." My words come out choppy and frail.

"Do you have the means to secure your own counsel?"

"My parents do, sir." I wonder how much that will cost.

"I see you have no previous charges. You may return to court in sixty days, providing that you agree not to consume any alcohol or drugs."

I have no idea how I'll pull off not drinking in the fraternity, but I'll say *anything* to get out of here. "I agree, Your Honor."

"Your bond is set at two thousand dollars. The sheriff will show you where to take care of the paperwork."

The room blurs. Two thousand dollars. Dad thinks it's only going to be one.

Chapter 3

Outside the county lock-up, everything feels so normal. People drive by on the adjoining road, ignoring the tension, the hatred, and the dysfunction occurring inside the jail. While Dad and I walk to the car, a small plane takes off from the airport.

I inhale the fresh scent of pine. It cleans the stagnant jail air from my lungs. A light breeze blows my hair around.

Dad's dressed for work in a white-and-blue checked, long-sleeved shirt that's too tight around the middle, with khaki pants. He hasn't said a word, and his mouth is downturned. His tight, stubborn curls won't budge with the soft breeze.

"Thanks for coming up here, Dad. For… you know, getting me out."

"I was only a grand short," Dad hisses, his blue eyes blazing.

My stomach twists. "I'm sorry. What did you do?"

"I had to call a bondsman. He charged me dearly to buy an insurance bond." He points his keys at his red Buick sedan.

I follow his line of sight, searching for Mom. The only movement visible is that of the door locks when they stand at attention.

"Where's Mom?"

"We decided she should stay at home to find you a lawyer. That way, she only has to miss a half-day of work." Dad hurls himself into the driver's seat.

"Is everything okay with her?"

"She's rattled by all this crap you pulled, but she's fine." He slams his door shut.

"I really want to get into med school, to see what can be done to help. I never want to see her as sick as she was again."

"You're certainly getting a good start, aren't you? You'd better hope this doesn't screw up your chances."

I scramble into the passenger side and move the map they gave me to find my car to the top of the stack of paperwork. My phone is dead, so I'm glad to have it. But I feel like I've climbed out of one cage and into another.

"Which way?" Dad pulls out of the parking spot.

The seatbelt connects with a loud snap, a warning to brace for a rough ride. "Turn left at the street and take Weaton to United."

"You're lucky your mother talked me out of hauling your butt home because I don't think you deserve to stay." Dad clenches the gear shift.

Prep for my rebuttal churns through my brain, in case he changes his mind.

"How could you be so stupid, David? Why were you even at the pool?"

"I didn't have a key. I had to find Zane."

"It never occurred to you to unpack before you took off with your roommate?"

I tuck my fingers under my legs, like a dog with its tail, and inhale. "I figured we were just going to the liquor store and I'd be back in ten minutes."

"You could have just said no when he asked." His knuckles are white against the steering wheel.

"I have to live with the guy. I thought it would be nice to show a little goodwill."

Dad's exhale is shrill through his nostrils. "You mean that all your stuff is still in your car?"

Little knots chew at my stomach. "Yes."

"Your new laptop and everything?"

Here we go. I rub the sweat from my palms into the fabric seat and stiffen myself against the onslaught. "I didn't unpack anything."

Dad rolls his eyes. "Figures. You better hope it's all still there. That laptop's only a week old." His frown lines are digging in so deep they look like permanent scars.

"I know." It's all I can muster while buildings, girls, and students on bicycles speed by in a blur.

The only reason he's up here for the start of school is because I ended up in jail. When Eric went off to Penn, Mom and Dad both went… with fanfare. The last-minute emergency of Mom's client was legit for her not to come with me. Dad's golf excuse was worse than lame.

A sigh slides out.

I have to figure out a way to get him to lighten up.

An idea tweaks in the far side of my brain. I'll take him by the fraternity house. That will make us both feel better. He won't know his way from this side of town. I check the map.

"Take a left and go down Thirtieth."

A few blocks later, he rounds the corner. I cross my fingers.

"The old stomping grounds." The corners of his lips make a directional change. His furrows all but disappear.

Yes.

Dad slides his foot off the accelerator, and he gapes at the two-story, red-brick frat house. Its distinctive front gable says "Mu Gamma Delta" in giant, white block letters. His face sags.

"You haven't even been to the fraternity house, and you're in all this trouble. It used to be that you'd be a hero for something like this. Times have changed. I hope they let you in now."

I look past him to the building, where the memories of his years at U of Mann are cemented in its mortar. "I hope so too."

He rolls down his window and takes in a big breath. A sigh whistles through his teeth—the pitch of fingernails on a blackboard. "You know, I wanted both you and Eric here at MGD, but I guess one of you is better than none."

The knots in my stomach form a big lump. I swallow, hoping to chase it away. I know how important the fraternity is to him and, therefore, to me. It's my ticket to med school. The map is soggy in my hands. I try to steady the cadence of my words.

"Turn on Ninth. Follow the road to Storehouse Drive. The yard's down there."

The compound is surrounded by a tall chain link fence with barbed wire on top. A little shack which could use a coat of paint sits out front.

"This better not take long. I want to get back on the road." Dad reaches over and knocks loudly on the office window.

"Can I help you?" a voice emerges from a box on the wall.

"We're here for a silver Honda Civic, license number R2M 0T1," Dad says to the speaker.

"That'll be a hundred and fifty dollars. I'll need to see your driver's license and registration." A gray metal drawer slides out and opens its mouth.

"Good thing your mother researched this." He scowls and pulls a folded-up copy of my registration from his back pocket.

The steel mouth comes back with my keys. A chain link gate rolls open outside.

"Go on. The car's in back."

I spot my car just beyond a lineup of bruised and battered vehicles—discarded bodies left to rot, like in jail.

Running ahead, I yank the door open, and dig for my laptop. "I found it." I clutch the laptop to my chest and scan the rest of the interior. "Everything has shifted, but it's all still here."

"Good thing." Dad wanders to the back of the car. "Well, it looks like my wallet's not the only thing that got gouged this weekend."

Stale dirt clogs the back of my throat when he wipes away a heavy layer of dust, exposing two gashes on the bumper. No way. *My ride's ruined* is what I almost blurt. I hold back, try to downplay it.

I run my fingers over the bumper, sensing the depth of the jagged scrapes. I'd like to sue the jackass who towed this car. Doesn't he know how to do his effing job?

"A little touch-up paint will take care of that," I say, hoping to convince myself as much as him.

Dad squats down to take in the damage at eye level. "It's going to take more work than that. You might be able to fix it yourself with some Bondo. You can't just hide it with paint."

"I'll try that. Thanks, Dad. Thanks again, too, for coming up here to help me out today." I roll a rock over with the edge of my shoe.

He puts his foot up on the bumper, then leans over his knee. "You've got a long way to go 'til you graduate. Your mom said to make sure you meet with the learning disabilities coordinator. You'll be fine if you get into the medical fraternity and start hanging out with decent guys."

"I know." I roll the rock back to its original spot in the dirt, but the hole has changed, and the rock doesn't quite fit.

***

My grumbling stomach sends me looking for a drive-thru once Dad heads home. It's twelve thirty, halfway through what should have been my last class of the day. At least I'll be able to get to the fraternity for Rush.

In Dad's head, if I try harder and hang out with his kind of people, my dyscalculia will fade into the background. I wish it would. He doesn't get that numbers flip in my head like words do for someone with dyslexia. At least Mom gets me.

While I wait to order, Maria comes to mind, with her warning to watch out for Zane. He sure has gotten me into a ton of trouble already. Maria gave me a get-out-of-jail-free card. That was bizarre. Did she know? Is she a weirdo like Zane said, or was that a joke?

I inch the car forward, my brain toggling between moving in or bolting. Should I head to the apartment and unpack or look for somewhere else to live? The problem is, when I looked for housing, this was all I could find at the last minute.

"That's $12.39," the girl at the window says.

I pull out my wallet and hand her a ten.

"That's not enough. It's $12.39."

I shuffle through the bills, stalling while my mind scrambles for the answer to this simple arithmetic.

"You need $2.39 more." There is a bite in her voice while she watches the line grow behind me.

The difference doesn't register. My mind spins. I'm glad I'm not with anybody. Even if they know, they don't understand how I can function so well with other things but cannot add numbers. I hand her a twenty, hoping it'll cover the difference. If I had longer, I could figure it out.

She gives me a handful of change, along with my ten and other bills. I dump it into my center console—I don't want to look at it—then hurry to take the bag of food so I can get away.

My mind returns to Zane.

I felt lucky when a friend told me about someone who needed a roommate at the last minute. The guy seems to have a way with girls that I need to learn. Plus, the apartment complex is so chill. Who could find fault with keg parties on a pool deck full of hot babes, right out the front door?

My parents, that's who. The back of my throat sours.

Half a dozen guys wearing golf shirts in MGD red, yellow, and black are heading into the restaurant. They are giving each other friendly shoves and laughing. That's what I want more than anything. The fraternity brothers will be my tribe. What does it matter where I live?

I don't have to like Zane, although he could be fun, especially with girls by the pool. He doesn't think I'm an epic failure, like my dad does. I turn the car away from campus to head back to the apartment.

***

At the fake mahogany dining table, I check the school's Eaglechat board and my waitlist for room availability—still none.

I step back to observe my new castle.

This place is so much nicer than a dorm. The living room's sage green couch and fake mahogany coffee table, along with gray and sage chairs on either side, make it feel more like a home.

I sink into one. It is comfy. This is so cool. I'll make new friends and avoid the dude. Besides, what am I going to do, sleep in my car?

I jump up and check out the kitchen. White cabinets with

a countertop hanging over into the living room, where two gray barstools slide in on a floor of wood planks. They must have renovated recently because the building appears older. I love that my room and Zane's are on opposite sides. It gives me more privacy. Time to make it mine.

I dump the green Eagle comforter on my new queen bed and stash my fishing rod in the closet. My phone rings.

"Hey, Mom. How are you?"

"Fine. I spent the morning calling all over to find an attorney. Mark Solter was nice enough to say he'll see you this afternoon at four thirty."

The elation of moving in is swallowed by regret. "Got it. Thanks for setting it up, Mom." I grab my backpack and dig in it to find my phone charger, stabbing my finger. "Ouch."

Blood wells up.

"Are you all right?"

I peer into the backpack and spot the culprit. "Yup. It was my fish filleting knife. I must have forgotten to take it out when we went fishing last week."

The shower scene in *Psycho* flashes through my head, but it's at a gas station. Freaky.

"I packed a first aid kit in the box that has blue tape on the outside."

"Okay." The bleeding won't stop. I find a half-inch gash on my fingertip. After stacking on some tissues and holding them tight, I bury the knife in the back of my closet.

"I'm sorry I'm not there to help you, David."

I dig out the pack of bandages and rip open three. "No problem, Mom. Your job is to take care of your clients."

"I've been worried about you. Have you talked to the LD coordinator?"

"I will. Don't worry. I'm good, Mom." I pull the bandage tight across the cut, then do another one beside it.

"Don't forget… It's the coordinator's job to orient you to modifications and services."

"I'll get in touch this week." I find the phone charger and plug it in. "Mom, I'm excited about getting into MGD as a leg-up for med school, but what if I can't cut it with dyscalculia?"

"You've always had good study habits. I've heard that as long as you get through organic chemistry, you'll be fine."

"I hope so."

"Okay, tell me about your new roommate." Her voice is softer.

I know what she's going to say, but she puts it so much nicer than Dad does, and I don't mind talking to her about things. "His name is Zane Maddox. I'd only met him about twenty minutes before we got arrested. I haven't seen him since." I put the third bandage around the other two, and the bleeding stops.

"I'm concerned about you living with this boy. Maybe someone canceled at the last minute in one of the dorms."

"I checked a few minutes ago, Mom. All the dorms have waiting lists, and I'm way at the bottom."

"How about a house near the fraternity? I'll pay for you breaking your lease. I want you out of there." Her voice is strained.

Here she goes again.

"I checked the university site, the local newspaper, and online rental listings—nothing. The apartment is big, Mom, and our bedrooms are on opposite sides. The living room, dining room, and kitchen separate us. We each have our own bathroom, so I don't have to see much of him. I'll be at school or the frat all the time."

"You don't realize how much of a negative influence someone like that can have on you. I see it all the time with my clients."

My finger throbs, but the bandages hold. "Your clients all need a shrink. That's why they're there to see you. I'm not twelve, Mom. You raised me to make my own decisions, and I'm making one now. I'm going to stay."

"This is no joke, David. You need to get away from the guy." Her voice is rising.

"I'm good, Mom."

"That's what your classmate said before committing suicide."

"That's ridiculous. I'm not going to kill myself over this, Mom. Besides, you would know. If you ever detected one ounce of depression, you'd be hiring drone scans of the apartment complex."

"Stop it, David. I'm serious."

The voice of her assistant comes through, saying her next client is there.

"I have to go. Please reconsider, and don't forget your appointment with Solter."

"Thanks for arranging it." I hang up the phone.

Blood seeps through the bandage. I slap on another one and hold pressure, telling myself she's wrong.

***

I head for the parking lot, past a dozen sweet-looking babes reading textbooks by the pool. How could a guy ever move from here? While I am climbing into the car, my phone rings.

"Hey, Eric. How are things?" I ask my brother.

"Mom wants me to check on you."

"Tell her I made an appointment with the LD coordinator the day after tomorrow. I told him what my classes were, and he emailed me a color-coded map. Or, Mr. Spy, is she worried I'd forget about the appointment with the lawyer?"

"No, no," he lies, but I know she asked my faultless brother to call his unworthy younger sibling because that's her way of being less intrusive. "She's freaked out about the situation. I did some damage control and reminded both of them about Jessy McGee. You remember her? She got arrested for underage drinking in her first semester at UNC. Her parents were worried she'd lose her scholarship. Now she's the CFO of Rocke Industries. That put things in perspective a little bit."

I laugh, relieved my parents aren't checking my schedule.

"Thanks, bro. Hey, did you take a full class load your first semester? I'm thinking I could drop one and take it over the summer. They require you to take a couple of summer classes here. This way, I can kind of ease in, you know?"

"The problem with that is the selection of summer classes is limited. You might not get what you want. You'll be fine."

"You're right. I'll be fine. How's work?"

"In two more days, I'll be done. I don't go back to school for a week after that. Do you want me to come up and help you look for a place?"

I want to say, *How nice that you have a free moment from your way-too-perfect life to come and arrange my living situation*, but decide to go with, "Did Mom put you up to that?"

"I agree with her. This guy's a problem already. You don't know what he's going to pull. Why don't you look online and call me when you find something?"

I switch my phone to speaker and put it on the console. "My complex has a pool the size of Dad's office building, with hot babes in bikinis lined up around it every day. If you come here, you're going to want to transfer out of Penn so you can take in the Florida scenery."

"Yeah, right."

"You said you hate the winters up there."

"There are only two years left. I'll deal. So, what's up with the roommate?"

Not again. He needs to learn I can make my own decisions.

"I haven't even seen him today. It's Rush week, and I've got to get caught up with what I missed in my first classes. Let me give it a few days. If it's bad, I'll call you."

"Fair enough. I'm happy to come to rescue you on the weekend if you need me."

Like I need to help make him more of a hero.

"Gotta go. I don't want to be late." I hurry into the building where I'm directed to the office on the right.

"David Everest?" A tall, thin man older than my dad approaches. His pure white hair and pinstriped suit make him look like an erasable pen. Will he be able to wipe this out? "I'm Mark Solter." He clasps my hand between both of his.

This guy seems more politician than a criminal attorney.

"Have a seat." He indicates one of two tufted chairs in front of a desk backed by wooden bookshelves and leather-bound books.

The sound of my footsteps disappears into the plush burgundy carpet. What conversations has it absorbed? What confessions?

"My assistant was able to obtain a copy of the police report since we spoke earlier today. It states things pretty much the way I expected. There is one problem that you didn't mention."

I lean closer. "What's that?"

"Zane Maddox is a minor. His birthday is just over a month away."

"Yeah... I found that out when they hauled him off to

juvenile detention and left me alone in that hellhole." I fall back into buttery leather. It comforts me. "So that means I'm the adult. Am I going to get blamed for this whole thing?"

"It shouldn't be a problem. You can demonstrate that you only just met him and didn't know his history."

The word pulls me upright. "What history?"

"It turns out that he's been arrested before."

"Lucky me. What for?"

"Petty theft from a drugstore. It appears that Zane has a way with the ladies. He was caught stealing condoms at age fourteen."

A loud groan slips past my throat. "He'll probably be stealing them from my room now."

Solter bursts out laughing.

I shift back into the softness of the chair and think about telling him this isn't funny.

"The information at hand will work in your favor, David." Solter clicks his Silver Cross pen and sketches a crude figure of a bird.

What's with birds everywhere?

He starts to color it in. "We should go before the judge in about sixty days, unless the court is backed up. I'm glad you came early. It can take a month or more to gather documents."

I look at the rows of books lined up and wonder if he has read them or if they are for show. "What happens if we don't win?"

"I've never lost one of these."

"What if we don't?"

"There could be a fine and a few months to maybe a year of incarceration." Solter tilts the scratch pad and starts drawing squares.

It creeps me out. Makes me think of being penned in a

box. A vision of Mullet at the jail, scowling at me, flashes by. My jaw tightens, and my hands start to sweat.

Solter taps his pen on the desk. "I presume you'll be attending school. Keep your grades up. It looks good before the judge."

I wipe my hands on my pant legs. "You are going to get me out of this, aren't you?"

He sketches out a rectangle.

It looks like the black bin in the jailhouse. I see myself putting my phone, my wallet, and my keys in it, all over again, and my heart starts to race. He's told me everything. Time to get out of here.

I stand and tug my phone from my pocket, cradling it in my hands. The chair tips, crashing into a giant black-and-gold vase, knocking it into the wall. The vase cracks and falls to the ground, spilling tall, gold-painted bamboo sticks across the room.

"I'm so sorry," I sputter, shoving the phone back into my pocket.

Solter runs to the vase and eases it off the floor, supporting it with care while he examines the crack.

"I'm sorry," I say again, gathering the sticks.

Solter raises his head real slow. He glances at me and back to the vase.

"I'll buy you a new one."

He rolls his eyes. "You won't be able to."

There's a *thud* in my stomach. I want out of here. "Okay… Well, thank you for seeing me."

His eyes go back to the vase.

"I'll show myself out."

I can't do anything right.

Chapter 4

The oak-paneled door of Mu Gamma Delta looms before me. I've been through it so many times with my dad for his alumni weekends, and it feels like home. The connections I'll make here will give me the edge to get into med school, especially if there is anything math-related on the MCAT. I can't wait to belong.

I step inside and inhale the familiar scent of dirty socks and bleach. After all that's happened with Zane, I'm hoping I won't have any problems being accepted as a pledge, thanks to Dad's legacy.

A guy in an emerald-green golf shirt thrusts a paper toward me. "Put your name and hometown on the sheet. Put it on a name tag too."

I follow his directions and approach a couple of brothers, sporting matching MGD shirts, leaning against a white-washed wall. When I get closer, one of them looks familiar.

"Aren't you an officer here? You did the food for the alums at homecoming last year."

"I remember seeing you. I'm Brandon Wickham. I'm Rush chair this year." He pushes away from the wall and extends his hand.

I shake it. "David Everest. My dad was class of '78. He'd sleep on green sheets if my mom would let him."

Their laughter lifts me out of the funk from the previous day.

A built guy studies me. "Didn't you play football? You beat out my friend for a spot as a receiver at Elon."

"What was his name?"

"Mel Spring."

"Oh, yeah. They said he didn't have enough spring in his step." I laugh.

No one else does.

"How'd you end up here?"

A twinge in my shoulder reminds me. "I separated my shoulder a few weeks ago."

Built-Guy crosses his arms. "My buddy took a spot at a lesser school because of you."

My mouth dries up. This isn't going well. I look at Brandon.

"Elon took back their offer?" Brandon asks.

The armpits of my shirt are damp. Dad said some guys will be intimidating.

"It was the second time it happened in two years. My doctor told me if it happened again, I'd need a shoulder replacement this year and possibly one every ten years after that."

Brandon's eyes scrunch up. "Nasty."

"Football was the only thing I was ever good at. Now it's gone," I mumble.

"Where you from?" a short guy with a round face asks in a deep voice.

"Delray Beach. In South Florida."

"I *know* where it is," the short guy snaps.

Brandon elbows him. "Robert's having a bad day. He got his car towed last night."

My cheek twitches. I wonder if that's a dig at me and the arrest. Will I not get in if I don't say it upfront?

Brandon's phone beeps. He starts down the hall. "I'll be right back."

"Where'd your car get towed from?" I smooth down a roughed-up corner of my name tag.

"I was at the gym. I didn't see a no-parking sign that was behind a branch. When I came out, it was gone."

"That sucks."

"So…" The guy looks at me. He clears his throat.

I hold my breath, thinking I messed up and here it comes.

"You're a legacy," he says in a deeper tone. "Got any sisters or brothers here?"

I exhale and shove my hands into my pockets. "I have a brother at Penn. The only thing acceptable, other than U of Mann, to my dad is getting a scholarship into an Ivy."

He laughs. "Your dad's Frank Everest? What's he do now?"

"Other than drive me nuts, he sells medical equipment."

Robert coughs. It sounds like one of those where a guy covers his mouth and coughs out "loser."

My chest tightens. Dad warned me some guys might be jerks about the fact he didn't go to med school after being in a medical fraternity. My dad may be a hard-ass, but he's still my dad.

"What'd you say?"

"Nothing."

"Oh, I thought you may have been calling him a loser," I reply, masking my distaste for the dude.

"Food's here," Brandon says. He puts big platters of wings out on the tables.

My stomach grumbles, and I follow the scent of wing sauce, which smells hot enough to burn. "Nice talking to you."

Robert bangs his fist against the wall and looks past me to a guy down the hall. "I'm in charge of the pledges, so good luck."

***

I'm still so pissed at Zane for the arrest that, on my way home, I figure I need to work it off.

Inside the apartment, it is quiet. A good study atmosphere. This place will work for me. I change and head straight for the workout room. It's smaller than a regular gym but has the usual black rubber floor and equipment. I spot a large punching bag hanging in the back. A smile creeps to my lips.

"Here's for getting me arrested." I close my fist and smash it hard at face level. It jars my wrist but feels so good I do it again… and again. "This is for getting my father on my case." I whack it with one elbow, then the other, and keep going until the skin tears. "This one's for only being seventeen." I hold on tightly and slam my knee into it with every ounce of strength I have.

A horrible stench filters in when a couple of girls enter the gym. It's not them.

I look for the stupid vulture that's been in the courtyard every time I walk out my apartment door. It's gawking at me through the large glass windows. I find it unnerving, having the thing stare at me. I grab my towel and head back to the apartment.

The bird's beady eyes follow.

"I should complain to the office," I mutter. I close the door on its stare and sit down to respond to an email from my mom about Solter.

The desk is white, with a wood top and a drawer under

it. It's just big enough for a laptop and an open textbook. A small bookshelf is built into the side of the desk, facing the bed. It doubles as a nightstand.

Zane spots me at my desk, making me wish I'd closed my bedroom door.

"Hey, bro. Just wanted to say I'm sorry for what happened."

"You're a next-level asshole." I don't look up but notice his head drop out of the corner of my eye.

He strides past the high-top stools into my room. "I know, man. It was a stupid thing to do. I'm sorry."

I can still see him through the reflection on the computer screen. "Don't try to weasel out of this. You took off to juvy and left me to deal. What kind of a person does that?"

"Sorry, man. I had no choice." He presses his lips together.

I crank myself in the chair to face him. "You *had* a choice. You didn't need to steal the Tequila."

"I meant about getting dragged off to juvy."

"Dragged? You were thrilled to be able to get out of there. Then, you don't even come back 'til nighttime, when they let you out in the morning.

"I had to have my uncle come and get me 'cause my mom's in Paris."

"I don't care about your excuses."

Darkness covers his face. He looks at his feet.

"What the hell is your mother doing in Paris?"

Little lines form on his upper lip. "She moved there with her boyfriend when I started here in the summer semester."

I lower the screen with the e-mail to my mother. "What about your dad?"

His shoulders sag, and he sits down on my bed. "He was a charter boat captain. He and the people on his boat went missing when I started high school. The boat was found sunken off Haiti. The Coast Guard figured they were killed and the boat was stolen for smuggling people. You know, when people jump ship off the beach, swim in, and scatter."

The back of my neck twitches from the creeps. "That's nasty. They never found anything?"

"They found his wallet on the boat. In the spot we told them he used to hide it."

I swallow hard. "I'm sorry."

"My dad was valid fun."

I run my thumb along the edge of the laptop, not sure what to say next. While I understand the feeling of abandonment and feel bad for him, I'm still really pissed.

"Anyway, I thought I'd buy you a beer over here." Zane points to the refrigerator, and his face gets brighter.

"No, thanks." I reopen the laptop, and cc my dad.

"Come on, bro. It'll work out."

"How do you know? You been to see a lawyer yet? 'Cause I have."

Zane backs to the doorway. "How'd you manage to do *that* so fast?"

"I wanted to know where I stand, so I made a point of it."

"Mister Organized."

"That's why I want to get into a fraternity. They plan ahead."

"Fine, but you don't need to buy your friends, Dude. Look out the window. There are hundreds of people right here you can meet."

A list of things my dad has told me all my life runs through my head. "The brothers teach you leadership and fundraising. Working on projects, you build a network of lifelong friends. The best part is that they have events with sororities."

"That's something I'd go for. Enough of the sales pitch. Have a cold one with me. It's not like you have to study tonight." He walks to the fridge and fumbles around.

The *tssst* of two beers popping open filters over. A beer would taste good right now. I should put all this behind me. I thrust myself away from the desk.

What am I thinking? This guy's a disaster. I slide the chair back in while the slap of his flip-flops comes this way. Instead, I stay focused on my computer.

"Told you, I don't want one."

"You can't stay holed up in your room forever. Monday Night Football is on. Here." He nudges my arms, holding the beer close enough for me to get a whiff of sweet hops.

I tell myself I should wait to have a drink until after we go to court, but the scent tugs at a place that wants to be chill and forget about everything that's happened. I'm in my own apartment. Who is going to notice?

The screen of my laptop flickers, like the power is about to go out. I reach for the beer and slam the laptop shut.

***

The scent of Maria's perfume filters through my nostrils while I drive to the MGD house. I must have gotten some on my folder today in physics.

I'm glad we're in the same class. She remembered I struggle with math and offered to study with me. I managed to get her to admit she dated Zane until he messed around with another girl. No wonder she doesn't like him.

The red brick and white columns of the house loom ahead. Dad told me to be sure to come here every day. He said to look for guys I haven't talked to yet and to smile, nod, or throw a *hey* to the ones I have. I grab a name tag at the front table.

A stocky guy with hooded eyes looks up from behind the table. "I remember you from the last alum function. I'm Og. Are you here for Rush?"

"Yeah. Dave Everest." Our palms connect. A vague memory spins in the back of my head. The dyscalc makes it hard to recall names, but there's something else about him I'm not remembering. "Can't imagine being anywhere else but MGD."

"I know what you mean. It would be cool to be in the same fraternity as my dad. Welcome to the house."

"Thanks."

"Hey, guys," he says to the others at the table. "This is Dave. He's a legacy."

I make some small talk with the other guys, then move on. A dude in a T-shirt, which has an eagle sitting in a beach chair, is holding a beer by a campfire.

"Great shirt."

"I made it last year for the Fielder." He smooths the front of it.

"Sweet. What's a Fielder?" I check his name—Evan.

The dude's head is flat. When I see him I'll think of *even*, then I can associate it and maybe connect it to his name.

He rolls his eyes as if it's the stupidest question he's ever heard. "A bonfire on a farm."

I don't remember Dad ever mentioning those.

An image forms of the time in fourth grade when I went camping with my friend, Collin, and his family. Collin had tripped and fallen into the bonfire, burning his hands badly. I remember his screams, his skin peeling away. I shake it off.

"How many of you went?"

"A busload."

"So, it's a social event with a sorority?"

"Yup."

It feels like I'm having a conversation with a signpost. "You must've had a blast."

"Yup."

I comb the tiny black flecks on the linoleum floor for ideas, coming up with something else to talk to him about. "Where you from?"

"Tampa."

I fall against the white wall. The guy's personality is as flat as his head. This dude *has* to give me more than a single word.

"Hey, Dave. What's happening?"

Zane's voice.

Dread floods my veins when I spin around to face him. "What are you doing here?"

"You were so infatuated with this place I figured I'd rush."

"I don't think you'd like it," I say.

"Why?"

Guess he didn't catch the hint. "It's for pre-meds, and it's expensive too."

"I'll deal," Zane replies.

"There's one I haven't met yet," the short guy in charge of pledges says. His baritone voice volleys off the bare walls of the hall.

I want to bolt the other way. "Hey, Robert. How's it going?"

He looks at my name tag. "Oh, you again."

Great. He doesn't like me already. I need to get rid of Zane. "Come on, Zane. They have pizza over there."

Zane turns to the guy with the one-word answers and slaps me on the back. "Dave talks about this place like you're all some kind of heroes or something. Where's the party? I thought this was the hottest place on campus?"

Robert eyes Zane up and down. "Who are you?"

"Zane Maddox." He sticks out his hand.

Robert ignores it.

Zane's hand twitches, then he stuffs it back into his pocket. "What are you guys, a bunch of mad germaphobes?"

Robert's face darkens.

I nudge Zane's arm. "You need to eat."

"You gotta be kidding, Dave. You talk about this place like it's the best thing on Earth. These guys are assholes."

"We should go." I grab Zane's arm and turn him toward the door

"What's wrong with your mouth?" Robert says.

Zane shrugs off my grip to face him. "I got in a knife fight with a surgeon and lost," he shoots back, refering to a tiny scar on the edge of his lip.

I laugh. So does Zane. Nobody else does, though.

"This place sucks," Zane says, loud enough to turn all heads in the room. "Nobody has a sense of humor. The place is old and dingy. It smells like an old jockstrap. I'm not hanging with this bunch of dicks." He stomps through the door.

Their eyes turn to me.

I wish I could crawl into one of the patched-up holes in the wall. Instead, I give a weak smile, wondering what to do.

I head for the pizza.

Robert's glare follows me toward the food. When he thinks I'm out of earshot, he mutters, "Not on my watch."

***

The map the learning disabilities coordinator sent me shows his office is in the Fine Arts building. Maybe that's because a lot of folks with LDs go into the arts. I hope he doesn't tell me my current track in science is inviting craziness.

The red-brick building looks like most of the ones on campus, but inside, I'm greeted by a huge, white, abstract sculpture of an eagle's wing. I spot an open door down the hall, where it shows his office is, and I rap on the side of it.

"Stan?"

A fortyish guy with what's left of his dirty-blond hair approaches with an outstretched hand. His Eagles green-and-yellow checkered shirt is rolled up at the sleeves and tucked neatly into pressed khakis. "You must be Dave. How are you?"

"Good, thanks." I return a firm grip.

He closes the heavy oak door, then ushers me to a cushy, forest green chair. I'm glad the door is thick because I don't want anybody to hear our conversation. Talking with adults has always been easy enough. It's my friends I can't always relate to.

When he sits behind his oak desk, I notice the office has shelves with books about every learning disability that exists on the top and one-inch binders in a multitude of colors in perfect rows below.

"Wow, you're organized," I say, not knowing where to start.

"It's imperative, or I forget where I put things. I need to manage my own LD. Have a seat."

He has it too. No wonder he got the job.

I sink in the soft chair. It feels as warm and welcoming as he does. "Nice chair."

"My brother-in-law has a furniture store. There's a rip in the cushion, so he couldn't sell it. I flipped the cushion over, and we're good." He laughs. "Remind me what your classes are."

"Psychology, history, English, and physics. My biggest concern is physics."

"That one *will* be a challenge. You'll be able to get double time for your tests and quizzes. You may want to think about dropping one of the other classes so you only have three this semester."

"I've always done well in my classes other than math. That's why I avoided it this first semester."

"You can get a waiver for math with dyscalculia, but you'll need to take an alternate course credit option, substituting a science instead."

My breath lightens as if he just opened a window. "Really? That's awesome."

"Do you struggle with spelling and grammar?"

"Yes. Writing is okay for me, but I definitely use spellcheck, and I have a grammar program. Commas are what I have the most trouble with."

"We have vouchers for proofreaders you can use, if you have a paper to do. Make sure you finish it early enough for them to go through it and have time for you to make corrections."

"Got it." I fish through my backpack, retrieve a piece of looseleaf, and make notes.

He holds up a six-by-nine-inch notebook with "Planner" on the front. "I highly recommend that you get one of these organizers. They sell them in the bookstore. I use it because I have trouble planning and structuring time. I put my entire day in here—things to remember to do, to bring to work, to remember while I'm here, to do at lunch, my workout when I leave, and things to do at night. I keep them from year to year because I may not remember the exact dates, but I'll have an idea of when something occurred and can look in that date range for information I've written down. It's more efficient for me than an electronic calendar."

This dude is legit. He has all my issues down.

"That's amazing. People think I only have the LD when I have a textbook in my hand, but it spills over into everything. I feel like a fraud when I have good grades in other classes but can't figure out when to get to a class or where it is."

"Did the map I sent help?"

"Eliminating unimportant things and color-coding my classrooms, the library, and the bookstore is a lifesaver, but I still got lost on campus."

"Everyone does in the beginning. Don't tell anyone I said this, but you can note the people in your class and see if they're in your next class, then follow them or follow people from your class going in the direction of your dorm."

"I'm not in a dorm. I was supposed to go elsewhere and play football. I'm on a waitlist."

"I can put a word in and get you to the front of the list."

My mind races. I wanted the dorm so much, but after being rejected by everyone I asked out in high school, I want to learn techniques by the pool from Zane. "Thanks, but I'm already settled in a nearby apartment."

His phone rings. "It was great to meet you, Dave. Come back any time. I'm here to help you."

Outside his office, I dig out the map to find the bookstore. When I get there, only two planners are left. One has a forest path with a rabbit on it, and the other is Barbie on a college campus. Seriously?

I pay for the one with the forest scene, then head to my apartment.

Chapter 5

It's a hot, muggy afternoon. I'm in a full sweat before the car cools down on my way to the MGD house. The first week of school is over. I made it, and I can't wait to get my bid for the fraternity.

When I step through the giant doorway of the house, I feel like I'm home. A lot of the pledges have on Mu Gamma Delta shirts with a medical caduceus scrolled across the front. I stop to congratulate a couple of them.

A lot of the brothers I've talked to are here, but if I catch their eye, they won't look at me.

I spot Brandon in the crowd. He smiles and comes over my way. "Hey, David. How you doing?"

"Looking forward to a sick weekend." I grin.

His smile goes flat, and he leans in closer. "Listen, Dave… There's a bylaw here that if three brothers vote against a bidder, we can't let him in."

"It's just as well. Zane wasn't a good candidate."

He looks down and shifts his weight. "I know you're a legacy and all. I really wanted you in. I'm sorry."

His words float through the air like they're lost. My chest seizes. The black spots on the linoleum spin. I reach for the wall.

"Maybe you can try another house."

I stare at the floor, willing it to stop whirling. "There *is* no other house." It comes out thick, slower than I want.

"I'm sorry, man. I really tried. There's nothing I can do." Brandon takes my elbow to lead me to the entrance.

I follow along in numb silence. This can't be. They hate me enough to not let me in? Even as a legacy?

Robert slips away from a group he's talking to. He swings the door open wide, and a haze of humidity closes in around me, stifling my breath.

What am I going to do? It's too late to rush any other houses.

Robert nudges flat-headed Evan, who elbows some other dude. The guy looks at me and laughs.

I stop. They're the ones. But why? I don't get it.

"Come on, Dave." Brandon tugs on my elbow and steers me out into the street. "I'm sorry."

I force my feet to move, one step crashing after another, and follow the blur of gray on the sidewalk. The fraternity is everything—your friends, your dates, your ticket to med school. Your entire life. What am I going to do?

What's Dad going to say?

***

Shower, pizza delivered to my door, a beer, and I still don't feel better. What am I going to do if I don't have the frat? I wanted that extra boost to help me get into med school, even though most people say it's all about your grades. They don't want people like me.

Nobody wants me. I don't fit in anywhere.

My social media feeds show me how nice everyone else's lives are.

A shadow from outside darkens the room before the vulture lands on the windowsill. The darn thing is staring at my dresser. I wonder what it's thinking and how it got the scar under its right eye—another bird or ripping apart an animal? The thing is more alive than me. At least *it* can fly.

I close my blinds so I don't have to see it. My phone beeps with a text. It is Dad. Stellar. But I'm not talking to him. I know he's thinking that I was never going to make it anyway.

My hands are sticky when I put the phone down. I turn my attention back to the computer and stare at this year's football forecast, wondering what I'm going to say… eventually.

There are random YouTube videos of fraternity outings—parties with lots of girls and charity events with gorgeous women everywhere, guys doing insult contests.

The phone rings. There's no way I'm answering him.

But when I glance at the phone, my pulse quickens. Mom. How am I going to help her without the frat to help *me*? She encouraged it because she gets my struggle.

"Hi, Mom. What's up? How're you feeling?"

"We're getting ready for the game tomorrow. Your dad invited a bunch of people over."

"Are you okay to do that?"

"Today was a good day. I'll take it slow tomorrow. Did you get your ticket?"

A sigh slugs its way out of my lungs. "I don't have a ticket."

"I thought you'd go with some guys from the fraternity."

The pizza from an hour ago starts burning in my throat. I don't want to disappoint her. "Is Dad with you?"

"No, he's not golfing tomorrow so he can get set up for the football game. They went today. Why?"

I take a breath. "Because I didn't get into his fraternity."

"Oh, David." She gasps.

Silence.

My head pounds.

"What happened?" Mom asks.

I close my stinging eyes and put a cold hand over them.

"I got voted out. I know he didn't get into med school and it bothers him, but I couldn't even get into the frat."

"That must have been hard on you. I know you really wanted it."

I rub my thumb over the uneven edge of my desk. "Zane came to Rush 'cause I'd talked so much about it. He was hanging with me and pissed off some of the brothers. They got me kicked out."

"Can they do that?"

"All it takes is three guys to say they don't want you in, and nobody else can do anything about it." I pick at a loose thread on my shorts.

"I'm sure your father can do something. That's outrageous. You don't get in because someone else is a jerk?"

"I don't *want* Dad to do anything. It was the guy in charge of pledges who got me kicked out. If Dad makes a fuss and has them give me a bid, that tool would make my life miserable."

"I guess you can always join a different fraternity." Mom's tone sounds far away.

"It's too late. Rush ended." I tug on the thread. My shorts start to unravel.

"Zane is a disaster. You need to move."

"It's my fault, Mom."

"Did you invite him to Rush?"

"No, but if I hadn't said anything about it, he never would have shown up." The gap in the seam of my shorts widens, like the chasm between me and Dad. This was my only way to have something he'd like about me.

"Surely, you met other guys you got along with at MGD."

"Lots of them. The guy in charge of the pledges seemed to have it in for me, though. Maybe he would have blocked my bid even without Zane."

"I doubt it. You've got to do something to avoid being around that horrible creature you moved in with."

I want to tell her it's over-the-top cool being around someone who lives on the edge and can get a girl with a glance, when all I've done my whole life is follow the rules.

"The ogre that crawled out of a local cave is living with my son," I say.

Mom snorts. "Cut the innuendo about the school legend, Dave."

"His dad died, and I feel sorry for him. Yes, he made a stupid mistake, but I don't think he's all that bad."

"David, no matter how drunk you were, you'd never rob a liquor store."

No kidding. I'm too boring to do something that crazy. "You're right, Mom. So now I know to watch out for any dumb moves."

"You can still leave. I'm sure I could find a one-bedroom apartment somewhere. I have no problem paying for another place."

I crash onto my bed and grab my pillow to keep the light from my eyes. "And live by myself? Tucked away safely from all contact with people? Come on, Mom. It's bad enough I'm not in MGD."

"That's not what I meant." Her voice is jumpy.

"I'll be fine, Mom. Making decisions is what being an adult is all about, right? Isn't that what Dad always says?"

She doesn't answer.

"The complex here is huge. There are all kinds of guys I can meet out by the pool or in the gym."

A faint groan floats through the phone. "I hope you're right. I'll ease in the news about MGD to your father tonight, after he's had a couple of beers on the nineteenth hole."

"Thanks, Mom." I click the phone off, wishing I felt that sure.

Chapter 6

Zane bursts through the front door, then bolts to my room. His sun-bleached curls bounce with excitement. "I've got stupid good tickets for the game this weekend." He flashes them in my face.

I roll over in my bed, pretending I've been sleeping. "I don't want to go."

"What? Football is the best thing about this school. Well, that and the chicks."

I consider what I should say about the fraternity. They may not have liked me, but he really screwed me over. The dude knows how to get women, but he doesn't even realize he rubs people the wrong way.

"I'm not into it right now."

Zane leans over the desk. "Dude, you love football."

I look out the window at people having fun by the pool. "I got booted out of the fraternity."

He pivots my chair to sit on it backward. "Screw the fraternity. It's a bunch of snotty country club clones."

"Zane, you needed to be nice to the people there, not tell them off."

He snorts. "They were assholes."

I watch waves crashing against the side of the pool and feel like it's me being slammed into the walls. "You don't understand. My whole life I've heard stories about MGD.

'Mega Genuine Drafts,' Dad calls it. How much fun it is, the crazy parties… Mom said the associations could help me with getting into med school. But now, it's gone. I've failed."

"Who needs to buy their friends? You got me."

"Yeah, to help me rot in jail."

"Look out there." He points to the pool. "There are hundreds of horny girls out there. You can do a different one every night and still not do them all."

"You can, maybe. I couldn't even get a prom date." Movement from a bug dying on the floor catches my attention.

"Don't worry. I'll teach you. And I've got football tickets. I owe it to you. There's one catch, though." Zane kicks the bug into my closet, forcing me to look at him.

I'm afraid to ask. "What?"

"You have to forget about last weekend. Stop being mad."

How could I ever forget? I'm still pissed, but what else am I going to do? Everyone in the world is pledging.

"All right, man."

"I'm calling The Party Club to introduce them to a new member," he says, like there's someone else in the room. Zane digs out his phone and hits speed dial. "Come on over. I'm firing up the blender." He dials another number, says the same thing, and starts singing the Jimmy Buffet song about margaritas.

The quiet of the apartment is shattered by the loud *whir* of a blender. He leaves it running while he goes into his room. The noise is annoying. He left it on to make me get out of bed. I'm not giving in.

At long last, he turns off the blender. Someone hammers so hard on the door that it makes me jump.

Zane opens it. "Come on in," he yells.

A couple of guys I met at the last party march into the living room. Ian, a blond guy with big shoulders, stares at me on my bed.

"You can't get off your ass and answer the door when we knock you up?" he says with an Australian accent.

Zane laughs. Heat creeps to my face. I throw my legs off the bed, then dash to the living room.

"Sorry, I didn't hear you. The blender was on."

"So that these would be ready for you." Zane holds out a trifecta of red Solo cups. "And I've got some babes coming over for practice."

Everybody else laughs, which gets me off the hook.

I grab a hold of the frozen concoction. At least Zane is good for something.

"Step right up for your floater," he directs.

I follow them to the counter, where he grabs a handle of Tequila and pours another ounce on top of the margaritas.

"To the newest member of The Party Club." Zane slaps a sticker from a bottle of Tequila on me while he raises his glass.

"The official badge. What an honor." Ian laughs and lifts his glass, followed by the others.

I'm not in the mood, but I hold on to my drink, watching them slurp back the Tequila with mouthfuls of the frozen mix. These guys, like Zane, smell like weed. I didn't notice it at first. How can they smoke and study? I have enough trouble with memory and placement to have that affect me too.

Zane waves me away from the other guys and into the kitchen. "The girls will be here in a minute. Fix your hair. This is your chance."

"I never know what to say."

"Just ask questions and pretend you're interested in every little thing they say." He jabs me in the shoulder. "Stick your chest out and exude some confidence."

A girl pokes her head through the cracked front door, then marches in. Her friend follows behind her, and I lose the grip on my glass. The second girl's waist-length platinum blond hair flutters across her turquoise shirt when she walks. Her emerald eyes dance toward us, then dash away.

"Damn, she's hot," I mutter.

"You're just in time for another batch," Zane tells them. He dumps Tequila into the mixer.

I head over to help him, forcing myself not to stare. "That girl is sooo hot," I say breathlessly, dropping handfuls of ice into the blender.

"Elusive Lucy? I've been working on her for a while. She doesn't want me. She must be a lesbian."

I turn away to sneak another peek at her twinkling eyes and stunning curves. Where to start? I wish the words would roll off my tongue like they do off Zane's.

"That girl's definitely a smoke show," I whisper to Zane.

It goes unheard when he rekindles his stainless steel blender. I pour some green slush to take to the girls.

"Watch this." Zane grabs both glasses and does a butler bow to them. "Would you ladies like a nice topper for that?"

Lucy steps back. "It's good. Thanks."

"Dave, this is Rachael and Lucy."

"Hi." I stand straighter, remind myself not to stare. No words flow. I'm not feeling it today. Instead, I stay chill and take a seat on the couch.

"Come on, mate. You're falling behind there." Ian nods at my drink.

I look at the drink perched beside me. The Tequila would loosen the knot. I take a big gulp. The salt tingles on my tongue, and the sour tang glides down my throat.

Zane steps up by Lucy. "You're looking particularly fine tonight."

"Save it, dog breath." She hikes it over to sit by me.

Kind of aggressive. "That bite almost tore flesh, girl," rolls off my tongue.

She doesn't laugh.

Ugh. I blew it.

"Zane thinks every time I see him I should fall all over him, like the rest of the girls in this place. I don't know when he's going to learn that I'm not interested." She crosses her legs.

"That would've given me the hint."

Lucy giggles and adjusts her skirt. "It *was* a bit strong. He's such a creeper, but he's friends with Rachael. Mind if I use your bathroom? I don't want to be near his."

I grin, happy she likes the comment, and nod in the direction of my room, hoping the mess in it doesn't bother her. "Go right ahead."

After she gets up, Zane bends over from behind the couch, his head next to mine. "What did she say?"

I spin the margarita glass between my hands, wondering if I should tell him. "Nothing much."

"Gotta keep working on that one. I know this'll loosen her up." He takes a seat on the other end of the couch and then lights a bong.

Geez, that reeks. Maybe she doesn't like the smell either. Should I get up and talk to her in my room? Nah, that would be too obvious.

"Sure smells good." Lucy sits on the arm of the sofa next to me, avoiding the space beside Zane on the couch.

Glad I said nothing. Warmth radiates from her arm, down the length of her leg. The Tequila starts kicking in.

Zane gets up to pack and relight the pipe. He hands it to me and sits down closer, at an angle where he can see her. I pass the bong to Lucy.

"You first," she tells me.

I hesitate. "It's not my thing."

"It'll help you forget about the damn frat," says Zane.

I feel the crushing pain of rejection and picture the look on my father's face.

"He can't get up to open a door or get on with a bong," the Aussie says to his friend. "What's wrong with this guy?"

"He's a real rager, all right." Zane sniggers and leans in toward me. "C'mon, Rager."

Lucy's green eyes gaze into an empty space inside me. She wraps her hands around my faltering fist and turns it in my direction.

I raise the bong to my lips and breathe in. The smoke is sweeter than I'd imagined.

Chapter 7

"Hello?" I catch my phone on the last ring.

"David, it's Dad. We won't be able to make it to the game today. Your mother has some kind of stomach flu."

I bolt upright in bed. "Is she all right? Can I talk to her?"

"She's fine. It's just a stomachache. She's sleeping right now." He inhales slowly. "I heard about the fraternity."

I roll to the side and lock my feet on the floor, trying to focus on a ray of light peeking in through the blinds. "A couple of guys were kind of abrasive. I did my best to roll with it… but then Zane showed up. He pissed off the guy in charge of pledges."

"That was the preceptor, David. You don't talk back to him."

I want to say, *Yeah, you'd throw anyone under the bus.* I take a deep breath and tug at the sheets beside me. "I didn't. I tried to get Zane to leave."

"I knew this would happen." He breathes heavy through the speaker.

My stomach knots. "I'm doing fine, Dad, without the fraternity."

He sighs. "How are you going to get a decent date?"

"There are plenty of nice girls and functions around here, Dad."

"Where will you find a respectable function to attend? If you can find one at all?"

"There are games and concerts and lots of events around here."

"Right," Dad says. "How's school going?"

I stand up, spotting the psych quiz I got a B on, instead of the A I'd wanted. "Good." It comes out squeakier than I'd like. I hate myself for not staying on top of my grades.

"Don't mess up your chances for med school."

Like you did?

"At least your court date is the day before homecoming. I have to go. My tee time with the boys is in half an hour."

"What about Mom? You're playing golf when Mom's sick?"

"She's fine. She's asleep right now."

"Golf takes a long time. What if something happens while you're gone?"

"She's sleeping. Nothing is going to go wrong."

For you, maybe. I hang up and stare at the floor. He's such a dick. What if it happens again? The space around my room feels thick and heavy. I can't get my mind off Mom. I need some air.

When I step outside to the courtyard, there's no sun, and the air is heavy with humidity. I spot Maria beside the pool, in the shade of a couple of palm trees. The aqua water shimmers while I slide up a lounge chair.

A pink hibiscus flower grabs my attention. It's like Mom's favorite one at home. Pictures of her in a hospital bed roll through my head. I grip the chair tighter.

"What's bugging you?" Maria puts down her book.

"Nothing. Why?"

Maria's rich brown eyes radiate kindness. "I don't know. You look kind of sad."

My gaze wanders back to the pink flower. The image of Mom reappears, shriveled up in a wheelchair, her weakened voice commenting on the shape of the bud and the depth of its color. I nod toward the hibiscus.

"That's my mom's favorite flower. She asked me to plant a shrub just like that by her bedroom window when she was sick for a long time."

"What happened?" Maria's tone softens.

I hesitate.

I've known Maria forever, and she seems like she's the kind of person I can say anything to. Maybe because she's kind of plain.

"She got myasthenia gravis a while back. It's where not all the nerve signals get through to the muscles. She was holding on to things when she walked. Then her face drooped, and she had difficulty swallowing. She got so weak she was on a respirator from pneumonia."

Her feet sink to the ground. She lays her hand on my arm for a beat. "Yikes. That's scary. Is she better now?"

I slip my eyes away from Maria, back to the hibiscus. Dread seeps into my bones. "She is, but they said it could come back with extreme fatigue, a cold, or the flu."

"Come on, Rager. It's time to get your party on!" Zane yells from the doorway.

I wave my arm so he sees me, and he heads toward us.

"I really want to go to med school, Maria. The hospital here does a lot of research. I'm hoping they'll find something to help cure the disease she has."

"Maybe we'll have more classes together. I'm in indigenous studies, but I may change that to my minor and work toward nursing school." Maria smiles and lifts her brow.

I look at her book. "Is that what you're reading about?"

"No. I was reading about Zane."

"Huh?"

I glance behind her. He's almost in earshot.

Maria laughs and shifts the book from her lap. "It's by a psychologist who says you open yourself to possession with substance abuse."

"What? Like the Devil's coming into you?" I whisper.

"Not that harsh. More like a lost soul. Too much partying facilitates it. Zane would be a good candidate."

"For what?" Zane looms over her.

Maria straightens and clears her throat. "I was telling Dave you party too much."

Zane sets his jaw. He starts tapping his heel on the ground.

I leap out of my seat to stand between them. "A lot of people like to party, Maria. It's part of college life. You work hard, and you play hard."

Maria zeros in on him. "Don't get me wrong. I like to get out and have a few drinks too. But you, Zane, go overboard."

"You need to mind your own fucking business," Zane growls.

I want to tell her she is going overboard with this craziness, but I keep my mouth shut because I'm happy I had the chance to talk about Mom.

"Dave, let's go. Everybody's partying already," Zane says.

"See what I mean?" Maria asks. "I've got to go over something for my Spanish class before I leave to tailgate." She gathers her things.

We head for the apartment.

"I'll talk to you later," I say.

"What're you talkin' to that bitch for?" Zane snaps.

I square off against him. "She's got some weird thinking, but I've known her a long time, and she's in one of my classes."

"She thinks I'm in league with Satan."

"So do a lot of girls when you never call them back."

He grabs my shoulders. "She's a crazy religious freak. Stay away."

"Knock it off." I shake him loose.

Zane shoves his face toward me. "You need to ditch that bitch." He stomps to his bedroom, sandals slapping.

"You can't dictate to me. Give me five minutes to get ready for the game." I slam the bedroom door. My picture of a packed Eagles stadium clatters to the floor.

I towel off my hair after a quick shower. "Just putting my shirt on!" I grab a green shirt with a yellow Eagle emblem. "Okay, let's go."

Silence.

"Zane, you ready?"

I look in his room. The surf T-shirt and board shorts he was wearing are on the floor, and an empty hanger is on the bed. From the window, I can see that his truck is gone.

"I don't believe it." I grab the keys, then head to my car.

The traffic all but stops when I get closer to the stadium, cars bumper-to-bumper, inching along. The faces inside search for a place to park.

When I get to the road which'll take me to the tailgate spot I've heard him talk about, it's blocked off. So are the parking lots—all marked full. I look past the barricade and see Zane's truck, but everybody's gone.

A cop bangs on my window. "Move it along, buddy. You can't stop here."

The crowd roars from the stadium. I'm the sap on the outside.

"Damn it." I smack the steering wheel, then head back home.

The courtyard's deserted. I walk by the clubhouse to see

if anyone is watching the game there. The lights are out. There's not a soul in the building. It's completely dead.

Dragging myself into the apartment, I flop onto the couch, and stare at the blank TV screen.

I never thought college could be this lonely. I need to listen to Zane.

***

A week's gone by since I missed out on the game. I haven't met anybody, I have nothing to do, and I bombed the first test I've had in this place. My life sucks.

I slam the test paper on the desk, then bury my head in my pillow. "C+ in History. Ugh." Why do we have to memorize dates? Facts are important. Dates suck. I'll have to work twice as hard to bring this grade up.

After hurling the pillow at a wall, I grab the test and rip it to shreds. Maybe I should have stayed home and gone to FAU. I would hate being stuck with my grumpy dad for four more years, but at least I wouldn't be so lonely.

A girl in a red bikini saunters past my window. I tell myself to suck it up, that I don't need Zane to create a party. Hot women in tiny bikinis will cheer me up.

I head for a lounger on the far side of the pool, where she has joined a group of girls. What would Zane do?

I tug off my shirt and lie back in the chair. "Hello, ladies."

Red Bikini rolls the other way. Her friend beside me opens a political science textbook.

There's a jab in my chest. Ouch. This is not only embarrassing; it's not fair that she can study with all this noise around, when I need silence so I don't get distracted.

I search the courtyard for Ian, Jack, or any guy I've seen with Zane so I can strike up a conversation. The only thing familiar is the stupid vulture that's always clicking its tongue from the craggy oak tree.

I flip over and watch a trail of ants follow each other across the concrete, down into the dirt. *They've* got someone to hang out with. While I watch them trek along, the warm sun lulls me to sleep.

***

A sharp jolt against my chair forces my eyes open.

"Dude, whatcha doing sleeping on a day like this?"

When I roll over, my reflection in the clubhouse window shows red strips across my entire body. They look like prison stripes, like I'm imprisoned in solitary confinement, where Zane is my only friend.

"Dude, you took off without me for the game, then disappeared for days," I say. "You've got a skills issue there."

"I live in the moment, man. That's the way it is."

"Bullshit. Next time, if you can't wait a few minutes for a shower, tell me before I get in it."

"Fine." Zane peels off his shirt, then drops it on the chair beside me. He's sandy and two shades darker.

"Where'd you find sand around here?"

"I went surfin', bro. The hurricane that went up to Carolina left insane swells. I checked the surf cam and took off. Crashed with one of my high school buddies. We were out there at first light. Best way to spend my birthday ever."

"It's your birthday? I thought you were just out with one of your skanks last night." I check over my shoulder to make sure no one heard me.

"No way, man. Don't you remember Zane's hierarchy of needs? Surf first, party second, babes third. The rest is… whatever."

I try to think about something to do for his birthday.

The broad shadow of the vulture circles over the courtyard. It lands on the back of a chair about thirty feet away. I've never seen it this close before. It creeps me out.

Zane jumps into the pool, then hops out in front of the girls. He looks at the bird and flicks his head. It's an odd move. I wonder what he's up to.

"Hello, ladies. Looks like you're really workin' the color today," Zane says.

"Not as good as you." Red Bikini flashes a smile.

The vulture squats, and with a grunt, it takes flight. The chair topples to the deck with a bang, and the bird flaps toward the girls.

The other girls duck, but Red Bikini has her back to it.

The bird extends its claws.

"Watch out!" I yell.

The girl screams when a wing brushes her shoulder and the bird grabs the strings behind her neck.

I rush to shoo it away, but I trip, hitting the deck like bird shit.

Her bikini top falls to her lap when the bird takes off.

The girl's face is as red as her bikini while she scrambles to reattach the strings.

Guys around the pool burst out laughing. I don't know if it's at me, at her, or both.

Zane tries to help her, even though she has it tied. "You make a hot mermaid."

"Really?" she asks.

I can't see her well enough to tell if that means she's ready to slug him or if she liked what he said.

Zane leans in so they're shoulder to shoulder. "We need to talk about love at first swim."

She giggles. "I like the sound of that."

How does he do it? Two corny lines and she's ready to jump his bones. Meanwhile, I'm over here with skinned knees and my ego splayed on the pavement. I don't even get a glance of pity.

"Have you met my roommate, Dave?" he says to the friend beside her.

The two girls swap glances. My lounge chair's prison stripes darken. I grab my shirt and hold it in front of my face, taking extra time to find the armholes.

"We heard you snoring over there," a girl down the line says.

I slip the shirt over my head and give a weak grin. She must be the nice one.

"I'm thinking that we need to get a little party going here tonight." Zane gives me a thumbs-up behind his back.

"I hear ya," Red Bikini agrees. "Problem is, I went through this week's funds already."

"Mine are pretty bad too," the nice one says.

I think about the credit card from my parents, the harassing they'll give me. But it is Zane's birthday, and I need some homage paid to me. I leap out of the chair, standing tall next to Zane.

"If you can get a keg, I'll spring for it."

That'll make them look at me differently.

Chapter 8

The shelves at the school bookstore, overflowing with school supplies a couple of weeks ago, have been filled with stacks of caps, T-shirts, and mugs. The sweet smell of cocoa floats from a rack of chocolate bars.

"That's one hundred and forty dollars." The clerk drops a thick text on the counter in front of me with a *bang*.

I flinch, my mind returning to Saturday morning—the stench of a mound of undigested pizza all over my physics textbook and notes, the room spinning. Why did I buy that keg? What if the judge finds out I bought it? How could I be so stupid?

"Do you have any used textbooks?"

"Nope. They're long gone."

My mouth dries. I glance at the stacks of shelves behind him. The book I found online will take two weeks to get here. I hand over the credit card. Dad's going to freak.

I breeze along the gray concrete sidewalk outside the bookstore. Maria's familiar figure is ahead of me, in a pair of wide linen pants and a white, V-neck tee.

"Maria, are you going to physics?" I call out, remembering what the LD coordinator said about following people to where I need to go.

"New textbook?" she asks.

"I puked all over my old one on Saturday night. I had to throw it away."

She laughs so hard she has tears in her eyes. "Your notebook too?" She eyes the new blank pages.

"Yeah." The brick in my throat about telling my parents returns.

"Partying is Zane's solution to everything. Did he tell you the pot will show in your bloodwork for thirty days?"

My lungs spasm.

The judge.

My heart pounds. How could I be so stupid? Will I go to jail?

"Wait," I said. "How did you know that? You weren't there."

"Sometimes, I just know things."

"What do you mean?"

"I get a strong feeling, such as the judge saying you shouldn't smoke or drink."

Goosebumps rise on my arms. I haven't told anyone what the judge said.

"You're guessing."

"It's more than that. Sometimes, things pop into my head. Even things I may not want to know."

"What, are you psychic or something?"

"I don't know if that's what you call it. That's part of why I'm taking religious and indigenous studies. To figure it out."

I sigh, not knowing what to say. Zane warned me about her.

Maria turns at a crosswalk, and I follow, glad I can tag along with her and not get lost.

"What'd you do this weekend?"

"I went to church in Saint Augustine. I'm taking a class about the history of religion. My professor raved about the basilica. She said we'd get extra credit for going to the old chapel."

"Did you like it?"

"It was nice. I love the architecture in big churches. The most interesting thing was a conversation I overheard."

"About what?"

The broad shadow of a vulture blocks the sun for a beat. The bird swoops into a tree beside the physics building. Could it be the same one from our courtyard? Do those things have a territory?

I squint to see its markings.

"What are you staring at?" Maria asks.

"That's the vulture from our apartment building. It has a scar under its right eye."

She looks at the bird and keeps on talking, like it's nothing.

"The Vatican is increasing the number of exorcists being trained because requests have tripled to more than half a million a year in Italy alone. For some reason, problematic entities are getting into people. The entities are cunning and clever, so the priests are being trained on how to deal with them."

This stuff is bizarre. Zane is right about her. I don't know if it's her talking points or the bird, but I feel all crawly.

"That's weird," I say, unsure how to respond.

The vulture is staring at us.

"It's not as strange as that thing following you around."

I shiver, even though it's ninety degrees outside. "I wonder why it's here."

"I don't know, but we're studying the Sumerians in my class." Maria pushes forward like she has intel that will expire.

"Who?"

"Guys in the Bible who believed that all disease was caused by evil spirits." She scans my face.

I'm not sure of any of this, so I don't give her anything to work on.

"They had two kinds of doctors," Maria continues. "One applied splints and salves, and the other rid people of unwanted hitchhikers—or spirits—that were causing them problems."

This girl is so frigging strange. I wish I'd stayed in the bookstore longer.

"Sounds like you could do a paper on the whole thing." I yank on my backpack's zipper, but it's stuck.

"I'd rather do fieldwork on Zane."

"What?" The zipper unlocks and flies open. It catches my fingernail, tearing it off at the quick.

She swings around to face me. "I think his *you only live once* philosophy makes him a prime target for attachment through his partying."

Here we go again blows through my mind. I shove the new books into my backpack. "Be real, Maria. That stuff doesn't happen."

"Then why did the church start a class to teach it?"

"So some poor priest stuck in a third-world country can pretend he's doing voodoo with his unruly parishioners."

The vulture starts its *chkk-chkk-chkk* sound.

"Americans are learning the ritual. Apparently, you talk to the trapped entity and tell it to leave."

"That's insane. Why would you ever want to do something like that?" The creepy feeling snakes its way under my skin again.

"It's why I took this class. I want to prove my theory of what happened to my cousin before he died."

He probably jumped off a bridge to get away from her. I'm sick of the weird shit around here.

"Get lost." I wave my arms at the vulture.

The bird hurls itself off the branch and swoops, with its black wings spread wide, toward me. Its gray legs thrust forward, black claws extending.

"Look out!"

Maria ducks but steps in the path of the bird.

It grabs her hair.

She screams.

I shove it away, and the vulture takes off.

"Are you all right?" a girl nearby asks.

Maria is as white as a ghost. The girl picks up notebooks covered in rivers and trees, which are scattered on the ground. She puts them in Maria's thick canvas bookbag.

"Yes. Thank you." Maria pants. "It scared me." She fetches her purse, then drops it into the bag.

"No kidding. I don't think it was after you, though," the girl says. "It wanted him."

***

I'm working at my desk when my phone lights up.

Dad.

I close my laptop and go to the window. It'll make me feel better to check out the eye candy at the pool while he lectures me about my upcoming court case.

"Hi, Dad."

"I called to let you know that we'll be leaving early tomorrow morning."

No *Hello, how are you?* Typical Dad. "Mom's doing all right?"

"She's fine. We should be there by eleven, and we can go for lunch. That way, if there are traffic problems, we can still be at the courthouse by one o'clock."

"Gotcha."

"E-mail your professors and tell them that you have a family matter you need to attend to with your parents."

"Will do." I swallow. Man, I'm dreading tomorrow.

Dad clears his throat. Something bad is coming next.

"What are these charges on your credit card, David? One is a hundred and forty dollars. The other is almost as much."

A flush of heat zips through my face. "I uh… had to buy a new physics book."

"It's an awfully expensive one. I thought you got all your books at the beginning of the semester?"

His voice is tighter. It's making me nervous. I've never lied to him.

I hope he doesn't back me into a corner.

"I did."

"What happened to your other one?"

"I, uh… It fell in the pool." I glance at the women sitting poolside and spot Lucy. My heart races. "I was studying outside, and I put it down on the edge. The pages were all wrinkled up. Then the binding fell apart 'cause it was old to begin with. I had to throw it out."

Dampness forms in circles under my eyes.

"Now you're throwing away textbooks? What about the other hundred plus?"

I don't have an excuse. There is nothing legit to tell him.

"It looks like it's from a liquor store," he says.

Now I know there's no getting out of it. "I bought a keg, but other people gave me cash, so I won't have to use the card for any food next week." I lie, thinking I can score some free pizza outside the student building on Tuesday.

"What do you think you're doing? That credit card is not for kegs. Don't you think that this lawyer is enough of a financial burden?"

His voice is loud. It pounds in my ears with the sound of my heart.

I touch the quick of my finger, healing from the zipper tear the day I bought the book. "I know. Sorry."

"Well, straighten up. You need to be more responsible, young man. We'll call you tomorrow when we get off the highway."

"Okay." I hang up and toss my phone onto the kitchen countertop.

"You look thrilled," says Zane from the hall.

"That was my dad, reminding me about our stupid court date."

"Damn, he's all over you. I still haven't met my lawyer."

My legs go numb, and I grab the countertop. "I thought you saw him two weeks ago?"

"That was when the waves were really good, so I canceled."

"And you didn't reschedule?"

"The guy's been calling me, but I don't really like to think about it."

"Mark Solter said it takes a month or more to gather documents. I'm screwed."

"We're not being tried together. You'll be fine," Zane says with such nonchalance I can't stand it.

The reaming from my dad, the ruined book, and my bad grades that the lawyer said to keep up all come screaming at me. I slam my fist against the countertop.

"Eff you. My ass is on the line. You're out surfing and partying. *I'm* the one who'll get thrown under the bus."

Zane opens the fridge and shoves in a fresh case of beer. "Dude, you're spiraling. Relax."

Chapter 9

I try to quiet my nerves while Mom, Dad, and I climb the courthouse steps toward the giant columns guarding the threshold like sentinels. A nearby church bell rings on the three-quarter hour. *Gong*—will Solter get me out of this? *Gong*—will this ruin my chances for med school? *Gong*—if Solter bombs, will I go to jail? The sound shakes me to my core.

We slip past the heavy oak doors.

Inside, the same cold radiates from the polished gray stone as it did from the damp concrete walls of the jail. I shiver when I hand over my wallet and belt to go through security. We're all so wound up no one speaks.

Zane is nowhere in sight, causing the burger from lunch to rise higher in my stomach.

I spot Solter down the hall, wearing the same pinstriped suit from when I first met with him, and hope his erasable pen get-up works.

"David. Mr. and Mrs. Everest, I presume. I'm glad you're here to show support. This should be straightforward, with few ramifications." He does a quick handshake with each of us.

The muscles around my throat tense. He said *few* rather than *no* ramifications.

Mom is rocking from foot to foot. "Is David dressed appropriately? I brought a suit for him."

"We've been assigned a good judge who is fair and evenhanded with people. David looks like a student should, in his dress shirt and slacks. All will be fine if everyone shows the judge respect in his courtroom. We are the first case this afternoon. That's to our benefit."

Solter swings open the door of a large courtroom with a granite backdrop behind the bench. He leads us down the center aisle, past dozens of people.

"Mr. and Mrs. Everest, you can sit here." He indicates the first pew-like row. "David, we're upfront." He holds a short swinging door open for me.

There are two four-foot oak tables side by side on the left and an eight-foot table with four seats on the right. Solter points to the second seat on the left. He takes the far end.

The sour smell of sweat mixes with heavy layers of cologne, making me wonder what other people are trying to cover up.

How did I ever get here?

Officer Gallow appears and sits opposite my parents. The prosecutor arrives with the shopkeeper. They take a seat at the eight-foot table.

Thin, dark, clumpy hair and deep frown lines make the prosecutor look mean. I think about the number of people he must have put away and swallow hard, trying to fix the sudden dryness in my throat.

A young guy in a charcoal suit, white shirt, and blue tie pushes open the gate.

"Is that Zane?" Solter whispers.

"No. He looks younger than Zane. Could Zane have hired a student?"

"Must be a new grad. A student would need an attorney with him."

The guy goes to the four-foot table to our right. He sits

in the chair closest to me and gives Solter a nod. The bailiff, the clerk, and the court reporter are all ready to go.

I check over my shoulder. Still no Zane.

"Your friend *is* planning to be here today, isn't he?" Solter asks.

"He told me he was going to be here. And he's not my friend. I'm stuck living with him."

Zane's attorney coughs. He re-arranges the papers he brought with him.

Zane better be here because I don't know what will happen if he doesn't show up. I wipe my damp hands on my pants and check my phone: 12:59.

Solter lowers his voice. "Make sure that thing is off."

"Yes, sir. It is."

Solter drums his fingers against the table. "That kid needs to get here."

Zane's attorney seems panicked. His fingers fly across his phone screen.

A guy in uniform tells everyone to rise.

"Wait, my client…" Zane's lawyer waves at the bailiff.

Dread chokes my throat. I check the doorway one more time.

No Zane.

"The Honorable James G. Richards presiding."

The judge's black robes flutter behind a quick step to his bench. With his silver-streaked hair and kind face, resembles a minister. I hope he's as forgiving.

"You may be seated," he says.

His voice is so deep it's scary. I glance at the doorway again and tuck my fingers under my legs.

The courtroom stills when loud, slapping footsteps echo off the bare granite walls. I spot Zane running down the aisle in flip-flops, buttoning his shirt. His hair is wet and three shades darker. He has plastered it straight down on his head, eliminating all the curl.

"Unbelievable," mumbles Solter.

My fingers grind into my chair. What is Zane trying to pull? I want to yell at him for being late, for putting me, my family, and especially Mom through all of this.

Solter shoots me a glance while Zane's attorney ushers him into his seat.

"I should hold you both in contempt." The judge says to Zane and his lawyer.

"I apologize, Your Honor." The young guy is still standing. He locks his hands together behind his back.

I wonder if it is to keep them from trembling.

"Sit down," the judge says.

The attorney drops into his seat.

I stare at Zane, with his slicked-down hair. He winks at me and grins. Will I get nailed for his stupidity again? I straighten and face front, not daring to move.

Solter starts drawing circles on his notes.

Judge Richards opens a file and scans the first page. "The state has charged David Everest with being an accessory to theft and the possession of alcohol under the legal age. The prosecution may begin."

The heavy-set man in a navy suit steps up to a podium near his table. His frown lines deepen. "The afternoon of August twentieth, Greenville Police Department received a call at 5:43 p.m. that a theft involving two bottles of Jose Cuervo Tequila had occurred at Last Buck Liquor. The store clerk stated he had seen the alleged thief get into a silver Honda Civic and the vehicle made a right turn out of the parking lot onto Arch Avenue. David Everest was arrested at 5:48 p.m. on Arch Avenue, a mile from Last Buck Liquor. Two bottles of Jose Cuervo Tequila were found in his vehicle, along with an empty can of Hell energy drink. There was a receipt from Last Buck Liquor for the energy drink only.

My ears pound. This *has* been hell. I hope Solter's defense works.

The judge nods to the prosecutor, who clears his throat. "The prosecution calls Donald Martin to the stand."

The smell of stale liquor follows the shopkeeper when he walks past, then gets sworn in.

"A blond kid came in the store and asked me for this new energy drink called Hell that we got in. I had to go hunt for it. When he was pulling open the door, I saw the profile of two bottles under his shirt. I ran outside and saw him getting into a Honda Civic. I got the license number, then called the police."

The prosecutor turns away from the witness stand to face us. "Is that person in the courtroom now?"

The shopkeeper points at Zane. "That's him. His hair looks different, but I recognize the scar by his mouth."

Zane twitches in his chair. I study the judge's face for clues. The prosecutor asks the store clerk a few more questions.

The judge motions to Solter and says, "He's up."

Solter walks to the stand. "Mr. Martin, since we've established that David Everest was not in your shop, do you have video evidence that he was at Last Buck Liquor that day?"

"The video camera broke the week before and wasn't fixed yet. So, no, I don't."

"Did you get a look at the driver at all?"

"No. I only saw the car before they took off."

Solter backs away. "No further questions, Your Honor."

"The prosecution calls Officer William Gallow to the stand."

Gallow settles in.

"We got notification of a robbery, with a description, and we were only a couple blocks away. After pulling over the suspects, we found two bottles of Jose Cuervo Tequila in the back of the silver Honda Civic with license R2M 0T1. The driver's license stated that David Everest, the driver, was under the legal drinking age, and the passenger had no ID."

The prosecutor clears his throat. "Is the driver of that car here today?"

"He is right there." Gallow points at me.

I wonder how that can be fair since I'm the only other person at the table. The prosecutor sits, and Solter gets up, tenting his hands in front of him as if to hold in his ideas.

"Was David Everest cooperative when he was in your custody, Officer Gallow?"

"Yes, he was."

"Did he give you any indication that he was ever in the liquor store?"

"No, sir."

"Thank you, Officer Gallow. No further questions, Your Honor." Solter nods at me when he sits back down. "Going good. You're up now," he whispers.

"The defense calls David Everest to the stand."

My legs are rubbery. I take the oath. When I look up, I feel like a goldfish that's been dumped in a bowl. Sweat trickles in slow motion down my back. My gaze stops on my mother's worried face.

She fakes a smile.

Guilt seeps in like an IV infusion. I'm sorry, Mom.

Mark Solter lifts his chin and gives everyone a big smile. "David, how did you come to know Zane Maddox?"

"I decided to come to the University of Mann at the last minute. I needed a roommate, and a friend of a friend knew Zane."

"Did you talk to him before you arrived?"

"I contacted him through Eaglechat."

"What happened on August twentieth?"

I take a deep breath and remind myself to just chill. "I got into Greenville in the afternoon and went to the apartment, but it was locked. I found Zane at the pool. He asked me to drive him to the liquor store for this hard-to-find energy drink they had. I stayed in my car and talked to my dad on the phone. Driving back to the apartment, the police pulled us over. That's when I found out he'd stolen the Tequila."

"You had no idea there was a theft occurring in the store?"

Are you crazy? I would've left him there. "No, sir. None."

Solter steeples his fingers in front of his chest. "When you found out the liquor was stolen, what did you do?"

"I yelled at him."

Someone laughs from the rear of the courtroom.

"Were you aware of Zane Maddox's intentions while you waited outside the liquor store?"

"He said he wanted an energy drink, not Tequila."

"How long had you known Zane Maddox when he entered the liquor store?

"A little over twenty minutes."

"Did you know that Zane Maddox was seventeen years old at any time before he entered the store?"

"No."

"Thank you." He turns to the judge. "No further questions, Your Honor."

I look at Mom. She nods approval.

The prosecutor comes toward me. "David Everest, were you at Last Buck Liquor on August twentieth?"

"I was in the parking lot."

"Did you enter the liquor store at any time?"

"No."

"At what point did you learn that the liquor was stolen?"

"As the cop was pulling me over, right before he came to the driver's side window."

"But you drove Zane Maddox to a liquor store *knowing* he was not of legal drinking age."

"I just met him. I didn't know that."

"You had both been drinking. You wanted to continue, and you drove him there so you could keep partying. You were aiding and abetting a minor, and you knew it."

My throat tightens. I don't know what to do, so I gawk at Solter.

"Stop!" Zane jumps up. "I did it."

His lawyer grabs his arm and drags him back into the seat, hissing into Zane's ear. The attorney stands. "Your Honor, will the court take a recess so that I may speak with the prosecution?"

The judge checks Zane out, whose eyes and mouth are downturned like a misbehaved child. "The court will take a five-minute recess." His gavel slam makes me jump.

I glance at Solter. He looks at the bailiff, who motions me off the stand.

"Take a break. Talk to your family. We'll be fine," Solter tells me when I'm back at the table.

When the judge leaves and the prosecutor and the other attorney huddle, I go to see my parents. Mom is blanched, and Dad red-faced.

"Solter says we're still okay," I tell them.

"I hope so," Dad says. "I'm looking forward to a double whiskey after this."

I laugh, fishing around for something to say. "Are you warm enough, Mom?" I rub her back.

"Are you kidding? I'm sweating after that," she replies.

"I thought I was the only one." I check for sweat marks on the armpits of my shirt.

"Did the judge look really mad up close?" Mom asks.

"He wasn't happy with Zane's outburst, that's for sure."

Dad looks toward the bench. "Hopefully, this is over soon, and we can all move on."

I swallow hard and nod in agreement, then check out the other people in the courtroom. "I'm glad we got to go first. I'd hate to be waiting all afternoon in here."

Dad jingles the change in his pocket. "That's the privilege of having counsel that's paid for."

"Thanks, Dad." I do appreciate it, but he never misses a chance to make a dig.

"They're back." Mom uses her elbow to discreetly point at Zane, his attorney, and the prosecutor settling into their seats. "Good luck." She gives my arm a squeeze, and I return to my seat next to Solter.

The judge and everybody else gets settled before the prosecutor starts. "The State is dropping the charges against David Everest for accessory to theft, Your Honor."

Relief floods in.

The judge looks at me. "Mr. Everest, if you will accept the charge of being a minor in possession of alcohol and choose to do one hundred hours of community service, I will have this incident expunged from your record."

Solter smiles and nods.

"Yes, Your Honor. Thank you." I turn and grin at Mom and Dad. "He did it."

Mom claps her hands silently.

"What's going to happen to Zane?" I ask Solter.

"The judge will probably call the juvenile system, and they'll decide what to do."

I can't stop grinning, but I feel bad about Zane. "Should we wait for him?"

"His attorney, the prosecutor, and the judge may want to

figure out some things. I'll follow up with the return of the bail monies and send you the receipt. We need to clear out of here so they can set up for the next case." He opens the little gate and shoos me into the aisle.

Mom and Dad are already on their way. I look back at Zane.

"Do you think they'll let me talk to him a second?"

"Go find out." Solter forges ahead with his long stride.

I walk back toward the tables. The judge is talking with a sheriff's deputy while Zane, his attorney, and the prosecutor wait.

I lean over the fence. "Hey, man… thanks."

Zane meets my gaze with nonchalance. "I take care of my friends."

Chapter 10

"Hi, David," Mom yells over the background noise. "Are you coming to the fraternity house to eat? There's a big buffet."

I don't want to go, but I don't want to leave her stuck with Dad when the liquor starts to make him stupid and obnoxious.

Dad's laugh echoes in the background. It's the wild giggle he gets when he's had too much to drink. The phone clunks.

"That you, David?"

Dad must have grabbed it away. It pisses me off when he does that to her.

"Hey, Dad. I want to make sure you're behaving yourself with your old fraternity brothers."

"We're having a great time." Dad's words are loose. He's had a few.

"I'm calling because you said you wanted me to come over there for dinner."

"Did I say that?" He pauses. "Well, you don't have to."

My chest tightens. He's having second thoughts.

"It's just a bunch of us old guys. You probably wouldn't have any fun."

He doesn't want me. I want to see Mom. After all, I'm the one she came up here for, not Dad's friends.

I do a lap around the couch.

I can't go there. I'd have to face Robert and the entire pledge class who *did* get in.

I open the fridge. The only thing in it is beer. "Can I talk to Mom a minute?"

"No problem," Dad hollers.

"David, they have a great spread here. Come get something to eat." Mom's voice strains above the crowd.

"I don't know, Mom. It sounds like Dad doesn't want me to."

She clears her throat. "Of course he does. He's just preoccupied with his friends."

Zane comes down the hall, opens the fridge, then cracks open two beers. One pops loud, spraying the kitchen wall. "Just like champagne." He laughs and hands it to me.

"What's that, David? It's loud in here. Come join us!" Mom shouts.

The front door swings open. Ian and Jake, each with a case of beer under an arm, precede six hot-looking girls in tight shorts and T-shirts, carrying bottles of vodka and Tequila.

"Mom?" I rub the hollow of my cheek that's never grown any hair. "Would you mind if I catch up with you tomorrow?"

"We'd love to see you, David, but I understand." The disappointment in her voice sends a wave of guilt across my chest.

I wonder if I've done the right thing. It's obvious Dad doesn't want me.

"Thanks, Mom." I end the call and take a long pull on the beer.

***

There's a sea of green and yellow on U of Mann Drive the next day. We flow with the tide toward the stadium, excitement rising with each step. The game's sold out. It's going to be awesome.

Dad was too hung over to tailgate. We had lunch by ourselves, but Key Lime House was packed, and we are running late. I am happy that I get to spend time with Mom, but I feel like a loser sitting with the alumni.

The street is closed to traffic, and there is no shade. Waves of heat waft from the pavement. While we weave along the packed sidewalk, a man steps out of a rickshaw. He reaches over for his young son, face streaked green, hair the color of carrots.

I stop to make room for him on the curb.

The boy looks at me with eager eyes. "I wanna go to school here too. I wanna be a doctor," he announces while his father tips the runner.

I feel his excitement, remembering the trips with my dad at that age. "Me too." I laugh.

He holds up his hand. I give him five and step off the curb, jogging up to my parents.

"It was nice of you to stop for that little boy." Mom smiles.

"I didn't want to plow him over."

"He cares more about a stranger than his legacy," Dad mumbles to Mom.

"Knock it off, Frank," she says.

We jostle forward with the crowd, and I try not to think about the dig. When I get into med school, his tune will change.

Dad plucks out his tickets when we reach the booth. "Couldn't you find student tickets from somebody?"

My jaw tightens. "Not this time." I shift my gaze over

the mass of people funneling into the stadium and spot Brandon with some other house officers. Something thumps my chest, in the cavern that had once held MGD.

We stop for a jam-up at the base of the stairs. Dad lifts his sunglasses to wipe his face. His eyes are still red and glassy.

"I need some water before I climb those steps. Want some?"

Mom and I nod. She fans herself with her program. I spot Maria, in a tight Eagles T-shirt and bright green shorts, picking her way through the crowd.

Mom sees me looking. "That's a cute girl."

True, but she's a party-pooper. Should I wave Maria over, or will Mom think she's another freak living way too close to me?

"She lives in my complex. You might not like her. Her ideas on religion are… different."

Maria spies me and slips out of the crowd to join us. "Hey, David. You melt yet?"

"Hi, I'm David's mom, Lynn," Mom interjects with an outstretched hand before I can introduce them. "David says you live in the same apartment complex."

"I'm across the courtyard." Maria's hand connects.

"So, you know his roommate." The corners of Mom's mouth turn down.

"Zane is a piece of work. I've been trying to enlighten Dave about him."

"I tried everything but a crowbar to get him to find a new roommate." Mom looks at me sideways.

"See? I didn't need to move, Mom. There are lots of nice people around."

Mom puts her foot on the bleacher, then leans toward me. "Except the bad apple *just happened* to fall out of his tree next to you."

"Now, *there's* an expression." Maria grins. "Personally, I think Zane is a bit crazed."

"Crazed enough to require treatment?" Mom says hurriedly.

"Not quite that crazy, but close." Maria smirks.

Mom is wide-eyed. She locks her gaze on me.

"You're only saying that because you used to date him," I say, hoping to calm Mom.

Maria frowns. "Not for long. I'm saying it because I got duped by Zane's charismatic, impulsive behavior, and I don't want you to be."

Mom's attention returns to Maria. "David said you're interested in religion?"

"I'm studying religious traditions of indigenous cultures and how they're pertinent in our world view."

"What faith do you follow?"

"I don't particularly have one at the moment."

"Oh." Mom fans herself faster with her program.

Maria lifts the hair off the back of her neck, then knots it on top of her head. "I need to get some water."

"I hear ya. Good to see you." I grin.

Maria winks at me, then merges back into the crowd.

Mom does a little sigh.

"Are you all right?" I turn to face her.

"I'm getting hot, that's all," Mom says, fanning at full speed. "I don't know how the players manage when it's over ninety degrees out here."

Dad returns while I am watching Maria stride into the tunnel. "Here's your water. Let's go," he says.

Maria's hips move in a sexy sway I never noticed before. With my eyes still on her, I stick my hand out for the water and miss. Dad drops it on Mom's foot. I lurch forward to grab the water from the steps.

After catching my breath, I stand up to deep, deliberate sniggers. Making their way to the student side are Robert and his mousy friend, with a bunch of guys wearing MGD logo shirts.

Dad spots them, and his face broadens. He opens his mouth to say something, then looks at me.

I dig around for the courage to meet his gaze but don't quite muster it.

Embarrassment crosses his face, his mouth shuts tight, and he walks on.

The echo of cruel laughter rings through my ears. I'm done feeling bad I that didn't get in. I hate the frat.

We climb the stairs to our seats. The stadium is packed. Dad spots his frat boys waving at him ten rows up. They're mostly balding and overweight. Every one of them is in an Eagles jersey.

Dad surges ahead, files down a row in front of them, and sit next to a guy who looks familiar. I'm on the end, farthest away. Good.

I glance across the stadium, wondering where Zane and Ian are sitting.

"Hey, Frank, Lynn. Good to see you," a guy in front of me says.

There's a row of them there too. I'm surrounded. Great.

Kilometer, the Eagle mascot, is on the field, working the crowd.

"Yellow!" The students on the sunny side of the stadium chant for the animated mascot.

His female counterpart spurs the alumni side.

"Green!" forty thousand of us scream, sending a ripple across a bottle of water someone left on the floor.

"Yellow!" The noise comes at us like the reverberating footsteps of a monster.

We return it. The sound travels faster until the thunderous

volume of ninety thousand ecstatic fans shakes the concrete bowl like an earthquake. The team runs onto the field. A thrill courses up my spine when a roar from the crowd escalates to one giant, undulating scream. It permeates every inch of my body. I laugh when a little girl across the aisle covers her ears.

College football is the best thing ever. This is why I'm here.

"We won the toss. We're on the move." Dad's voice quickens. "We've got to score right away." He's all smiles.

The ball gets down to the end zone fast, with the quarterback passing to the wide receiver for a touchdown. Screaming high-fives abound. Dad's slapping the hands of everyone in the rows in front of and behind us.

He's so happy at these games. His mood has done a one-eighty, and he's like a kid again.

The Eagles maneuver the ball down the field in bits. The quarterback fakes a pass and runs it in.

My arms fly up. "Touchdown!"

Dad hugs Mom. There's a tangle of arm slapping all around us.

"Damn, it's hot," Dad moans.

"It doesn't matter. We're ahead," I yell above the crowd.

He raises his hand for a bump. We connect. I love everything about football.

As halftime approaches, Mom looks like she's wilting.

"Are you all right in this heat, Mom? I can go get water."

"I'm going to the men's room. I'll get it." Dad pushes past me, then heads down the aisle.

I watch my chance to escape for a few minutes descend into the tunnel.

"Hey, David," an unfamiliar male voice says from behind me.

My back muscles tighten, thrusting me upright. How

does this guy know my name? I know the regulars. I've seen them all my life. This is someone new.

I turn the best I can within the tight bench seating. "Hi." I extend my hand.

This guy has hair, and it's still brunette-colored. This, along with his normal weight, makes him appear much younger than the rest. His palm connects.

"I'm Doug Foley, Brandon's dad."

My muscles relax. His face is kind, his smile genuine. He seems to be decent, like his son. "Nice to meet you, Dr. Foley. Brandon's a nice guy."

"Thanks. How's school going for you?"

"It's going well. Thanks for asking."

"You're not going to flunk out like the old man, are you?" the dude next to him blurts.

I don't recognize him either. He's round and balding, with a face covered in faded acne scars.

"Figured I'd try something new." Sweat runs down the inside of my leg and puddles under my foot.

"What, you don't want to follow the good example set for you by F-man?"

I've never heard any of them call Dad that before. They usually call him Frat-man.

"Mom always says that college is a time to discover yourself, so I figure I'll give it a chance and see how it goes."

A grin creeps onto Mom's face.

"Lynn, how are you?" the wife of one of the regulars calls from down the row.

Mom stands up to join her in conversation.

"Is that why you decided not to go into MGD?" Brandon's dad gives me a generous smile.

A picture of the raccoon we caught in a live trap after it spread garbage across our yard years ago comes to mind. I remember the fear in its eyes, the bloody paw from trying to claw its way out.

"I *did* go to Rush."

"Oh." Doug recoils. He toggles his eyes back and forth, like he's looking for something to say.

The bald guy's lips turn south. "He brought in some jerkoff."

"I didn't invite him. He showed up on his own," I say.

His whole head reddens. "Then you got mouthy with Robert."

The crimp in my neck sharpens. I stand up and face him. "Robert's your son?"

"He certainly is."

"Well, that fits," slips out of my mouth.

"What do you mean by that?" Bald Guy challenges.

"Robert had it in for me from day one, no matter what I said. It's like his decision was predetermined."

Doug gawks at the guy. "You *didn't.*"

What did he mean by that? Could the other guy have had it out for my dad?

"People need to pay their debts, even if it takes a long time," the Bald Guy snaps.

What debt?

Mom sinks to her seat, brushing my arm. Her face is red. Is she upset about their conversation?

I squat down beside her. She's stopped sweating, and her skin is hot.

"We need to get you in some cool air, Mom. I'm taking you downstairs."

She doesn't complain while I help her up. Mom leans heavy on me, and we descend to cooler air.

I don't know if that guy was joking or if the heat was getting to his head, but I'm happy to be out of there.

I lean Mom against a wall in the air-conditioning.

"Hey, bro. What's up?"

Zane's voice.

"Hey, man. What are you doing over on this side of the stadium?"

"They're out of water over there, so I came this way."

Mom's eyes widen. She doesn't speak.

"She overheated, so I brought her down here to cool off," I say, trying to explain away the silence.

"There's a clinic around the corner for people who overheat."

"I'm not going there," Mom says.

Zane's phone beeps. "Here, take this. I gotta go." He shoves two bottles of ice water into my hands, then heads off, tapping out a text.

***

Dad's car crawls along Arch Avenue. The post-game traffic is bumper-to-bumper. The people who are on foot are moving faster than we are, but at least we have air-conditioning.

"I'm glad we won. What did you think of the final touchdown?"

"Great. Damn traffic." Dad leans on the horn.

Mom points over her shoulder from the front seat. "David, reach in the cooler and get us all some water, would you? It was nice of Zane to give me his when I needed it. It really helped."

One of her strategies with Dad is to not disturb him when he's stressed in traffic. I wonder if she's changed her attitude about Zane. But I better not ask that question.

"I'm happy we went to the bar across the street to watch the rest of the game. It was so much better to sit in the air-conditioning and have a beer," says Dad.

96

Mom raises an eyebrow. "I wish we'd left twenty minutes ago. It's a long drive home, and I'm worn out."

I lean in and try to get a read on Mom. "You could stay in my room. You don't want to become exhausted. I'll sleep on the couch so you can rest."

Dad shakes his head. "I have a golf game in the morning. We'll be fine."

"Dad, take the next right. There's a shortcut to the apartment down that street."

He makes the turn. "Make sure you do that community service, David. We don't need any more problems. By the way, we won't be able to come for any games in November. A guy in my office is getting married on one of the game weekends, and I have a golf tournament for work."

"But we'll see you at Thanksgiving," Mom says.

She brings out the good things, always looks ahead. I think of my high school homies, spread out across the country.

"I'm looking forward to being home for a few days and seeing everybody out of school."

"Speaking of school, how are you doing with your classes?"

Shit. I adjust my seatbelt while I think about the C posted for me on an English test after one of Zane's epic parties.

"Okay." It comes out squeaky.

"That doesn't sound too good." Dad steps on the brake, then turns to give me a look.

Mom twists in her seat. Her flattened smile tells me she's pierced my thin disguise.

My face gets hotter. There's no way I can tell him. He'd pack me up and make me go home *tonight*.

"No, they're fine."

"What does that mean?" Dad presses.

He knows I'm lying. I run my fingers around the tight neck of the plastic water bottle.

"It means… they're good."

"You gave me your login and password, but I can't find anything that shows your grades." Dad eyes me in the rearview mirror.

It feels like a lime wedge from a Corona is stuck in my throat. If I push it out, it'll be so sour my tongue won't work. If I suck it in further, I'll choke.

I take a sip of my water. "I know, it's just that… we don't find out 'til the end of the semester."

"Don't they post your ongoing grades online?"

"No." Thank goodness. And I'm glad they can't see my heel bouncing off the floorboard.

"You can tell by the tests and quizzes they give back to you, David," Mom says.

"I only have a couple of them so far, and they're okay." Water drips from the bottle and splatters onto my leg, running in a jagged line as my leg bounces.

Dad's mouth flattens. "Give me a number, not a generality."

I lean in on my elbows, holding my leg still. "I have a B in psych and a C in English."

Dad's jaw tightens. "What are you doing? Those are two of your best classes. It should be easy for you to have 3.0 in everything. You said you'd be carrying at least a 3.75." His thumb beats against the steering wheel.

Mom's worry lines are deeper. "You know that we're here to support you and help you through any tough times." Her words are curated, tempered.

My heel starts to bounce again.

"You've already had enough trouble this year. I don't

want to hear about anything else." Dad stomps the brake harder than usual when we pull up to the apartment.

Mom and I lurch forward. I jump out fast, open Mom's door, then drop to my knees.

"You okay?"

She nods. Her eyes have puffy lines underneath. Are they from fatigue or worry?

Mom loosens her seatbelt and draws me into a hug. "If you come home, I can help you manage the offshoots of the dyscalculia," she whispers.

"Thanks, Mom. I'm all right. I can do it." I exhale in her ear.

"Ask if you can start the community service after midterms," she says quietly.

"That's a good idea. I'm going to ace those midterms." Hope I can make it happen.

Chapter 11

I plod my way to the apartment, making a plan for study. An hour of psych, then switch to English and go to bed. Zane won't bother me. I'll put headphones on and ignore him.

"Parental units gone?" Zane calls from across the parking lot.

Jack, Ian, and Zane are unloading empty coolers and folding chairs from their tailgate party. Zane's green Eagle T-shirt has sweat marks down the back, and he seems a little wobbly, like he's drunk. I wish he'd ignore me.

"Yeah, I can get on with life now," I respond and keep walking.

"Oh no. It's the local hag," Zane hollers toward Maria when she climbs out of a white Volkswagen Jetta.

Maria's legs look sweet. She jogs over in her high-cut green shorts. "Hey, David. Your mom is really nice."

If Mom knew more, she'd think you're a little weird. I glance over to the boys and wonder if their thoughts are the same.

"Thanks."

"Oh, look. It's Frank the Tank and his entourage," Maria mumbles, loud enough for Zane to hear.

Zane's mouth goes south. "What are you doing here?"

"I happen to live here." Maria swings a big tote onto her shoulder. The bag slips. She catches it in front of her.

Zane circles her with a stare as cold as a jackal's. "That huge black bag makes you look like a heifer. Heiferwitch— the ultimate title. Now that's next level." He tosses out an exaggerated laugh.

Maria's cheeks are blazing. She may have odd ideas, but that was brutal.

I step between them. "Hey, man. Knock it off. You don't talk to girls like that."

Zane throws his head back, laughing. "She's not a girl. She's a fugly witch. If you're so sold on the ho-bag, why don't you pack up and move your ass across the courtyard?" His words rebound off the concrete walls and hover in the air.

Ian pretends to be examining a nearby plant with Jack.

Rachael throws Zane an icy glare. "Get a life, dude. Maria talks about that stuff because of the class she's in."

"Let's go. This is a waste of time." Zane slaps Ian on the back, then heads for the apartment.

Jack shoots an apologetic glance at Maria and falls in line behind Ian.

I take her by the elbow. There's a tremble in her arm while I steer her toward her apartment.

"Zane is wrong, Maria. You look great."

"Thanks." She takes an audible breath. "Your parents on their way home?"

"Yeah, and I promised to study." I glance at the guys filing into our apartment.

"Why don't you come in? We can review for the physics test next week."

"I don't know." I look back toward my place, thinking I'll never study there. A cold beer would sure taste good, though, and the guys will be jawing about the game. But I need to get my grades up.

"You'll be doing me a favor." Maria slides her key into

the lock. "It'll get my mind off what just happened. I've always thought Zane needs a filter, and he just proved it."

She cuts Zane down all the time. Do I want to listen to that all night? I hesitate at the door.

"I don't have my books."

"I have all the material." She ushers me inside.

Her apartment is similar to ours, but it's clean and all girlied up. Leather-trimmed green pillows on the couch match the colors of the pictures on the wall. Something smells like roses. There's a candle in a glass jar burning beside a picture of a guy on a side table.

Maria notices me looking at it. "That's my cousin who died."

"What happened to him?"

"My abuelo said someone got into him."

"What?"

"My cousin ran away and died two weeks later of an overdose. My grandfather said someone should have noticed when his colors changed because he was overtaken by another soul."

"That doesn't make sense."

"I don't know how to explain it, but I know it happens. Let me show you something." She flips to the end of the physics text. "This explains the colors."

The page goes into detail about various levels of vibration and how they are held and reflected by people.

"That's in our textbook?"

"Yeah. I hope we get to it later in the semester, but for now, let's get started on this string theory." She flips back to the beginning. "I read on Rate My Professor that he always tests on the first thing and the last thing he says in class, so let's start there."

"Geez, is that how you nailed the last quiz?"

"Yeah, *poof*! Magic. You goofball." She laughs and tosses her hair over her shoulder.

I catch myself staring at it falling in big, soft curls down her back. But I remind myself she's too weird.

"Let me move the dolls." She jumps up and zips away a bunch of fat women in shrinking sizes, all painted the same.

"You still play with dolls?" That was lame. Heat rises in my cheeks.

A little eleven forms between her brows. She cracks up. "They're Russian nesting dolls—a decoration. Although… my grandmother always said they show what Tequila does to you."

I laugh, stalling for a way to recover from my dumb question. "I wondered why they all looked like this." I puff my cheeks out, then realize how stupid it must look. *That'll* impress her. My face gets hotter.

"You need your babushka to go with it." Maria laughs, grabs a blanket draped over the sofa, and wraps it around my head.

She doesn't care how stupid I am. Heaviness lifts from my chest, and I burst out in a chuckle.

"A what?"

"It's Russian for *headscarf*. My grandmother on my mom's side was Russian."

"Oh, I get it," I lie.

I tell myself this is not a date. And I can say whatever I want because I'm not interested in her. The thought makes me feel better, as if someone tapped a valve and released some steam.

"I want to go over how all the different particles and forces and expressions of reality tie together. He puts a lot of focus on that." Maria reaches for her notebook. A sweet scent wafts from her wrist when it goes by.

It smells so good that I have to remind myself she's the party nemesis and I'm only here to study.

"Will you read the text paragraphs from *The Theory of Everything*? I want to look up what he said in the notes about quantum mechanics and general relativity."

The sun has slipped below the horizon, and the concepts are starting to jumble. She doesn't know reading out loud gets my words flipping like numbers, and I'm not going to demonstrate. I jostle back my chair and stretch.

"That's it. I'm done."

"We're almost there. We'll take a break." Maria jumps up, grabs some glasses, and pours water from a pitcher in the fridge.

I don't want to show her I'm not understanding these concepts. If I go home, it'll be too noisy to study. I could go to the library, though… It's pretty far to go now.

"High-class water. We get ours straight from the faucet, chunks and all."

She giggles and puts the water down. While she's chatting away, I spot a single rose in a vase on the kitchen counter. Is there someone I don't know about? I decide to check it out.

"Nice flower."

"Thanks."

That didn't work.

There's an awkward silence. Is she thinking about him? I shove my chair onto its back legs and look around her apartment.

Wonder what Zane and the guys are doing. Having more fun than studying…

I should celebrate that I only got community service and that this weekend is over. My leg starts a nervous twitch, like it wants to run out the door. But I remind myself I really need to up my grades.

"Doesn't Zane ever study?" Maria asks, as if she can read my mind.

"Haven't seen him with a book once. He says he has girls write his papers and gets old tests from them too."

"Figures." She hurries to get more water, even though we haven't finished what she poured.

Maria seems hyper. I wonder if it is me or if she's always like this.

"Sounds pretty sweet to me." I take a gulp of my drink.

Maria's smile disappears.

Shit. I didn't mean that the way it sounded. "I'm not trying to do that with you."

"I know, Dave. Zane is such a user. It bothers me." Maria straightens the notes spread across her table.

"He does use women, but he's legit with the guys." As soon as it comes out, I know it sounds bad too. The guys laugh when I do something stupid. This is uncomfortable. How do I explain?

She looks away. The skin on her throat tightens. "How can you stand living over there with Zane?"

"He's entertaining. It blows my mind how he gets away with things that other guys wouldn't even attempt. Plus, I don't have much choice. I was late getting here, so I had to take what I could get."

"Come on. You know he gets over-the-top crazy all the time."

"He gets a little raunchy sometimes. It's part of his game."

Maria's forehead wrinkles. "How about when he uses your stuff without asking or he's playing music so loud you can't think?"

"He turns the music down when I ask."

"For five minutes, then cranks it back up."

"You're mad because of what he said."

Maria's hands fly to her hips. "B.S. If you disagree with him, he bites your head off."

She always cuts down our partying. I let the front legs of my chair fall to the floor with a bang.

"I need to head out."

Maria jerks her head back. "Don't you want to stay a little longer? We're almost done with this section." She follows me to the entrance. "I know you're tired. I can help you."

Maria stands close, almost touching. Her body heat radiates toward me. I wish she wasn't so weird, with the leather tied around her wrist and those long skirts. I wish she'd stop bashing Zane. The scent of her skin is mixed with rose. She smells so good. I reach toward her.

Zane's voice rings in my ear. *Witch.*

"Thanks for the study help." I grab the doorknob instead.

From the courtyard comes the vulture's *chkk-chkk-chkk.* Its silhouette shows on the sidewalk next to our apartment. The thing creeps me out.

"Go live somewhere else."

Zane, Ian, and Jack are chilling in the apartment, feet on the coffee table, watching another college football game. Their shirts show lines of salt, where sweat from partying earlier has dried. Their eyes are glazed like they're high.

Zane looks up. "Hey, dude. What took you so long?"

I would love to hang out, light one up, and forget about this entire weekend, but I gave my word, and I'm sticking to it. "I told my parents I'd catch up for a test I have this week."

"On the weekend?" Zane twists in his spot on the couch and faces me. "Grab a beer and have a seat."

I'm on a roll. I can switch to English, not have to worry about numbers, and be ready for my test next week. If I sit down with them, I'll never do it.

"I'm going to take a shower."

When I'm done, I ease the door shut and slip on some jeans. I think about going to the library, but I don't want to walk past all of them again, so I put in my earbuds and turn on some elevator music. After organizing my notes on the desk, I settle in.

Zane opens the door. "Do you know where the bottle opener is?"

My eyes shift to a picture of Mom in a drawer that's cracked open beside me. I promised to study, so I don't look up. "Dishwasher."

He disappears.

A minute later, Zane sticks his head in the door. "Can't find it. What're ya doin'?"

"Texting." I stay locked in my chair and reach for my phone.

He eyes the books that have slid out of my backpack and onto the floor. "You're not studying again."

I throw him an annoyed glance. "Is it against the law?"

He tugs my earbud out. "Whoa, Rager. What's eating you?"

"Zane, did you find that opener?" A girl's voice rises above the rest.

"Come on, Rager. Lucy's here. I'm trying to set you up."

He's probably BSing me, but if I don't get up, he'll keep bothering me. "Okay. I'll look."

The opener isn't in the dishwasher. It's on the counter behind a beer box. I reach for it, but it's snatched away by a French manicure.

"Thanks. I've been looking all over for that," a sexy voice says.

It's Lucy, the gorgeous blond. Zane *wasn't* BSing me. The seam on my jeans gets a little tighter.

"How've you been?" She pops a Corona, adds the lime, then slowly licks her fingers.

My lip twitches. The thought of being with Lucy tears at the emptiness in my chest. Stellar.

I turn away and open the fridge to cool down. Why does this have to happen now?

"There's a cooler of beer from our tailgate over there." Her slender finger points to the other side of the kitchen.

I force my mouth to open, my tongue to move. "I'm good." The words sputter out. "I was just getting some water so I can go back and study."

"It's Saturday night. Eagles have some celebrating to do." She sidles up beside me, heels clicking the floor.

The cadence is familiar. That *click, click, click* sounds almost like the vulture. Strange.

Lucy steals the bong away from Zane with a graceful swipe.

A PowerPoint of my parents starts in my head. Something in there shuts it off while I gape, wordless, at this amazingly hot babe who is somehow interested in me.

Zane waves from across the room. Gives me a thumbs-up.

Lucy smiles and slides her soft hand along my forearm. It's electric. She places the bong in my hands. "You have all day tomorrow to study."

The PowerPoint returns. A longing for relief from the painful weekend creeps in. With my arm around Lucy's back, I shut my eyes, press my lips to the glass, and inhale.

***

There's a heaviness on my shoulder, and my arm's asleep. Something smells nice.

One eye opens to a mass of golden hair. I stroke the strands and delight in its silkiness. Is this a dream?

Soft fingers inch up my chest. A bare leg slides over and rests on my junk. That's enough to make me open the other eye wide enough to see a French manicure.

Details of the night flood in. A tug of war starts between my gut and my groin, but there's a strong undertow from the leg that's camped there, rocking with each even breath. The physical overrides all thought while I re-explore the flawless naked figure beside me, studying, computing, and memorizing her personal data.

Lucy's body responds. Her eyes flutter, dreams still swirling around her.

She moans with delight, magnetizing me with her intense green eyes. "Hey, there."

"Good morning." I grin.

"It is. Let's make it even better." Like a panther after her prey, she shoves me down on the bed and mounts me.

***

Lucy emerges from the shower, a natural beauty in her wet hair and skin shining beneath her clothes. I can't believe I scored the ultimate babe. I made the grade.

"Here's some coffee for you." I hold out a steaming mug.

"No, thanks. I drink tea." Lucy runs her hand up my tingling spine. Her nipples tighten, showing their outline through her dress.

The throb in my head intensifies. I close my eyes, expecting a kiss.

The doorknob turns. She's halfway out the door.

I try to shout, "I'll call you," but it gets stuck before it leaves my mouth.

I broke my promise.

***

Zane heard about a youth football coach who needed an assistant, which can be used as community service hours. He wasn't interested, so he told me. I don't know how he plans to fulfil the hours the juvy judge gave him, but this is an awesome way for me to get mine done.

My phone call is picked up on the first ring.

"Hi. I heard you were looking for an assistant coach?"

"I am. What do you know about football?"

"I played receiver in high school. I was accepted to play at Elon until I got injured and came here instead."

"If you have patience with eight-year-olds, you can start today."

"I heard you give community service hours. Is that correct?" Good thing schools always encourage community service. I don't have to explain why.

"Sure is."

I think of what Mom said about starting after midterms. That's late in the season. There will never be a coaching position open then.

"What time do you need me to be there?"

A couple of hours later, my phone rings. It's Mom. A wave of guilt washes over me. My head's still not clear enough to focus on books. I click off Instagram and put the phone on speaker.

"Hi, Mom."

"How are you?"

Through my window, I watch Maria leave her apartment and head for the parking lot.

"I'm good." A weighty breath works its way out.

"Then what's wrong? It's not that worthless roommate of yours, is it?"

My words hang in the air, somewhere between manning up and hiding behind her apron. "Zane and Maria are at each other's throats all the time."

"That's got to be hard," she whispers. "What happened?"

Mom's not ripping Zane, so she must be practicing her shrink crap on me. "They're like opposite poles. Every time they get near each other, they butt heads, and I get caught in the middle."

"That's a tough spot to be in," Mom coos in her most soothing voice.

"No kidding. It's driving me nuts."

"Well, just remember to focus on your studies, and you'll be fine."

She's right. I'll mind my own business and let them duke it out all they want.

"I registered to teach football to eight-year-olds in a youth league." I check the time on my phone.

"I thought you were going to wait until after midterms to register?" Her voice is tighter.

"Yeah, I know." I pick up a pencil and start to doodle in my notebook. "I just called to ask about it, and the coach said I can start today."

"I'm happy you found something you like." Her words are slow, controlled. "Did you ask him if you could start in two weeks?"

"I studied physics with Maria last night, so I'm getting there. And you always say when an opportunity arises, seize it."

"I do, but not when it gets in the way of your grades."

Lucy and her friends walk through the courtyard. Being with her last night was like a victory in front of Zane. My chest puffs. I can handle this.

"I can manage study time and coaching."

"If you explain the circumstances to him, the coach might let you start later. Coaches are parents too."

She's treating me like a child. "So, I can say, 'Hey, Coach. I'm a delinquent with lousy grades, working with your kids. Do you mind if I postpone this great opportunity?'"

"You're exaggerating, David. Keep your priorities straight."

"Mom, I was able to play football *and* keep up my GPA in high school."

"Your GPA was never this bad. This is college. You need to think about your grades."

"I am, but staying out of jail is a little more important, don't you think?"

"That's obvious. Don't be sarcastic."

Don't interfere. I stand up and bang the lid of my laptop shut.

"I need to go. The kids' football practice is across town. I want to make sure I have enough time to get there." My gaze drops to the sheet of paper in front of me.

I've drawn a ghost.

Halloween isn't for two more weeks.

Chapter 12

The next day, storm clouds pile on each other, creating a barrier which holds in a layer of stifling humidity. When I arrive at the library, it's cool inside—a break from the heat and bustle on the sidewalks.

The long rows of books absorb the sound and make me think of all the people who have studied them and gone on to do great things. The library is almost empty. Ten thirty on a Monday morning seems too early for most.

I scroll through the psych section for books to reference for a paper. A lot of them are checked out, so I head for the periodicals, start rifling through, but realize I've run out of time before class. Maybe Mom can help me.

"Hey, goofball." Maria's voice lures me into a one-eighty.

I grin at the silly name while she's packing her things from a study table. Maria looks good in a form-fitting, moss-colored T-shirt. I'm glad she's not a flashy, label-chasing girl, like so many others I know.

"Hi. How was the rest of your weekend?"

"Fun," she says in a library whisper.

I wonder if the "fun" was with the guy who sent the rose. I offer a smile back.

She hefts her backpack over her shoulder. "I meant to ask, how did things go in court?"

"Zane pleaded guilty, and we got off with community service."

"That must have made everyone happy."

"Everybody but Zane." I chuckle. "He wanted to pay a fine, not do any work."

Maria slides a reference book across the counter to the librarian. "That sounds like Zane."

"How do *you* know what sounds like me?" Zane's voice booms.

We swing around.

He's barreling down upon us, his clothes wrinkled, his yellow mop a total bed head.

I've never seen the guy read or study anything. "What are you doing here?"

"I was taking a shit," he roars.

That's crude.

People nearby look up.

"*Shhh.*" The librarian hisses.

Yellow rings of foam gather at the corners of his mouth. It's like he doesn't hear the librarian. He remains locked on Maria. "You think you know me, and you have some unreal, wild urge to interfere with my friends, which interferes with me."

"Are you okay?" I ask him.

He doesn't answer.

Maria stays cool. "I might know somebody who can help you with that anger."

Zane's eyes bulge, showing long red streaks. "That's what I mean." He shoves his face in hers. "Go dance in the woods with the other witches."

Damn, that's nasty.

Everyone is staring.

The librarian leaps to her feet. She appears panicked. "Get him out of here."

"Calm down, dude." I steer him for the door.

Zane swivels his head past me. His eyes latch onto Maria. "I'm not kidding. Stay away."

The librarian reaches for her telephone.

I hold open the heavy front door and shove his shoulder. "Take a chill pill."

Zane wobbles on the stairway, then catches his balance. "Lose that bitch," he barks at me, then turns back to Maria. "You stay away from this guy, or I'll have the baseball team come visit you and your car."

The color drains from Maria's face.

"Get outta here. You can't talk to her like that." I slide my arm across her shoulders, trying to shield her.

Zane merges with the crush of bodies on the sidewalk and disappears around the corner of the building.

The smell of lemon from Maria's shampoo drifts by. If she weren't so hippie-ish…

"He didn't mean that. He doesn't even know anybody on a baseball team."

Maria shivers. "He's not usually that aggressive. Do you think he's on something?"

"The thought crossed my mind." I glance at the corner of the building where Zane just disappeared. She may be strange, but he shouldn't treat her like that.

"Maybe he's brought on an entity." Her eyes widen. "No. Like you said, he's on something."

That's sketchy. Maybe Zane is right. Suddenly, the heat of her next to me is overwhelming. I wiggle farther away.

Maria checks her phone. "We better go. We'll be late for physics."

"Zane's comment was seriously lame. You should ignore him."

"I've tried. It doesn't work."

"I wish he'd quit calling you a witch."

She points to the symbol on her back. It's a guy in a circle, with arms and legs outstretched. "He's talking about my shirt. Some people associate it with witchcraft or devil worship."

My throat tightens, so I swallow. Zane does have her pegged.

We're at the steps. I want to run.

At the top, I swing open the door. "Wait a minute. I've seen that guy."

"The Vitruvian Man? He's the symbol of physical therapy and body mechanics. PT students were giving them out last week before a lecture."

While she smooths her shirt, I shake a whole other set of body mechanics from my head and refocus on the subject. "What does that have to do with witchcraft?"

"If you draw lines around him within the circle, it makes a defined pentagram." Maria settles into her seat.

The lump in my throat swells. I gulp down my thoughts before they form.

***

"Some of you did well on this test, while others"—the professor looks up from his open laptop on the desk at the front of the lecture hall—"need improvement."

Is he looking at me or the guy behind me? There are a lot of seats in this place. The professor gave me double the amount of time because of my dyscalculia, but the graphs were a bear. I hope I did all right.

"Your grades will be posted at the end of class, according to your previously assigned number."

Part of me wants to see my grade, but another part wants to turn and run. I twirl the pen Mom and Dad gave me at graduation. It's a nice pen. It came full of expectations. I reach for my notebook, and the pen clatters to the floor.

"I need to do better," I mumble while I retrieve it.

The professor starts a discussion on a quantum algorithm to optimize the feeding rate of alcohol fermentation, but it feels like my brain is fermenting when I get any math components. Why do we need math we'll never use again?

A guy in front of me chuckles. "Sounds like a fraternity social."

I think about the fraternity and the lost opportunities. How could I have blown it? Sometimes, I just don't fit in my skin.

Suck it up, Dave. I focus on the professor as if I'm wearing horse blinders. I can get through this.

At the end of class, Maria is using different colored pens to mark things in her notebook.

"What are you doing?"

She drops the pens in her backpack and scoops it up. "It helps me remember where I put things. Come on. Let's check our grades."

There's a rush out of the class. People craning their necks. Smiles, hi-fives. I hope I can do the same.

I find the letter grade beside my number. It's a C-minus. Phenomenal. Panic drums its way up my spine. The heavy classroom door slams shut behind us.

Maria grabs my arm. "I got an A. How'd you do?"

I plaster a happy look on my face. "Not quite as good as that."

"You should come join our study group next time. We have fun."

"Sure."

People are laughing. Someone says "B," and someone else adds, "Me too."

I fumble with the strap on my backpack.

Maria rolls her hair off her shoulder, then swings up her knapsack. "I've got to run. My next class is across campus."

There's something about her smile, the curve of her neck. I recheck the assigned number I have written down.

"Better hurry."

I retie my shoe, allowing the crowd to dissipate. Perhaps the dyscalculia has me seeing someone else's grade. I put the edge of my notebook under my number to make sure it's the correct line.

No doubt this time.

Can it get any worse?

***

"Do you have to throw your shit all over the place?" Zane tosses my flip-flops at me. They hit me in the chest and fall to the ground.

I swing my backpack off my shoulder, then close the apartment door. "What shit?"

The pizza box he left out yesterday is in the garbage, and the shoes he leaves by the door are gone. He reaches over the couch from behind and grabs a sweatshirt.

"This." He wads the shirt into a ball, zips over, then thrusts it at me like a quarterback handoff. "All that shit in the sink's yours too. Can't you put any of it in the dishwasher?"

"You're the slob around here. I leave a few things out when I'm trying to work on a paper and you freak out? What's up your ass?"

"I'm sick of tripping over all your stuff." Zane speeds to the kitchen and starts wiping the counter.

"I've never seen you like this. What are you doing?"

He squares off in my face. "Mad clean. It's time. You got a problem with that?"

His breath is rank. My mind scrambles for neutral territory while I break away.

"Hey… thanks for giving my mom your water at the game. You really made some brownie points there."

"Like I give a shit about your parents. I was going to get some pussy, like you with Lucy."

My lip twitches, and I search for words. There's a knock at the door. I swing it wide to let some air in.

Maria stands in the doorway with my sunglasses in hand. She's changed into a white peasant top. I guess she doesn't want to prompt Zane into any more insults.

The vulture lands on the concrete walkway behind her. It flaps its dark wings and inspects the inside of our apartment.

Maria spins toward it. "You may *not* bother us," she says directly to the thing, like it'll understand her.

The bird flaps its wings again.

"Time to go," she tells it, like it's someone's pet.

The bird flies off.

"That thing *listened* to you. Amazing." I watch it fly out of the courtyard.

"I won't tolerate the negative energy it carries."

I'm not sure what that means, but I'm not going to ask.

"I stuck these in my bag by mistake." She holds out my sunglasses. "I thought maybe we could review today's physics lesson? I want to understand quantum theory better."

I take my shades, then prop them on top of my head. "Thanks. Come on in."

"Well, if it isn't the local witch." Zane storms into the living room.

Maria smiles and keeps her cool. "Hello, Zane. How are you?"

"I was fine until you got here." He zips to the dining table, snags his backpack, then darts into the hall.

"I'd like to draw him out. We'll see what happens," she whispers. Maria shoots her gaze to Zane and studies him. "Well, if it isn't the face of evil," she replies in a loud voice.

Zane halts at his bedroom door. He gives her a cold stare. "Looks like the wart on your nose is growing."

Maria's chest spasms. Her hand flies to a tiny zit on the side of her nose.

I think about how nasty Zane's mouth can get. "Chill, man. You're making me tired with all that running around. Why don't you come out here and sit down?"

Zane chucks his backpack into his room and dashes over to roost on the back of the couch. I watch his jaw tighten and his face clouds. "I thought I told you to stay away."

"She brought my sunglasses back, man. Who cares?"

"Hiding his shit in your bag so you can get over here is pathetic." Zane glares.

Maria knots her fingers together in her lap. "I thought maybe we should try to get along better."

Zane twists so his back is to her. "I don't want to have anything to do with your fat ass."

Maria's closed lips squish sideways. Her grip tightens.

I feel sorry for her, but I don't get why she's here. "Come on, Zane. She just wants to talk."

"Go eat a baby, witch."

"From the mouth of the town druggie." Her jaw clamps while redness floods her face.

"You're in college, *girlfriend*." Zane stands and slaps a hand on his hip, then shoves his hip way out to the side. "Isn't it about time you came out of your innocent little box?"

Maria's eyes are blazing. She thrusts her face toward his. "So I can fly around jacked-up all day? Get a life."

Little red veins pop up on Zane's forehead. He slams his fist on the counter. "Get outta here!"

I wonder what she's trying to pull. "What is your point, Maria?"

"Forget it. He's a lost cause."

Zane is breathing harder.

I don't know what he'll do, so I place myself between the two of them and lock my eyes on her. "There's nothing wrong with a little partying."

"He's so messed up his eyes are rotting in his head."

"Screw you, witch." Zane growls, throwing a pillow onto the couch.

I remember the pentagram T-shirt. It *is* weird. A shiver travels through my backbone.

Zane may be a jerk, but he's a blast to be around, and he threw himself on the sword for me in court. I don't need this aggravation. "You should go. Thanks for bringing my shades." I take her by the arm and lead her outside.

Maria grabs my hand, eyes pleading. "Wait. What about studying? I saw your face when you got your physics grade. It wasn't good."

"Don't worry."

"Tell me I'm wrong," she says.

"I'll manage." I go to close the door, but the vulture is back again. It's trying to hop into the apartment. "Go away." I shut the door in a hurry.

Does that thing have something to do with Maria? It always seems to be around her.

When Maria marches past the window, I spot the pad of paper with a drawing of string theory I attempted. "You're an idiot." I stomp past Zane.

The graph paper is cranked sideways, and everything's skewed. I feel lightheaded and off-balance.

"It's about time you unloaded that bitch." Zane rises from the couch.

My foot bumps something. It's Zane's bong. I touch the glass. It's smooth between my fingers, and a strange longing clamps onto my bones.

I need to think about my grades. After shaking off the sensation, I hand the bong to Zane. "Here, you forgot something."

He snags the bong before stomping down the hall.

The chill in the room stays. The graph paper wobbles when the AC comes on, waving in my face the failed attempt of my brain that doesn't know how to work any better. I snatch the pad of paper and throw it against the wall.

"What's up with you?" Zane shoots down the hall like nothing happened.

"I got a C-minus on my physics midterm, that's what." I wind up and kick the pad. The papers scatter.

"That sucks. Here." He shoves a blunt in my hand, then flicks his lighter.

I push his hand away. "I hate cigars."

"The cigar tobacco is only on the outside. It's flavored so you don't notice. Go ahead." He lowers the flame under the end.

I think about my lousy grade and look at the mess of papers at my feet. Where to start to figure out the solution to my problems?

"It'll make you feel better, dude."

I snag the doctored-up cigar, filling my lungs to capacity. He is right. It tastes like some kind of fruit. The tension ebbs, and my limbs loosen. *Ahhhh.*

"You need to find some girls to give you their old tests." Zane pockets the lighter.

My thoughts return to Maria and her offer versus Zane's threat. "I don't know any."

"You know Lucy." He clomps back to his room.

Zane set me up with her. Is he pissed that it worked? I look at the blunt, then take another long pull. It smells different, like the scent of cornstalks burning. A chuckle breaks out when I realize this is Zane's stuff and he's not sticking around for any.

"Hey, where'd you go? Don't you want any of this?" I ask.

"No. I've got a meeting with my buddy Aaron over on Elm St."

"Where's that?" I poke my head into his room.

"Next to the pancake place."

Zane has a digital scale on his desk, with an airtight canister of herb and a line of thirty blunts beside it. "You keep it," he tells me.

I wonder if he's dealing. I haven't heard about Aaron, and I don't think I want to know.

"What?" I say. "You always want these things."

"So do you, it seems, but only when it's on my tab."

The truth hits me hard. He's right. The painful thought gets under my skin and sticks in my bones. I don't want the expense of buying those things.

Smoke dances past my nostrils, tempting just one more inhale to relieve the hurt. I take another hit, and my lungs sing. Sweet smoke reaches far into the crevices. I exhale slowly and look at the burning roll in my hand.

"How much are they?"

"The cigars are only two dollars. It's what you put in them."

"So, how much?"

"Ten dollars."

The sound of *chkk-chkk-chkk* fills the room. I don't even see the damn vulture. I want to turn off the sound, let my brain rest.

A plume of smoke drifts by. It sure does help. It'll wear off in a bit, then I'll study again. And if he's dealing, I'll get a good rate.

I snap my wallet shut and throw my money down.

Chapter 13

"Eagles are gonna chomp your Pitbull ass," Zane screams when a pickup truck loaded with guys dressed in red and blue inches past.

Our tailgate in Johnstown for the Eagle-Pitbull game is set up, with others from our apartment building, in a big field five minutes from the stadium. People have brought ping-pong tables and horseshoe games. There's even an above ground swimming pool, making me wonder how they got the water out here. Gotta love the "biggest tailgate party in the world."

"Chomp this!" A guy drops his shorts, then so do his homies beside him. The song "We Are the Champions" blares.

"That guy's ass looked like a Pitbull's." I laugh.

"That's how you're gonna look when the Eagles wipe your ass!" Zane screams. His face is painted yellow and green.

"That guy had the hairiest ass I've ever seen." Jack stares. "No, really."

Ian's doubled over, laughing so hard his eyes are wet.

"Have you seen Lucy? I heard she's crashing at the beach house tonight too." I pat my front pocket, feeling the outline of the packaged circles beneath.

"There she is." Ian points to a tent a few spots over.

I holler at her and bang on the beer-pong table.

Lucy waves and heads our way.

"Hi, Dave." She pecks my cheek. "Isn't this party great?"

A huge grin etches my face. It wasn't a kiss on the lips, but it wasn't stand-offish either.

"It's sick fun razzing Pitbull fans."

"No kidding. My whole sorority is over there, thinking up fun insults."

My mind churns with ways to get her alone. "I heard there are some awesome boats tied up on the river. Do you want to go see them?"

"I'd love to, but we came with a fraternity, and I'm helping to put out the food in a few minutes."

"Lucy, you're up!" a guy calls from the direction she came.

"Got to go." She runs off.

Robert from MGD slides his arm around Lucy's waist when he hands her a ping-pong ball. He locks eyes with me while he guides her over to the beer pong table.

"Jerkoff." An overwhelming urge for a stiff drink takes hold. I search the tables, the truck bed, for something stronger than a beer, finally spotting a bottle of Jack Daniel's. It doesn't matter who it belongs to. I turn my back on Robert, pour myself a Solo cup full, then chug it down.

Zane is sliding cold cans of beer into a long, insulated tube. He zips the top shut and puts the strap over his head. It looks like a quiver of arrows on his back.

"What are you doing?"

"Huntin' pussy. Let's go."

"Great idea." I follow while he weaves through the crowd toward a bar on the river.

A peek inside The Dockings reveals big windows showcasing the river, with a beige tile floor and a bunch of high-top tables, which I heard get moved out later for a dance floor.

"Whoa, look at that Jumbotron." Zane takes off in the

direction of a twenty-by-fifteen TV screen that's set up outside in a brick paver-lined courtyard.

The Jack's kicking in. I'm feeling way beyond mellow. No running for me.

Zane circles back, then heads for a bartender behind a granite-topped bar. "You're walking awfully slow."

While my body needs a glass of water, the picture of Lucy and Robert still hasn't dulled. I dig out my wallet, my fingers thick, while I order a beer.

"Now, that girl's definitely not fugly." Zane points like he's a dog flushing out a pheasant. He lays down a ten for his drink, then takes off in her direction.

I spot a girl who looks like Lucy in the distance. There's a thump in my chest, so I make my way over. I can't wait to touch her amazing ass. Zane says I need to be more aggressive with women. Now's my chance.

"There you are." I grab her by the hips and spin her around.

"Get away from me," the girl screams.

"Get your hands off her." A guy shoves me hard.

My beer bottle crashes to the floor. I fall back against a wall and hold onto it for support. "Sorry. I thought you were someone else."

Zane appears out of nowhere. "This party is stupid good."

I shove myself off the wall. The room tilts. I grab his shoulder.

"Whoa, Rager. You're nuked."

"Am not." I let go of his shoulder. It doesn't go well. I grab the wall again.

"Come on, Rager. Let's check out the water toys." Zane pulls me off the wall.

There are about fifty boats tied up, bow to stern, in a row along the seawall. Some small skiffs. Others are sixty-foot yachts.

"Look at all the teak on that one." Zane ogles the only sailboat in the line. He runs his hand along the gunwale.

My cheeks are starting to burn. I'm overheating out here in the sun and need water. When I spot a dispensing machine, I reach for my wallet. My heart starts to pound. I rifle through the bills.

"My ticket's gone."

Zane stops short. "I saw it in your hand when we got beer this morning."

I empty my pockets. My ID, my phone, a credit card, and two ten-dollar bills. It's the best game of the season, and I can't even go. I'm such a loser.

I need a drink.

The boat owner climbs out of the cockpit with a sweat-covered Corona. He's about to drop it into the garbage, but I extend my hand.

"Hey, buddy. Help a college kid out?"

The guy hesitates. "Looks like you've had enough today." He drops it into the garbage.

As soon as the guy disappears on his boat, I fish the beer back out. "Still cold."

"You're stooping low, dude. Get rid of that thing. It's just about game time. Go check the truck. Maybe your ticket fell out in the cab. I'll meet you at the stadium."

I turn and stagger back toward the vehicle.

***

"Dude, wake up." Zane shakes me. "Whatcha doin' down there?"

When my eyes focus, I realize I'm in the grass under the tailgate of the truck. There's a pile of empty beer cans beside me, and everything is fuzzy.

"It was hot. I needed some shade. I must have fallen asleep."

"More like passed out, judging from that pile of beer cans beside you." Zane pops open a beer.

"Drink some water." Lucy squats down beside me and hands me a cold bottle. "It's a shame you missed the game."

I want to say something intelligent, but my brain won't work, so I take a sip of water. Pieces of grass fall into my lap. When I touch the side of my face, there's grass stuck all over it. I knock it off in clumsy swipes.

"It's time to P-A-R-T-Y." Zane tosses his now-empty beer can past me into the truck. "There's a hot bitch that smells of skank waiting for me at The Dockings." He takes off, with Ian and Jack in tow.

"You're not staying here, Dave." Lucy hooks her arm under my armpit and drags me to my feet.

My body sways. I grab the tailgate.

"Drink more water and eat this." There's disgust in her voice.

I swallow large gulps while she shoves a sandwich into my hand. I start after the others with small steps.

Lucy dances past me, hips swaying to music off in the distance.

We return to The Dockings bar, where the tables are cleared out and a four-piece band is cranking out fast-paced dance tunes. The light outside is fading, and the small boats have left. People must be crashing overnight in the big ones with cabins.

"The band's got 'em raging already." Jack taps his foot on the dance floor.

"There's my sorority." Lucy takes off in the opposite direction.

I watch her disappear into the crowd. Ditched. All

around the room, everyone's partying, having a great time. I am alone again.

"Maybe I should go back to Greenville. I've screwed up enough tonight," I say to Jack.

"Ef that. You can't leave now. Besides, where you going to get a ride?" He starts moving in time with a girl beside him.

"Look who's out there, dancing with not one, but *two* bitches?" Zane hollers above the band.

"Alex. You're the man!" Jack screams.

A huge guy of pure muscle turns toward me and Jack. His arms and neck are way too big. He must be a juicer.

"You know that guy?"

Jack tosses his head with a nod. "He's one of my best friends. I thought you knew Alex?"

"I saw him in the gym once." My gut tightens when I remember Alex bullying a scrawny guy at the gym.

"Come on. We'll buy him a beer since it's his beach house we're staying at tonight."

My stomach turns. The last thing I want to do is buy that 'roided-up jerkoff a beer. "He looks busy."

I feel like shit, and I'm *not* staying at the juicer's. My eyes search the raving dance floor. *Some*one must be going back to Greenville tonight.

I spot Zane working his score.

"I meemember you," she slurs.

Zane flashes a thumbs-up behind her back.

She drops her head on his shoulder.

It's like Zane hasn't ever been the polite gentleman, and I can't get past it. I want to tell her what she's in for. That she's the flavor of the week. That he'll do his best to avoid taking her phone number, and if she succeeds in getting his, he'll answer in lame texts or not at all.

Lucy appears out of nowhere. "Zane has quite a nose."

"What do you mean?"

"He's already found Jessica, the Delta Mu girl that guys call Pass-Around."

"You know her?" I watch Zane slip his arm around Jessica when she stumbles.

"Yeah, and Amber—the other one who sat here all afternoon and drank. That disgusts me." Lucy nods to the other girl Zane was talking to before the game.

I wonder if she thinks that way about me. But I hadn't planned to get so drunk. It snuck up on me. I need to make a play, like Zane said.

"I love this song." I grab Lucy by the hand, then draw her to the dance floor.

She's swirling, grinding, around me, erasing every thought of my leaving to go anywhere.

My moves are sloppy, but I'm working it. All of a sudden, my arm swings too wide and hits Lucy in the jaw. There's a shriek. Her hand's over her mouth, and blood seeps between her fingers.

"I'm so sorry. Are you okay?"

"I'm fine. I bit my tongue."

One of her sorority sisters hands her a cocktail napkin, then yanks Lucy away from me.

I follow, hating myself for being so drunk. "I feel so bad. You're sure you're all right?"

Lucy clamps the napkin over her tongue and nods.

The girl gives me a dirty look before ushering Lucy toward the ladies' room.

I don't know whether to stay or bolt. I feel like such an ass.

"Dave," a voice booms from behind.

I swing around. Jack is standing shoulder to shoulder with Maria. My stomach tightens. Are they together?

"You know Jack?"

"He lives in the apartment next to me. What happened to your hair? It's sticking up like you've seen a ghost." Maria wipes some moisture off the side of my beer bottle to reshape my hair.

Her voice is riveting. It surprises me.

"We're packing up for the beach house. You ready to go?" Jack says.

"*You're* going?" I gape at Maria. The shrill pitch exposes my surprise.

"No." She laughs. "I rode up here with a couple of girls who want to go back. I'm going to study for physics. You need a ride?"

An hour ago, I wanted out, and here she is. As if she knew. I think about the bad grade I have in physics, the promise to my mother.

Lucy appears at my side, smiling like nothing's happened. Her heat radiates toward me, and I remember the smoothness of her skin. It's like they're both magnetic and I'm a lopsided hunk of steel caught in the middle. My eyes dart between the two. My mouth opens.

"Thanks, but I'm going to the beach house," slides out.

***

Rachel's driving the truck, and Alex is in front to give her directions to his family's beach house. The rest of us are piled in the truck bed. Good thing we're on a back road.

Light from a full moon highlights Lucy's hair. My pulse quickens.

"This water is rusting my pipes." Zane tosses the bottle over the side. It disappears in the darkness.

"Hey, no littering," says Jessica.

131

"Sorry, I forgot." Zane's hair blows forward over his face, masking his lie.

"You really shouldn't do that, you know. Not only is it bad for the animals, it looks ugly."

"Will this make you feel better?" He slides a giant joint out of his backpack. "I'll light it for you."

He leans close to the cab, out of the wind.

"We're dying of thirst back here. We need to stop and buy beer," Zane calls through an opening in the back window.

"Both fridges at the beach house are already stocked up. We're ten minutes away," Alex says before winking at Lucy.

I can't stand that guy. I want to yell out, "Save it, jack-off."

We hit a bump, and Ian slams into Amber. He rubs her arm. "Sorry, love. Didn't mean to nail you like that."

Amber slides closer to him. "Your accent's so cute. It reminds me of that little lizard on TV."

That's because his lizard's looking for a workout.

"He turns green and gets all slimy after midnight, though," I joke.

"Whereas you're slimy all the time," Ian says.

Amber's eyes lock on Lucy. I wonder what's going through her head. Is that some kind of warning?

"Look at the bird." Amber points when we turn onto a gravel side street.

Fifty feet behind the truck is a vulture, black wings spread in a wide V. A chill spirals down my spine.

Lucy squints into the darkness. "That's weird. I've never seen one at night before."

We turn into a driveway, and the vulture follows. Its shadow blocks out the moon when it does a loop over the house, then disappears.

I scout the trees and rooftops while everyone else heads to the house. The damn thing followed me here.

"I love this house." Lucy gawks and dashes up the steps of a wide wraparound porch. "Look at the hammock, Dave."

Can't wait to get you in it.

"Perfect spot for chilling." I scramble to catch up with her.

"The house is huge." Rachael peeks in through a multi-paned window, past the stained board-and-batten siding.

"Four bedrooms and a den, with a pull-out couch." Alex swings an old wood door open. "You can crash wherever but…" He looks sideways at Jack. "I get the master bedroom."

Alex flips on a light, and there's a collective *ohhh* when we enter a large, two-story room.

"Look at the stacked stone on the fireplace." Lucy crosses the wide plank floor.

I follow like a puppy, racking my brain for conversation.

"This is amazing." She runs her finger over an antique spinning wheel that's fireside.

"Help yourself to the beer." Alex beams while he strolls around, lighting the place up. The seductive sound of "You Earned It" by The Weekend starts through hidden speakers.

"I'll get you a drink, Lucy." I rush for the fridge in a big kitchen with lots of wood cabinets.

"Thanks." She beams, her sultry eyes twinkling.

My heart melts.

Lucy runs her fingers along the thread, following it to the spool. "I always wanted to see one of these in person."

Zane is working Jessica. He's washed the green-and-yellow paint off his face and is wearing a fresh shirt. The guy thinks of everything. He shoots me a look that screams, *What are you waiting for?*

I chug my beer, hoping to get words flowing with Lucy. "I don't know much about antiques, but that thing is pretty chill." I lean close, trying to mirror her delight.

Alex appears at her side. "This grandfather clock belonged to my great-grandparents, Lucy."

The girl is spellbound, firing away questions about types of wood and place of origin.

Zane strides over, Jessica in tow.

"This stupid history lesson is taking too long," I murmur.

"Don't let Lucy's fall for his tour guide routine," Zane whispers.

"What do you mean?" I glance at them in my periphery.

"Alex will take her all around the house, showing her the fancy antiques and artwork on the walls. They'll end up in the main bedroom, where he'll offer her champagne from a loaded mini-bar, and you won't see them until morning. I've watched him do it twice this summer."

A spasm in my back throttles me upright. "Why didn't you warn me, man?"

Jessica rubs the front of Zane's chest. He switches his focus to her. "Sorry, man."

"Zane, you're good at talking to girls. I never know what to say."

"Compliment her."

"She hates when you do that. She says it's like you're trying to shoehorn your way in."

"Whatever." Zane slides his arm around Jessica. "Would you like another drink, gorgeous?" He shuffles her off to the kitchen.

I need to come up with something, a quick comment, anything to get her attention off Alex.

"I didn't know you were into antiques, Lucy." Alex beams.

"I'm amazed at the quality. There's no pitting on any of the brass in this clockface after all these years."

Lucy examines the clock. Its loud *tic* announces each second passing by.

I've known Lucy for months. Perhaps I should go say something funny.

You can do this.

I grip my beer and move into their circle. "You're looking mighty fine, Lucy, even after being out all day in the sun."

Her brow shoots up. "Has Zane been giving you lessons?" Lucy walks to the base of the stairs. "Alex, tell me about that painting."

"That one is a reproduction, but this one"—Alex climbs to the landing—"is an original oil painting by an old guy whose gallery used to be in town." He's all smiles.

Why did I say that? Why can't I make it work like Zane?

"Now, *this* painting…" Alex shows Lucy the next one up.

Lucy glances at me with a look of disgust before she disappears beyond the landing.

I'm toast, so I head to the kitchen to go find Zane. He's made some kind of fancy drink in a martinia glass for Jessica and is rubbing the rim with lemon rind. I yank the fridge open wide and stick my head in to cool off.

"Get me a Corona while you're there. I'll get the lime," Zane says.

"This is ridiculous." The refrigerator door squeals when I slam it shut. A box of Trojans falls from the top and crashes on the floor, sending a spray of them across my feet. I hurl them to the back wall so they all fall behind the fridge.

Zane laughs and cracks open his beer. "Meet you outside."

Rachel and Jack are making out in the den when I go by.

"What's up with that?" I jam the lime down the throat of my beer.

"Ef buddies. Didn't you know?" The screen door bangs behind him.

I gawk at the staircase on my way by. I should have said something sooner, been clever. If only I wasn't so damn awkward.

Thick fog, like a cloud, has formed over the grass. It spills through the bushes onto the porch.

Light from a room above shows Alex and Lucy's shadows on the blind. I wind up and kick the porch column as hard as I can. It hurts like hell, like my insides. This really sucks.

Zane lights one up, then hands it to me. "This is the best stuff I've ever had. It'll help."

My head's swimming with shitty images. I inhale hard, and my chest draws in a blur of relief.

Jessica calls Zane from an upstairs bedroom window. He steps to the porch rail and pees a proud arc into the flower bed below. "Keep it. I'll see you in the morning."

A horrible pain grips my head, like someone has their finger under my eyeballs, trying to pop them out. I crawl into the lone hammock on the porch.

The outline of the vulture glides across the lawn. It lands on a stunted tree next to the porch, with its *chkk-chkk-chkk.*

"Shut up." I turn my back to it and take a bigger hit.

The scent of burnt corn floats past my nose. I've never smelled weed like that before. I draw the smoke in deep and hold on to it, longing for company.

Faint rumbling laughter echoes around the hammock. A chill grips me, raising the hair on the back of my neck. The shadow of a face appears in the bushes.

I roll toward it and focus on its features. It looks like a guy with short hair and a tall forehead.

"Who's there?"

The murky blackness doesn't answer.

A cold wind puts the hammock in motion.

"Cut it out." I try to sit up, expecting to hear Zane or Jack crack up.

The laughter continues, like a whisper inside my head.

"All right, enough. Where are you guys?" I scan the porch beyond the railing.

Nothing but wisps of vapor.

The laughter of Alex and Lucy radiates from upstairs. A door slams shut. Zane slides the blinds closed in his bedroom.

A freezing blast of air cuts to my bones.

"Der'mo. It's too cold out here!" I holler at my shadow while I watch it shiver. "Der'mo? I meant to say *damn*. What's der'mo?"

The shadow follows me while I propel myself to the living room couch. How weird.

My head hurts so bad that I keep my eyes in slits to avoid the light. I curl up in a ball, cold hands cradling my aching chest. An eerie feeling wraps itself around and through me. Something fills the empty hole inside.

The grandfather clock bangs out the late hour with slow, painful gongs.

Chapter 14

I plug "What is addiction?" into the search engine while I sit at my desk, starting a paper that was assigned in psych class last week. The Wikipedia Disease Model of Addiction pops up and says it's an abnormal condition which causes discomfort, dysfunction, or distress to the individual afflicted.

But everyone has that stuff in abnormal conditions.

"The medical model also takes into consideration that such disease may be the result of other biologic, physiologic, or sociologic entities despite an incomplete understanding of the mechanisms of these entities."

I shrink it and plug in "entity."

"Something that has a distinct, separate existence. Not a legal entity or corporation. Spirits or soul fragments that have, for whatever reason, not moved on after the death of the human body."

I need help with this mess, so I pick up my phone. "Hi, Mom. How are you?"

"I'm fine. David, I've been thinking. You don't need a medical fraternity to get into med school. Yes, it helps, but you will just have to work harder."

"Okay, I can do that."

"Good. How's school going?"

"Not bad." Not great either. "I need to do a paper on addiction. I figured I should call my favorite shrink."

"What an honor," she mocks.

"I looked it up online, and they are talking about entities and soul fragments. I am totally lost. Can you help me out?"

"It's not exactly under marriage and family counseling, David." Her voice is more curt.

"I know you can come up with something. I am desperate."

"What's with your diction? Are you doing some kind of experiment with no contractions?"

"What?"

She shuffles papers on her desk. "You keep pronouncing words the long way."

I have been trying to ignore it, but Mom pointing out the fact gives me the creeps. "I noticed my lack of contractions yesterday as I was leaving the beach house. Guess I'm a little tongue-tied." I laugh and try to shake it off.

"Anyway, the latest thing they're using with addiction here in South Florida is a new type of scan that shows holes in the brains of addicts."

"Cool. The word *entities* keeps coming up in the stuff I have found. You know anything about that?"

"One of my colleagues went to school with Dr. Edith Fiore, whose theory is that entities are attachments people take on after having a traumatic experience that leaves them feeling like there's a hole they need to fill."

Hmm, sounds like what Maria said. "Okay."

"My personal feeling is that addiction is a chemical imbalance in the brain which, after detox, is best treated with antidepressants. When is this paper due?"

"Next week."

"I'll search for articles in my psychology periodicals. How is everything else?"

I know she wants to eke out some bad thing about Zane

so she can convince me to move out. "I talked to a girl from Delta Mu at the Pitbull game, but she got scammed by a grimy jerk, and I never saw her again."

"How did that make you feel?"

"Like crap." I look out the window, trying to see something new.

"Want to tell me about it?"

"No."

"It's me. You can talk."

"Mom, it is over. I don't care."

"It's good to get those kinds of things off your chest."

Deep menacing anger shoots through me. I thrust myself upright, crashing the chair to the floor. "Quit practicing your psych bullshit on me."

"Since when do you curse at me?"

"Like what?"

"You told me to stop practicing psych bullshit on you."

"I did?" I sit back down and take a breath.

"David, are you all right?"

Was that a blackout? I am not even drunk. "Just tired. Sorry if I was grumpy. All is good. Um… can you help me with reference material?"

"I'll send some right away."

"Great. Thanks," I tell her, trying to recall what she said.

"We can't wait to see you, David."

"Me, too." Guilt sets in when I disconnect. Why did I talk to her like that?

***

The youth football area is sixty percent the size of a regulation field. It shares the same park where baseball and soccer are played. Today, the sidelines are smattered with parents, some watching, others focused on younger siblings playing with toys or in small groups.

"Come on, Jamie. Run!" I yell to one of the kids.

He turns around to look at me.

"No, the other way, Jamie."

The five-year-old boy stops, only to get plowed by a kid on the other team.

Both kids are crying in a heap out in the middle of the field. Coach Brock and I jog through the soft grass, still damp from an afternoon rain.

"He's supposed to take my flag," Jamie sobs.

"I guess he couldn't stop in time." Coach kneels beside him. "Tell me what's wrong."

"My foot hurts." Tears run sideways into his thick, dark hair.

I pat his shoulder. "Hang in there, buddy. We will help you."

Coach sits Jamie up. "Let's get your helmet off. Can you wiggle the toes on that foot?"

"No, it's broken," he wails.

"Let me take a look." Coach examines it from a couple of angles, brushes the dirt aside, and then carefully slides off Jamie's shoe. "Can you draw a circle in the air with your foot?"

Jamie is still crying, but he does it. "It really hurts."

"I think you're all right." Coach turns to me. "Let's get him off the field, David."

"Hold on to your shoe, buddy." I scoop up Jamie and carry him over to the bench. "I have some water that we are going to put your foot into. It is going to be cold."

"Good 'cause I'm too hot," he puffs through red, tear-stained cheeks.

I open the cooler of melting ice I always bring to games

after watching my coach do it so often in high school. "Can you hold your foot in there like a submarine for two minutes? Should we make a bet?"

Jamie grins and takes the bait. "Betcha I can."

Something clicks down inside me. It feels like a pissed-off switch jolting my nerve endings. "Bet you cannot," I grumble in a gravelly voice.

Jamie sticks a toe in and catches his breath. He squishes his lips together, then plunges his foot in above the ankle.

"The cold hurts more than my foot." He starts to pant. "How much time left?"

A deep chuckle rumbles through the back of my mind. Why should I care about this kid? I can make him keep his foot in there until it turns blue. I fake a look at a watch I am not wearing.

"Another minute."

"Tell me when." Jamie takes a deep breath and holds it.

"Jamie, are you all right?" A man's voice.

I turn to see my history professor, red-faced and breathless. The shock of seeing him here is a jolt. Professor Taft drops to his knees beside Jamie.

Jamie's face has turned crimson, and his eyes are starting to bulge.

It is way past two minutes, but something inside of me finds the scenario funny. I chase away my mood change and tug the foot out to examine. "How you doing?"

Jamie rotates his ankle and wiggles his toes. "I'm all better. Dad, he got my foot fixed."

The professor looks up, blinking a few times while he gawks.

A wave of guilt runs through me. Why did I make the kid stay in the ice so long?

"Professor, I am David Everest. I am in your history

class on Tuesdays and Thursdays at eleven. I am assistant coach here." I glance away, wondering why the funny speech.

The professor clears his throat. "Yes, of course. Is he okay?"

"You might want to have it checked." I take some ice from the cooler, place it in a towel, and wrap Jamie's foot. "Best to keep it from swelling."

"Good idea."

"Jamie, put your foot on your dad's lap so it does not swell up big and hurt more."

Jamie offers his foot to his father. His dad sets it down with care, then eyes me. "Your grade is kind of on the edge, and you've missed some classes, David. Are you enjoying the class?"

No, but I need it to graduate runs through my brain. "I find it better than memorizing who won which battle."

He laughs. "History through the Renaissance is more interesting to me than war. We are going to be covering church and state in Europe next."

The grumpiness returns like a cloud. I let out a grunt.

"I see you're not fond of the idea."

"Church is not my thing."

"It's more about how medieval churches used architecture to ward off dragons and other entities."

That shit is not true rings loud in my ears. "Great," spills out louder than I wanted. I slam the lid shut on the cooler. "Entities is a foolish word."

Did I just say that?

Professor Taft furrows his brow. He looks at me for a beat, making me wonder if he will ask me what I am talking about.

"Since you're coaching here, I'd like to offer you help. Your grades need to come up, or you'll be in trouble at exam time."

***

I flop down onto the couch to open my mail. Late afternoon sun blasts through the window, making the room hot.

Zane emerges from his room, shirtless, in a pair of dirty turquoise board shorts, and heads to the kitchen. He carries the sharp smell of good weed with him. It makes me want to light one up, but I remind myself I need to work on my essay.

"What's in the package?" Glasses clink while Zane bumps around in the cupboard.

"My mom sent reference material for my psych paper."

"Nice. I was like my mom's babysitter. She was always scattered before my dad died. Then my brother died, and she fell apart. I don't like the guy she took off to Paris with, but he got her to pull herself together, and he took over managing stuff around the house."

He has not mentioned the brother before. I wonder why? "My mom is good about helping me keep up with my dyscalculia."

"Your what?"

My chest tightens. Shit. I wanted to ease into it. "I have this math thing, kind of like dyslexia but with numbers."

"Don't worry about it. I've got ADHD, so we're good."

I laugh. "I guess so."

A figure in the window blocks the pink twilight, then a knock on the door.

"Come on in," Zane calls.

A moth darts in the cracked door and heads for the light of my desk lamp.

Alex steps in with it.

Something snakes up my spine. Not *that* asshole.

"What's up?" he says, eyeing the envelope.

"My mom overnighted this stuff." I rip open the

oversized envelope, digging out a pile of papers and old issues of *Psychology Today*. "I need it for a paper." I thumb through the stack. She organized them into articles which look most helpful, as well as the ones I should enjoy reading.

"Is that Alex?" Zane sails from the kitchen, thumbing his phone. "The girl I banged last night is texting me. I've got to delete her number." He slides it into his pocket, then slaps Alex on the back. "Hey, bro. Where ya been?"

Alex points at me. "Doing that. I had two papers due this week."

"What's this?" Zane takes a bunch of papers from the "Helpful" stack. "*Stages of Addiction.* Oooh, sounds heavy."

I wonder if Mom sent it in a certain order. I stand to watch more closely.

"'Early stage,'" reads Zane. "'Preoccupied with alcohol or drugs.' Come on, that's high school stuff."

Alex steps in behind Zane and reads, "'Increased tolerance.' *Now* we're in college." He laughs.

Zane flips to the next page.

"Hey, I need that." I reach for the papers.

Zane turns to avoid my reach. "'Drinks or uses before or after social functions.'"

"Hello?" says Alex. "That's why they call it *pre-gaming.*"

I crack a smile. "I am serious. Those pages are in order. Give it back."

"'Blackouts'." Zane leaps away. "Does that mean when you don't remember or the passing out type?" He shrugs. "Either way, still high school."

"'Middle stages of addiction,'" Alex reads. "'Feels guilty about use.'"

"I believe you call it, 'I am never drinking again.'" I confess. "Having said it a lot lately."

They both crack up.

"This sounds like everyday life to me." Zane leans against the countertop. "'Neglects health and nutrition.' What? Three or four pizzas a week is healthy. Protein, carbs, and tomato, all in one delicious meal."

The juicer really laughs at that one.

I picture him with steroid-filled protein shakes clenched in his fists. *Jerkoff.*

"'Tries periods of forced abstinence,'" reads Zane. "Just call it exam week."

Another round of laughter.

Alex grabs the paper away from Zane. "'Drinks or uses alone.'"

The two of them pause.

Geez, they both do that.

I wait for a response.

"Nothing wrong with it." Zane sets a fixed gaze on Alex, who quickly nods.

"'Quits or loses job,'" Alex rattles on. "There's the first one that makes sense."

Zane glares at me. "This is a load of crap. You can't put that in an essay. It's incompatible with life." He snatches the paper back. "'Late stages of addiction: early-morning use.'" Zane throws his arms in the air. "Happens every time the TV networks schedule a twelve thirty game."

Alex and I burst out laughing.

"You are right," I agree. "This *does* sound ridiculous. How much is left?"

"'Tremors or shakes and unable to work.'" Zane lowers the paper. "We all know they both go away after you re-hydrate and eat. And the last one is…" Zane does a long, dramatic pause. "'Loses friends and family.'"

"You're not going to lose any friends. We're all here, doing the same thing," Alex says. "And we're *all* away from our families."

"So, other than losing your job, this describes the national lifestyle of higher education." Zane tosses it onto the floor.

"Hear, hear," I chant with an English accent, holding up an imaginary cup to toast.

They crack up laughing, and my heart warms with the approval.

"Dude, you got the stuff for me?" Alex asks.

Zane fishes a baggy of weed out of his pocket.

Alex reaches for his wallet, then hands Zane a fistful of bills. "That's for both." Alex points back and forth in the air.

Zane disappears into his room, then comes back with a jar of powder I assume is the stuff that makes Alex so jacked.

I lock my teeth together so I refrain from commenting while I retrieve my paper from the floor.

When Alex leaves, Zane counts his money. "Love the color green."

"Since when are you dealing?" I say, even though I saw him with a scale weeks ago.

He flinches as if I just speared him in the chest. "I'm *not* dealing. I'm just covering my expenses."

"Yeah, right." I gather up the stacks from Mom before anything gets lost.

Zane plucks out his wallet. The Velcro crackles as he rips it open. He stuffs the bills inside. "That slimy boyfriend of my mother's said she was giving me too much money. He made her cut me way back." He tugs out his one-hitter pipe, packs it, takes a long pull, and hands it to me.

"No, thanks. I need to finish this."

"When's it due?" His words come out in a billow of smoke.

"Day after tomorrow."

"You've got tons of time." Zane reloads the pipe. "Alex

said that Lucy was sweet." Too bad you didn't do her at the beach."

Heat climbs my spine. I try to shrug it off, but it gets into my head. My teeth grind, and I attempt to ignore the picture of the two of them together.

Zane lights the pipe and fills himself up.

My jaw pulsates with pain. The scene in my head of Alex wooing Lucy upstairs… thoughts of him kissing her… touching her… wrenches at my insides.

I take the pipe and inhale. The moth that got in earlier lands on the papers from my mother.

***

My assignment is due in the morning. I wish I had stuck to working on this last night. After all, I should be breaking big jobs down into small parts, like the LD people told me. I want to avoid getting into the "overwhelm" stage.

Searching "addiction cure" on my laptop, a couple of things pop up.

"Most substance abuse treatment in the western world is based on the assumption that alcoholism and drug addiction are diseases. Treatment uses the 'spiritual' twelve-step program, even though statistics show that only five percent of patients are alive and clean or sober seven years later."

Geez, that is a lousy statistic.

Click.

"The Israeli Medical Association found a ninety percent success rate for overcoming drug addiction using hypnosis."

I flip through the magazines Mom sent. This is too much. I hit speed dial. "Hi, Mom. How you feeling?"

"I'm fine, honey. Did you get the package of information I sent?"

"Yeah, thanks. You sent enough to do a fucking master's thesis."

She forces a laugh. "That's awfully strong language for you, David."

"This package is out of control." I sniff.

Mom stirs in the room on the other end of the phone. "I didn't know what angle you wanted to present, David, so I sent a bunch. Try to create sections and remember to take breaks in between."

I flip open another magazine. "I am trying to get through it all. There are a hell of a lot of methods for treatment."

"Have you come across the one they use in Bangkok? It has a red cover." Mom chuckles.

I keep flipping. "Here it is. 'Treatment in Bangkok includes chaining people to trees for three to six months and giving them herbs.'"

Mom giggles.

"'Thousands have been rehabilitated and never return to their old ways because they do not like being chained.' That is definitely going into my paper."

Mom laughs. "You're not using contractions again. Is this a test?"

A lump forms in my stomach. I do not know what to say about this weird new talk. "Yeah, *haha*. Mom, did you or Dad ever do that back in the day?"

"Not me. It doesn't sound like something your dad would do either."

"Not a game when I was a baby or anything?"

"You probably heard it on some game show or something. You always liked to test new words on Eric when you were young and tell him you were smarter."

I smile at the thought of tormenting my brother, but the brick in my gut stays. "That must be it."

"By the way, David, your dad says that your bank account has been going down fast lately."

"Did he tell you I had to buy a new textbook?"

"This is more than one textbook, David."

"The cost of living is a lot more than thirty years ago, Mom."

"I understand that, but your expenses seem unusually high, compared to the start of the semester."

Anger seeps into my bones. Dad is always complaining about something. "I am not in the fucking frat. I am saving you money. You should be happy."

"Your dad's had a few loud protests about it. I just wanted to let you know before—"

"Fine." I jump from my seat and slam the lid of my laptop down. "I will watch it." I click the phone off and throw it onto the bed.

Guilt swirls in mucky clouds around my room. Why did I snap at her like that?

Chapter 15

At my desk, I am hurrying to finish the psych paper when my phone rings. I consider not answering, but I notice Stan, my LD counselor, is calling. Maybe he has some new helpful hints.

"Hey! How are you, Stan?"

"Thought I'd check in and see how things are going."

"Good. I have memorized some landmarks to help me find my classes, and I do look for people to follow. Thanks for that suggestion."

"No problem. How are your classes? The accommodations helping?"

"I am struggling with physics, but the extra time helps. Right now, I have a paper for psych class to work on."

"Don't forget, we can set you up with a proofreader."

Except the paper is due tonight. The proofread program in my laptop is going to have to do. "Yeah, thanks."

"You know, you don't have to be in a medical fraternity to get into med school."

We have never talked about the fraternity. "How did you know I didn't get in?"

Stan pauses, and I hear a door close. "Well... your mother called today. She was worried about you and asked me to see how you're doing."

Heat builds in my face. He means well, but they both have no business meddling.

"I am fine. Thanks for checking. But I need to finish this paper, so if you will excuse me…"

"Sure. Stop by any time. We're here to help you."

"Got it. Thanks." I hang up, then throw my phone onto the bed. "That bitch. How dare she undermine me."

"Have you finished that paper yet? The concert starts in half an hour," Zane yells from the living room.

"Ten more minutes, then I just need to submit it."

When the proofread finishes, I save the essay. I click on my email, and the screen fills with the notice of an error. The server is down.

I glance up to see Zane.

"Let's go, dude. This concert is going to be stupid good." He tugs my sleeve. "You said you'd be done half an hour ago."

"Dude, spelling and grammar are my second biggest pitfalls, next to math. No rushing that stuff." I am kicking myself for not finishing early enough to get it proofread.

My hands sweat when I try the email again.

"Save it on a flash drive and bring it with you. If ours is out, the whole complex will be out. You can go send it from campus."

"Loading it on the thumb drive right now. And I need a picture of the email."

"You driving?" Zane asks.

"I am still burnt from the first time you had me drive this year. I will throw down for gas."

We climb in his truck, and I check my pocket. The thumb drive is there. I wish I finished this assignment last night. I hate doing a rush job.

When we pull onto Alacosta Drive, Zane shoots me a funny look. "Since when do you chew your nails?"

I tug my hand from my mouth. "I never used to. It just started this week."

He is still staring.

"What is up with you?" I ask him. "You look like you're going to do something weird, like pull out a gun."

Zane laughs. "My brother used to chew his nails, that's all. Anyway, you've been kinda bummed since the beach house, so I got you something."

"What is it? A 'How to Steal your Friend's Date' starter kit?"

The cab fills with riotous laughter. "It's too bad Alex hit on Lucy, but you should be thrilled you banged the hottest girl around. How was she?" He is salivating like a dog.

"Since when did you turn into a creeper?"

"Come on. Don't leave me hanging."

"She has some awesome moves." I play it up, which makes me feel better. I have never seen him like this.

"Next time, do her on ecstasy. She'll be even better." Zane rounds the corner onto Main Street, where the yellow glow of overarching lamps makes the street look like a ghost could walk down it at any time.

It could be good rumbles into my brain, and a strange ache travels up my arms. I try to shake it off by pushing my hands against the dashboard. The maneuver does not work.

"Looks like you need to stretch. I've got something that will help." Zane reaches deep into his jeans pocket, then hands me a pink pill. "Here, you dumbass. This is the perfect antidote for depression. You'll be feelin' sweet and lovin' the world."

"I do not agree." That wierd talk again. Why am I doing it? "I would rather smoke." I pat my own pockets. "Shit, I forgot to bring it."

"That little bit you left on the kitchen counter? I polished it off hours ago."

My face screws up. "Smoke your own, dickhead."

"Like you haven't been helping yourself to mine all semester?"

He is right. I cannot say anything. He has given me a lot. It has helped break down my walls and open new doors. Everything is more chill with Zane around.

"It's why I brought you that." He points to the pill.

"What is it?"

"It's the E, man. You can't get beer at the concert, but you can get water. You'll be a dancing fool, rolling with the bitches."

"I need to get this paper sent in tonight. I do not want to be all messed up."

"You won't be, man. I'm telling ya, the stuff is sweet. You'll be fine. You'll just feel like talking to girls and dancing. Is that so bad?"

"I am really not into it." *Do not be a pansy* rings through the back of my head. I have never heard that before. Is that my word?

"Lucy's going to be here tonight. You don't want to be tongue-tied and blow your chance again, do ya?"

"Well… no."

"Go ahead. It takes two hours for it it to really get rolling. You'll have time to take care of your paper."

I think of Lucy—her hot lips, her awesome shape. My left thumb and forefinger roll the pill while I think it through.

"If she's not feeling the spark, it's because you didn't create it. Flirt, tease, escalate. That hottie will feel even nicer this time, I promise."

I look at the pink pill and feel Lucy's touch. I think about the beach house. If I had just said the right things, maybe she would have been with me instead of Alex.

I am not making that mistake again.

I toss the pill way back in my throat and swallow fast before I change my mind.

"Now you're living up to your name, Rager." Zane grins.

"Drive by campus so I can send in this assignment."

"No way, dude. We're already late. You can drop me off and take my truck."

In no time, a warm wave rushes over me. "I thought you said this stuff has a delayed start?"

"It usually takes half an hour."

"You said two hours."

"That's when it's really doing its job. Right now, you're in the warm-up."

I check my phone. "It has only been twenty minutes, and I can feel it. Pull up to the front door and get out. I need to hurry and get this taken care of."

Zane stops the truck under the giant portico of the concert hall. The dude's eyes are twitching. He jumps up and gives me a chest bump. "Hear that music? It's time to go find some slam pieces."

I hop out, then zip to the driver's side.

"I thought my *dad* was crude. Your mouth is disgusting." The music filters into my bones, making me want to move my feet.

"It's a banger." Zane laughs. "Look, there's Lucy. If you don't get her this time, she's free game."

Lucy is talking to some girlfriends, headed this way. She is in a silky red dress which clings in just the right places. Lucy spots me, and her face lights up. She rushes over, throwing her arms around my neck.

"Dave, how've you been? I haven't seen you in forever."

I look at the flash drive in my hand and think about how my mom dissed me today, then shove the drive into my pocket. Lucy's fullness presses against my chest, and her tiny waist sits beneath my fingers.

"You look awesome in that dress, Lucy." And even better without it. I grin to myself.

"You're so sweet. I love this song." She steps back and starts dancing where she stands. Her eyes twitch.

Does she have the hug drug? Awesome.

Lucy narrows her gaze, then starts surging in spirals, like a snake charmer, toward me, drawing me into her spell.

My temperature is rising. I do not know if it is Lucy or the "love," as they call it, and I do not care. I give way to the heat and follow her motion.

"Dance for me, girl."

The crowd is an undulating mass funneling in. Some guy starts a freaky solo near us.

I do a bad job of imitating him, and Lucy laughs.

"There's a spot over here." She drags me through the crowd to a bunch of girls going past the ticket counter. They must be Delta Mu because they are smiling and waving us on.

I wonder if she is having me checked out, but I also do not care. I flow with her, as if we are attached by invisible strings, just us and the music. The music dissolves me.

My toes are tapping like they are possessed. Lucy's touch is electric. I follow her dance moves like a wave surging with her, riding the rush up, down, a tweak to the side, flowing free in another dimension.

The crowd thins, and the lights come on. All I want to do is touch her, feel her next to me.

I draw her close and kiss her long.

When we turn for the exit, the sorority clump is gone. My breath turns to a wheeze. The psych paper, the truck… My mouth goes dry.

"Shit."

"What's the matter?" Lucy slides in close.

I dig out my phone and find a text from Zane:

Got a ride. The truck is in row five, keys under the front seat. Go get banged.

I want to laugh, but the knot in my stomach holds it back. "I was supposed to send in a paper before midnight. Our server was down, so I brought it with me." I tug the thumb drive from my pocket. My eyes pitch side-to-side while I gawk at it in my hand. "I forgot," squeaks out in a whisper.

"If your server was down, it probably affected other people in your class too. Maybe service was out all over town," she reassures me.

"Maybe." I attempt a smile.

It fails.

Lucy runs her hand down my back, then across my butt.

There is a flash in my head, me holding my hand over her screaming mouth, ripping at her clothes.

I shove the thumb drive back into my pocket. "I need to go."

"Take me with you."

"That may not be a good idea," I hear myself say.

What am I doing? I have waited for this moment. I cannot just blow her off, but the picture in my head has me freaked out.

"Alex was a mistake. I should have stayed with you at the beach house." Lucy strokes my arm. Her hand is like velvet, her touch burning away the image in my brain. "You're so sexy."

No one has ever said that to me before.

I tug her close. The rhythm of her heart beats against my chest. My heart rate slows. I decide it will be all right.

Zane is not at home. A light under the microwave throws a soft glow across the living room. Lucy kisses me deep. My tongue tastes hers, remembering.

She slides a hand behind my shirt.

My back muscles respond like never before, one after another, a rising tide. The sensation is amplified a thousand percent. My cool façade has turned all warm and fuzzy. I glide my tongue to her earlobe, along the hollow of her long neck.

She draws a quick breath, and we sink to the sofa.

"You're amazing," Lucy coos when she catches her breath.

Her seduction is so intense it is luring thoughts into my head that do not belong. I have a ramped-up, fine-tuned awareness of every touch. I cannot get enough. I glide my fingers across her throat, and… they start to tighten.

A thrill runs through my chest.

I jump to my feet, ripping my hand away.

"What's wrong?" Lucy stands, then wraps her arms around me.

"I was choking you," I pant.

"You were just playing." She runs a finger along the inside of my thigh.

My mind goes blank, and my body takes over. I lift Lucy's perfect glistening form and carry her to my bed. The tips of my fingers have ESP while they tease their way around Lucy's breast. She arches, convulsing. I trace the line of her waist… her hips. I stroke a finger over her folds.

Time and space disappear.

***

Intense light hits me in the face.

I sit up in a daze to find the source. Sunlight streaming between a gap in the blinds spotlights Lucy's naked body on the bed beside me. I smile when images of the night before flood my memory.

Lucy's eyes flutter open. She reaches for her phone. "Just in time for class."

"What time is it?"

"Half past twelve."

My stomach jumps. "Shit."

"What's wrong?" She hurries to her feet.

"I was supposed to go for extra help with my history professor at noon."

"Can't you get the notes from someone else?"

"No. He set aside time to help me because I coach his son's football team."

"How sweet of you. Maybe you can still catch him. I'll hurry." She grabs her clothes and heads to the bathroom.

While I step into my shoes, the light through the blinds shines across my legs, like the bars of a cell. A flash of the jailhouse pops into my head. My shoulders twist with a shiver.

"I'm so sorry this happened," Lucy says when she climbs into the car.

I wonder if she means last night or because I am late. "Not your fault. I should have turned on the alarm clock."

"But, instead, it was me you turned on." She plants a kiss on my cheek.

The road blurs. Amazing sensations from the night before emerge, along with a satisfied grin.

My mind drifts back to my problem at hand. My grades suck. I need to figure out what to do with the paper. Do they block it from being sent? Should I print it and take it in?

"Have you ever withdrawn from a class?" I ask.

"No. Are you thinking about it?"

"Yeah, but if I do, my dad will scream until I land in the next county."

"Ouch." Lucy looks down and goes quiet for a moment. "Today is the last day to drop a class."

"I know, and the decision is tearing me up."

"Get in to see your professor and study like mad. You can pull it off."

Except it is not just one class.

We arrive at her dorm. She is out of the car before I can lean over to kiss her.

"I will call you," I blurt.

Lucy flashes a smile. I wonder if she likes the idea or if she is thrilled to get away.

While looking for the spot where Zane parks without getting caught, I watch someone extract their car from a space so tight I do not know how they opened the car door. I remember how my car got scratched from being towed, but I am desperate for time. I do another glance around. There is nothing else.

My shoulder blades draw closer when I squeeze my car into the spot.

I sprint up the stairs to the office and round a corner to find a tiny, wrinkled lady with curly yellow hair. Her sweater is such a bright pink it makes my eyes hurt. She is at a desk with a big paper blotter underneath her laptop. Her desk is perched in the hallway, narrowing the space where someone can walk to about two feet. Obviously, her purpose is to screen people coming into the department.

"I am here to see Professor Taft."

The assistant eyeballs me like my professor told her some lame student was due almost an hour ago. "I'm sorry, but he's left for his next class."

My hope sinks, delivered with a *thump* into the empty crater of my stomach.

"Can I tell him who called?" The assistant checks a printed calendar on her desk.

I clear my throat and try not to sound panicked. "Would

you let him know David Everest was here and that I apologize sooo so much for my poor timing?"

She looks over the top of her glasses. "I shall."

I hate to pull this, but I need to do something. Maybe she will stick up for me. I sit in a chair near the front of her desk and scoot it up close to her.

"Are you familiar with dyscalculia? It is a learning disability I have. It has mostly to do with math, but it affects telling time too… because of the numbers." Sweat forms at my temples while I dance around the truth. "If you would be so kind as to explain that to Professor Taft, I would be forever grateful."

She says nothing, just examines my eyes.

I hope they are not bloodshot. While I had no alcohol last night, I do not know how that other stuff affects you the next day.

"Would you happen to know when he will be due back?" I smile.

"This is his last class of the day. He usually returns to his office, but I can't say for sure."

"Thank you. You have been so kind," I add for extra suck-up points.

After my next class, I return to Professor Taft's office.

The secretary takes off her readers with a cold glare. "Haven't seen him."

"Can I leave him a note?" I arch my brows and smile, trying to appear innocent.

"Sure." She hands me a notepad.

I tell myself to be a kiss-ass, even though I hate the idea. I ask about Jamie, then say I am sorry and leave my phone number. I hand her the note.

"I'll make sure he gets it," she says, shedding her sweater. Her yellow blouse reflects on her skin, making her look ill.

I feel the same.

Back at the car, I find that someone has somehow managed to park two wheels on the grass behind me. The car sticks precariously out into the lane. I walk over to the passenger side to see if there is any way I can maneuver out, only to find a huge key mark down the length of the car.

"I do not fucking believe it." I kick the tire of the car blocking mine.

"Don't believe what?" Zane and Ian stride into view.

"This." I point. "I park here to hurry in for extra help, I miss the professor, and some tool runs a key shorter than his dick along my car." I kick the car tire two more times.

Ian squats down and rubs his hand over the scratch. "It is a nasty one, mate. You might be able to get it out with rubbing compound."

I bend over to look, then run my fingers over the scrape. "It went all the way through to the fucking metal. Shit." I kick the tire again and lean back on the car, surprised I am cursing this much.

"It's just a lousy fucking day." Zane throws his backpack onto the ground.

"Why? What happened to you?" Ian asks.

I walk around to check the rest of my car.

"I had to drop half my classes, and my mother called to say her jackwagon boyfriend has some important meeting in Brussels, and she won't be home for Thanksgiving."

I swallow my self-pity. At least I have somewhere to go for Thanksgiving. "Sorry, man. You can come to my place if you want."

A pair of lines forms between Zane's eyes. "I'm not doing that. Your parents hate me."

"What about your uncle in Fort Lauderdale?"

"I'm fine right here. There'll be lots of people around 'cause it's the FLU game."

"Damn, I forgot about that." I rub the side of the car, wondering if I can fix it before the holiday.

"You're not getting this car out anytime soon. Come on. I'm ready to spark one." Zane starts walking.

"Here?"

"Not right here in plain view. I have a nicely landscaped courtyard over there." He does a sweeping motion to the right, then walks away with Ian in tow.

Thirty feet from the car, Zane and Ian duck behind a tall hedge planted to hide a row of air conditioners.

I stop. "This is sketchy, dude. Campus PD will smell that shit a mile away."

Zane steps back in view, hands on his hips. "I'll stand out here and watch while you and Ian take a rip, then you be lookout."

"I plan to chill right here by my car."

"Whatever. Just whistle if you see someone coming." He disappears behind the bushes.

I head back to my car and run my fingers over the huge gash in the paint, thinking about how Dad is going to kill me.

A minute later, they are both looking at the gouge close up.

"It'll cost at least four hundred dollars to fix it," concludes Zane.

"I hope not."

"At least your car doesn't look like *that*." Ian points to a dusty beater with missing hubcaps.

"That guy would not have the same problem." I huff. "There is no paint left."

"I can see you driving that tank, Ian." Zane laughs.

Ian squats like he is behind a steering wheel. They both crack up.

"It'd be going *chug, chug*." He lurches forward and back. The two of them find this hilarious.

"You can always sell your sperm, Dave." Zane laughs. "Lucy seems to find it valuable."

There's mad belly laughter.

"Very funny." I scan the road in hopes of finding someone walking this way, perhaps the owner of the car blocking mine. My fingers go back to the scratch, feel its depth. Another scar I have endured since I got here. A long sigh seeps out. *Go ahead, you will feel better* echoes through my mind. "Where is that pipe?"

"There's my man." Zane thumps me on the back and looks over his shoulder. "Nobody's coming. We can all go."

We cram ourselves into the small hidden space, and I breathe out the last molecule of oxygen before inhaling. I pray it fills every tiny air sac I have.

A sick headrush hits me, followed by odd, rolling laughter.

I peek through the bushes but see nothing.

Footsteps on the road catch my attention while we emerge from the bushes. My heart rockets when the profile appears.

"Hello, Professor."

Chapter 16

Professor Taft is examining my eyes. I wonder if he can tell.

I squirm in the hot sun, halfway between my car and the hedge we were smoking behind.

"So sorry I missed my appointment. I parked my car here because I was late getting to campus, and not only did I get blocked in, but someone keyed my car." I point to the gouge in the paint.

He rubs his index finger across his lips.

Zane and Ian head in the opposite direction from him. "We'll catch up with you later, Dave. Let us know what happens with the car."

He knows. I need to kiss ass.

"How is Jamie's ankle?"

"The ankle is fine. I'm supposed to pick him up at four o'clock. My assistant texted me about your dyscalculia. I'll squeeze in half an hour with you."

That excuse sure backfired. I lift my chin and stretch my cheeks into a smile. "Thank you, sir," I say, trying to think of a way to get out of this.

"Shall we go?"

My mind races. Was I gawking? My hands mobilize before the words come, and I point. "Sure, sorry. My backpack is in the car. I will get it."

What am I saying? He knows I will get it. I need to walk

fast, show purpose. My flip-flop catches on a root. I go down in the dirt.

Professor Taft turns away and starts toward his building.

I brush off and run to catch up. It feels like I am walking into the lion's den. What if he is leading me into a trap, helping the campus police? Would that negate my community service? Bring the charges back? Put me in jail?

"The doctor said Jamie would have had a lot more pain and swelling if you hadn't iced it right away." The professor's pace is fast.

"Glad I could help." I spot Zane and Ian driving away, and I want to bolt to the truck, throw myself in the back, and get the hell out of here.

At the history building, he opens the door for me. I keep my head down, telling myself I am doing good. The secretary is gone when we enter the office, thank goodness. She would be like a bloodhound, sniffing as I went by. I spot a note on his desk and hope it is mine.

"Have a seat." Professor Taft points to a chair. He looms over me, leaning heavily on the desk. "I'm carrying out this session, David, because I'm a man of my word." He lowers his head and locks onto my eyes.

My chest tightens.

"I don't approve of your conduct on campus or the state in which you've arrived in my office. If I see you in this condition at school or on the football field, I will inform the registrar and the police."

The face of Judge Richards flashes before me with the cold, hard granite wall of the courtroom behind him. The air leaves the room. I open my mouth, but nothing goes in or out. I am not sure what to say, but I will not admit I am high.

The professor sits down. "What is it that you need clarified, David?"

My breath is shallow. I tell myself to play it cool and scramble to retrieve a paper with questions from my backpack. "The concept of gargoyles and lost souls is confusing."

He switches a desk lamp on. "Back then, people believed physical and mental problems were due to an incident like abuse, grief, or extreme fear."

It seems like there are a million eyes on me. I look around for a camera in the room.

"The pagans thought this could cause the soul to actually fracture, taking part of someone's life force with it."

The life is being sucked out of me. I scribble what he says in my notebook. "What does it have to do with gargoyles?" I ask.

"The gargoyle represents someone whose soul has been lost and now is in eternal torment."

My mind goes to the wispy face with the laugh from the bushes at the beach house. I want him to explain the strange laugh which followed me, but how do I ask? I focus on my writing. I am trying to go fast, but my fingers are slow. It is pissing me off.

"If that is true, how do they get it back?"

"That's what the rite of exorcism did."

Something inside me revolts, thrusting me upright. I slam my pencil down. "That stuff does not happen."

The professor glances at me with a strange look on his face. "Belief in possession was universal until the end of the sixteenth century, David."

"That is all I want to know. Thank you for your help." I shove the chair back and run out the door.

I hate that he made me go in there with him. Professor Taft knew I was buzzed. He should have left me alone. I want to smash his ugly face into a wall.

"This is bullshit." I slam my fist on the hood of my car and watch the metal beneath it crinkle.

***

I hit SEND on the psych paper that was due yesterday. The teacher's assistant instructed me to include in the email that our server was down. He told me it may not help me, though. I mentioned the dyscalculia and my problem with time.

I wish I had told the professor at the beginning of the semester, like Mom and the counselor told me to do. I should not have gotten pissed off at them—I need help. Especially after the Professor Taft episode.

Mom always had me taking supplements like Omega-3 and B vitamins to improve my focus rather than medication. Half the people around here take Adderall to study, and I need all the help I can get.

Zane is in the kitchen, rummaging through an open cabinet next to the sink. Glasses clink together while he shoves them around.

"What are you doing?"

"Looking for my keys."

"With the glasses?"

"I can't find them anywhere else. I figured maybe I went to make a drink and left them there."

He cannot be serious. "Before you slither off in the grass again, I need one of your study buddies."

A light pops overhead. The room goes dark.

"Damn cheap lights. That happened in my room, when I switched the dresser with the one in your room before you moved in."

"Wait, why did you switch the dresser?"

"Mine looked like it had been clawed."

I think about the scratches on my dresser. Perhaps I did not notice them because they are on the side away from me. His room is a mirror image, so he would have been looking at them more.

Zane continues. "Anyway, I didn't slither. I strode. Did your professor say anything?"

"He ripped the shit out of me, told me he would tell the cops. I think the only reason he did not is that I helped his kid. I was so nervous I hardly even talked."

"So, you pulled it off. Why're you bugging out?"

"He said some stuff about people in olden times, where they were in eternal torment because they were possessed. I feel like I am in eternal torment these days."

Zane laughs. "You couldn't possibly be possessed. Your head would be turning around while you projectile vomit, like in *The Exorcist*. It may have felt like the bed was levitating when you banged Lucy, but there were no unexpectedly strange noises coming from your room." He chuckles.

I smile while I picture Lucy naked in my bed. "Nothing like that. I have been speaking without contractions, and I have chewed my nails to the quick. I do not usually bite my nails."

"As for your no contractions thing… You're in college. You've improved your language skills, that's all. You're ahead of me on that. I'd chew my nails too, if I had to report to my mom like you do. You're in your head too much. Maybe drop a class and lighten your load. I bet it stops the nail-biting."

A flush of irritation runs through me. "Leave my mom out of this." The fact he and Ian snuck away unscathed has already dug its way under my skin. Now, he is telling me what to do. *Again.* "I cannot believe you made me go behind that bush on campus."

"I didn't *make* you do anything. Don't blame me that your professor came along. If you had a head on your shoulders, you would've seen him on time, and the whole thing wouldn't have happened."

Zane is pissing me off.

"You should not be smoking on campus to begin with."

"I'm not dumb enough to get caught."

"You are such an effing druggie. Get me one of those Adderalls you peddle to poor, innocent students so I can study."

"None of them are innocent. They're all of age, and, like you, they know just what they're doing."

"You are full of shit."

Zane clomps to his bedroom. "You're so clueless you don't even know time-released from instant."

I slam my backpack onto the counter. "Get me the biggest effing one you have. I need to stay up all night and ace this test. And I need to stay away from you."

He sticks his head out of his room and throws a pill down the hall. "Ten dollars."

I pick up the red-and-yellow capsule, then turn it over in my palm. "What a rip. You probably got it for two."

"It's the real deal, not generic. Read the side. I'm not making any money. I usually sell them for fifteen, which is what yours is going to be if you don't shut up."

"Here. Take your dead presidents." I stomp down the hall to shove the money into his hand.

"You sure you don't want the short-acting one?"

I swallow it, grab my backpack, then head to my room. "I am sure."

***

A couple of days later, I lift the screen of my laptop. It is time to log in to my psych professor's page so I can find the grade posted for my paper on addiction. I remember the comments I received when I fell asleep in class, after the Adderall had kept me up all night. I search for my assigned number and cross my fingers.

D-plus.

The food in my stomach sours, and rage courses to my fingertips. "Dammit." I slam my arm down, and my empty plate shatters through the notes on top of it. "Shi-i-i-t!" I scream, ignoring the pain.

"What's up your ass?" Zane appears at my door, hair all over the place, like he just rolled out of bed. He looks at the blood running down my arm, then spots the plate. "Sweet. I haven't done that since the walking L moved my mother to a foreign country."

"This is what I think of that psych bitch professor's face." I hurl the jagged plate fragments into the trash can. Bitter sweat seeps from my pores.

"You made a sick hole in it." Zane eyes the plate fragments in the garbage can.

"That paper was great," I gripe. Guilt fills my lungs, fuels my breath. "Nobody in this school could have dug up all the reference material my mom sent."

"She mailed a lot of stuff." Zane leans against the wall.

"It was only one day late." I turn my arm over to check out the damage.

"There are all kinds of assholes out there." A wicked grin slides across his face. He heads for the kitchen and laughs loud. "For this season of thanks, I got myself some over-the-top weed."

I follow and stick my arm under the sink tap. A new type of pain enters with the water, burrowing deep into the veins of my heart.

Zane opens a glass jar with a clamp-down lid and inhales a giant whiff of pot. "Gotta love the scent of flowers."

"I am going to need some of that for when my dad finds out my grade."

"Don't tell him."

"My mom will ask. She sent the references, remember?" I check out the gouges and rip off a chunk of skin which has curled into itself like a nautilus. The arm throbs and starts to bleed again.

The smell has filled the kitchen. It burrows its way into my lungs and starts a longing.

"Tell her you don't have it back yet." Zane disappears into his bedroom.

I grab a fresh paper towel to blot the blood. The open glass jar full of dank green herb lures me. *He will never miss any* rings raspy in my ears.

Not doing it.

The strong scent of good weed persists, drawing me closer.

The late paper was his fault because of the ecstasy enters my head in a gruff tone.

I snatch another paper towel, glance toward his room, grab a couple of buds, and drop them in. "I should not lie to my mom." I call to Zane.

He starts back down the hall. "I would."

"That smells amazing." I shove the bounty deep into my front pocket, then reach for my wallet. "How much is it?"

He puts a half dozen buds on a digital scale. "Fifty." He dumps it into a baggie.

I hand him the cash and put the baggie in my pocket.

Zane packs his pipe bowl. He takes a long draw before handing it to me.

I flop onto the couch, congratulating myself on a nice yoink, and cloak my pain in a thick blanket of fog.

Chapter 17

Anxiety flutters through me like a leaf loose in the wind while I drive down the palm tree-lined street to my parents' house. I know I need to be here for Thanksgiving, but the white stucco house with the red barrel-tile roof does not feel like home anymore.

I park on the far side of the circular drive, under a royal palm. If I am lucky, it will shed one of its giant fronds, and I can blame the tree for the new gouge and dents on my car. If not, hopefully, the car is far enough away that they may not notice.

A pressure is pushing on my temples, as if my ears do not want to hear the same old crap. I need to keep my parents happy. After all, they pay the bills.

When I open the front door, Touchdown, our old beagle, looks up from his favorite spot on the seagrass throw rug, then bolts under the matching ivory armchairs Mom has across from the charcoal leather couch.

"What are you doing under there?" I kneel by the chair. "Hey, TD, I missed you."

He inches farther away. Weird. He never hid when I came back from camp years ago.

"David, I'm so glad you're here." Mom rushes over and buries me in one of her overwhelming hugs.

I drop my bag and hold her warm shoulders. She has the

same rose-smelling lotion on her hands as when I was a kid. I melt into her embrace.

"How'd you get those cuts on your arm?" Mom cranes around my shoulder.

"I, uh, dropped a plate. The shards bounced up off the counter and cut me."

"Deep cuts, but they don't look infected. Come on." She pats my back. "Eric just got home from the airport."

As she shuttles me into the family room, I spot him, perfect as ever in his preppie plaid shorts and golf shirt, his hair smoothed with pristine placement. He was probably bragging about his 4.0.

A whiff of apples and cinnamon floats over from the kitchen. It smells so good. I want to love being home, but there is a layer of discomfort that was not here before.

"That sweet scent is definitely not you," I toss at Eric.

"You're right." Eric grins, slaps my back, and gives me a one-armed hug.

"You look even paler than last year, bro." I snort.

Eric forces a laugh. "I know. I can't wait to lay around all day tomorrow, soaking up the sun."

He will probably be sucking up to Dad, soaking his wallet for a game of golf, with free lunch and beers too.

"You need it if you plan to hang out with those Boca be-atch friends of yours," I say.

Eric rolls his eyes and opens his mouth to say something, but Mom clears her throat, so he shuts it.

"It's a long ride, David. Are you thirsty? I made some of your favorite iced tea." Mom rushes to the kitchen, opens the fridge, and pours a glass.

She knows me so well. I hope she will not just look at me and realize how bad my grades are. I turn my shoulder.

"No, thanks. I am going to put my bag in my room."

I duck around the corner and toss my bag onto the bed. I do not feel like sitting around, getting cross-examined about what I do every day. Perhaps I should climb out the window and light one up in the backyard.

"David is that you?"

Dad's voice. I have to go out there, but I do not want to deal with him. Dampness etches its way into my palms. I suck in a breath and step out into the family room.

"Good to see you, David." Dad extends his hand.

I stare at it. I should have expected his hand instead of a hug. Maybe this is better. I meet his gaze and his grip. "Hi, Dad."

Dad leans back and does a full body scan. His brows squeeze closer. "It looks like you put on the freshman fifteen and then some."

My teeth lock. Pellets of sweat sprout on my forehead. What does he expect—for me to show up and be the perfect son, like Eric? I should have smoked one before I walked in here. Then, maybe I could deal with his bullshit.

Mom shoots him a dirty look and gives me a smile. "I think you look good, David."

"Yeah, right," I say.

Dad grabs the iced tea Mom poured for me and takes a gulp. "Did you bring back my duffel bag?"

A twinge of guilt creeps under my skin because I did not write it down on my list. "I forgot. Sorry, Dad. I left it in my closet."

"I told you to bring it."

"I had it out, ready for you when you were in Greenville. You refused to carry it," I snap back.

"I need it for next week."

"Well, it is not here. I can buy you a new one."

He slams the glass down on the counter. "I don't *want* a new one."

Mom moves between me and Dad. "There's an old one in the attic that will do. Come sit down, David."

Tea has splashed onto the countertop and dribbled into the shape of an F. Everything in this house is against me, even the effing tea. I need to get out of this place.

"I need to go. Some high school friends organized a barbecue." I grab my keys and run out the door.

In my car, I reach for my stash, which I keep in a slit between the carpet and console. Life is easy for them. They do not understand what my life is like.

I inch down the street while I load my pipe bowl. At the end of the block, I flick my lighter, losing the vibe of Dad.

The barbecue is forty minutes west. I stop at a store, where they are loose with checking ID, to pick up a bottle of rum and some soda to go with it. Zane was right. This weed is good. It makes me want to chill instead of driving. The salt breeze surrounds me like a warm blanket while I return to my car.

I plunk down in my seat, thinking about the high school group. They are a bunch of kiss-asses who do not get high. That will create drama I do not need. I turn the car toward the beach.

I round a barrier of sea grapes. The sand feels cold on my bare feet.

A fishing boat pitches down in a trough, and a wave crashes over it. Water spills out the stern. The boat is getting nowhere in the rough water—like me with my family. I wish I was back in Greenville. The thought of being stuck talking to my parents and Eric all weekend is awful.

My mind goes to Zane and all the sick parties he has brought me to, the rush of hanging with him. I wonder what he is doing. Probably at some awesome bash right now.

I fish out my phone.

"Hey, Dave. You're missin' all the fun up here. I'm at this guy's house in Alacosta. He's got a pre-Thanksgiving feast of homemade hash brownies. You should be here, bro. They're nuclear."

"What do they taste like?"

"Like brownies, man, with hash in 'em." He laughs loudly.

I imagine the texture of a brownie and wonder if hash tastes nutty or bitter.

"The buzz is *siiiick*. You'd love it. What are *you* doin'?"

A cabana rattles like a cage of old bones in the wind. I look down the length of the deserted beach. "Nothing. This place is so boring. There is nobody here, nothing to do."

"Come back for the FLU game," Zane says.

"Yes." I jump up and kick the sand. It blasts back at me, pelting my face and stinging my arms. A bird shrieks from the dune, and I burst out laughing. "Get me a ticket."

"No shit? You're comin' back? I'll get you one."

A gust pounds the cabana. It teeters and collapses.

A girl in the background says something to Zane.

"Got to go, bro." The connection goes dead.

I am thrilled to find a good excuse. The idea will be easy to pass off on Dad. He is all about football. I will tell him the ticket was hard to get.

I cannot wait to go back to normal life.

The genius of Zane deserves a celebration. I reach into the pocket where I put my stuff. I pack my pipe and take a long hit, wondering how many girls are there and how they ever got a hold of hash. Leave it to Zane. He is always doing something new and exciting.

***

I slept in this morning, then had a long shower. No one has bothered me all day. I have not told them I skipped the barbeque. Mom is busy cooking, and Dad is screaming at football players on TV. The next few hours in conversation with him would have been brutal, so I sneak out my bedroom window and burn one.

"Frank, we have to leave for Aunt Susie's," Mom calls.

"Right after this offensive drive," Dad hollers over the television.

I check out my Eaglechat in my room. Zane posted a picture of a bunch of guys I do not recognize in front of an old barn, all doubled over from laughter.

Eric comes across the hall. "How's your first semester going?"

My foot twitches. I scroll down the news feed, wondering if I should tell him. He has never squealed on me before.

"Could be better."

"What do you mean?" He eases down on the bed.

I wrench around in the chair and stare Eric in the face. "I mean, my grades suck."

"You may not get As like you used to in high school."

I shift in the seat so my voice projects away from the kitchen and family room. "I would be happy with straight Cs right now."

Eric squints his eyes, and his mouth goes flat. "That bad?"

My head sinks to the chair back. "I have a C in English, a D in history, and Fs in physics and psych."

"Two Fs?" His shoulders contract, his voice shrill.

I glance at the door, hoping no one heard him.

"You withdrew, right?" Eric stammers.

"Two Fs?" Dad fills the doorway. "What the hell are you doing with two Fs?"

My outlook shrivels with each word. Why did stupid Eric have to open his mouth?

Mom arrives at Dad's side, then lays her hand on his shoulder. "We're late, Frank."

Dad snorts. "I don't care. I want to know what the hell is going on."

"Frank, it's Thanksgiving…" Mom gives him a look and dangles the keys by his side.

He grabs them and turns away, letting fresh air in the room.

"Come on, boys," Mom says.

I take the escape route she creates and follow close behind.

"What kind of moron goes from As to Fs?" Dad grumbles. "What do you have Fs in?"

"Get the sweet potatoes, David," Mom says. She is trying to help me, but I wish she would leave me alone so I can think up a defense.

I lug out the hot casserole and hold it in front of me as armor. "Physics and psych."

"Psychology?" She stops. "The paper we talked about sounded great. I sent you all that information."

"It was an awesome paper, but our server went down in the apartment complex, and by the time I got to school to email it, I was too late."

"Why the *hell* did you leave it 'til the last minute?" Dad's face is red, his eyes bulging.

"There was a lot of information."

Mom points us to the door. "Let's go. We can't be late. We'll deal with this later."

The heat from the bowl pulsates up my arms. I run for the car.

"If you think I'm paying for you to go to school and get

Fs, you're wrong." Dad's eyes sear into me through the rearview mirror while he backs out. "What the hell have you been doing all semester?"

I look for my seatbelt to avoid his glare. "It… just… got away from me."

"Got away from you, my ass. You decided that the party was more important than the degree." Dad's anger spills.

I think about opening the door and bailing. The scrapes and bruises I would get jumping from a moving car would be better than listening to this bullshit.

"Of course, it must be about me. 'Welcome home, David. Let us bash you nonstop.'"

"Let him talk it through, Frank." Mom rests her hand on Dad's arm—her nice way of telling him to shut up when my LD issues arise. "When did this start, David?"

Dad cranks his head to her. "Who gives a shit when it started? He knows all the tricks you and the counsellors taught him. The school gives him all kinds of breaks—no math, extra time, free proofreaders. With his smarts, he should breeze through these early classes." His burning eyes go back to the mirror. "What are you going to do about it is what *I* want to know."

Heat radiates from the casserole wedged between my feet. My head is ready to explode. I open my mouth to say, *I want to get the hell out of here.*

Mom turns in her seat and looks at me with kind eyes. "Let's take this one at a time. You just took a test in history. How do you think you did?"

"I have no idea how I did," I snap. This loud voice does not sound like mine. "I went for extra help with the professor, okay? Then I stayed up all night and studied. What else do you want?"

"Don't you dare speak to your mother like that. You're the one who's failing."

"Frank, let me talk," Mom snaps.

He is getting to *her* now. That takes a lot.

Dad shoots me another cold stare in the mirror. The asshole must have adjusted it for that purpose because it is angled straight at me.

"Did you submit the psych paper, David?" Mom continues.

"Yes, but there was a penalty for it being late."

"How big?"

"Two grades lower." I turn away and stare out the window to avoid her eyes.

"You knew what your grades were before this. Why didn't you do something about it?" Dad's voice booms.

"I can pull them up. I always have in the past," I shout.

"You'll never do it. You can't get to an A from an F with one test left," Dad says. "What the *hell* are you thinking?"

"Like you were a stellar student when you were partying with all your butt-paddling friends."

"At least I was good enough to get into the fraternity," Dad replies, seething.

The air freezes. My chest caves, like he ran over it with the car. "*You* are the reason I did *not* get in," I hiss.

"You're delusional."

"Your frat buddy had his lame son, Robert, block my bid. I paid the price for some eff-up of yours two decades ago."

We pull into Aunt Susie's driveway. Dad slams on the brake and reaches over, trying to grab me by the collar.

"Stop it." Mom waves her hands in the air. "This is not the boy we sent to college."

I escape from the car, rush to the kitchen with the casserole, and pour myself an extra-large glass of Aunt Susie's cheap wine.

***

Aunt Susie's house is old Florida seventies era, with the bedrooms on one side and an open living space on the other. Her living room is a gallery of stuffy antiques covered in scratchy fabric the color of blood. The house smells like she has had mothballs in the closets for fifty years.

Mom makes us endure it because she thinks cooking for the family gives Aunt Susie purpose.

Lucky for me, Dad goes straight out to the backyard since he hates the odor.

I plunk down onto the carpet beside my little cousins, who think I am cool and will not cross-examine me, figuring I can eat at the kids' table and avoid everybody else until I blow this popsicle stand.

"Is that my wonderful nephew, David? You're so sweet to keep the little ones from under my feet. Come here so I can give you a hug."

Aunt Susie's hair has shifted from black to salt and pepper. A large, pumpkin-y bib apron covers her rust-colored dress. She is still as thin as a skeleton.

I rise to my feet, bracing for a bony hug. Hopefully, the mothball smell is not in her clothes.

"Hi, Aunt Susie." I should say more, tell her she looks wonderful and all that crap, but I do not feel like talking right now.

"I'm a little bit behind today. Would you mind setting out the flatware for the children's table?" She hands me a fistful of knives, forks, and spoons.

"Sure." When I look at the table, I panic. Left and right flips in my head like numbers. I do not remember which side the fork goes on, so I close my eyes, trying to picture a formal place setting.

This is not working. I put the knives and forks down, hoping to use muscle memory for when I pick up a fork. No luck.

I will not embarrass myself by asking. The kids could care less. I plunk the forks and knives down one by one, saving the spoon for the spot with a booster seat. At least I know that one is correct.

"Turkey's carved. Come and eat!" Uncle Joe calls. "David, I want you to sit right here so you can tell me all about school." He reaches over his large belly to pat the chair next to him.

My stomach knots. "I figured I would sit at the kids' table. Someone needs to keep an eye on them."

His toothy grin is stained brown from years of black coffee. He runs a hand over his bald head to make sure his comb-over is in place. "They're big enough to feed themselves now. They'll be fine. Have a seat." He slides a chair with a red velvet seat out for me while everyone files in from the backyard.

"The fork is on the wrong side," five-year-old Lizzie calls out.

"Not to worry. We'll switch them around." My older cousin shoots me a look.

My cheeks heat. The damn dyscalculia screwed up a task so easy a kindergartener knows how to do it. I sink into my chair, wishing I was back at school, where no one cares about forks.

Dad takes the seat across from me, with Eric next to him. Mom's younger brother sits beside me. I pile food onto my plate, hoping that, when my mouth is full, I have an excuse not to talk.

"Tell me all about school." Uncle Joe digs into his food.

I need to stay as far away from the topic of grades as

possible. "The football games are great. There is nothing like being in a stadium of ninety thousand people cheering for your team."

"Don't you think you should knock it off on the gravy?" Dad says.

"Sure, maybe when you do," I reply.

"Ask him about his grades, Joe." Dad shoves a wad of turkey into his mouth.

My eyes lose focus. Leave me alone. "No matter what I say, it will not be good enough for you."

"You need to formulate a plan so you can get through this semester."

"I know. I need to study more."

"You think you might have figured that out before now."

You would think he might try using good manners at a gathering with Mom's family.

"Things are not like at home," I say, "where everyone is quiet when they know you have a test. Zane has people over, and I can hear them talking."

"Go to the library." Eric shoots a frown my way.

"You have *no* idea how hard my life is."

"Why didn't you get away from that jerk of a roommate when your mother offered to pay for a new place?" Dad persists.

I wriggle my butt back into the chair and sit tall. "Because Zane is a good friend."

"What kind of a friend gets someone arrested?" Dad snorts.

"You do not even know what it is like to have a friend. You golf with guys you say are your buddies, never bringing them over or going out anywhere with Mom and their wives. Friends come for dinners and graduation parties. At least Zane is there when it counts."

My father's face turns a dark shade of burgundy.

Mom waves her index finger in warning, where she thinks no one can see it.

"Which really isn't helping *you*." Eric shifts in his chair.

They will not stop pulling my strings. My family needs to leave me alone.

"You have no clue, Eric. You have always been the one who could do no wrong. Even when you went to Penn instead of U of Mann, it was all okay because you were in an *Ivy*." I make quotes around the word. "You have never had to struggle for anything."

Eric lunges toward me. "Do you think my classes are easy? Do you think they hand out grades for free? You've got to work at it."

"Preach to me, Mister Got-Into-Engineering-School-Perfect."

"That's enough," screams Dad.

"What? Am I upsetting your faultless son? The one who can do no wrong?"

"Come on, David," Mom calls from the other end of the table. "You know that's not true."

"Not true, my ass," I shout.

"Ass, ass, ass, ass." The kids start chanting, drumming their forks against their plates.

"David," Mom scolds.

"Stop it," their mother yells.

I turn to Mom. "You, with your fancy psychology degree, should have known better. You could have stuck up for me more. Instead, all my life, you have let Eric be the pet."

"Ass, ass, ass, ass," the kids keep going.

"David Everest, that's enough." Mom slaps the table.

"Now look what you've done." Dad slams down his fork.

The sound is deafening. My nerves want to jump out of my skin. I shove my chair back.

"Shut up," I scream at the kids.

Somebody starts to cry.

Uncle Joe launches from his seat and sticks his round, pink face in mine. "Don't you behave like that in my house."

"What? Am I disturbing the mothballs?"

Aunt Susie gasps.

Dad is on his feet.

I spot a bus coming down the road. *Get out while you can* rings in my ears. I run out the door, waving hard at the bus driver. He sees me and stops.

The bus drives away, with Mom at the front door, her fists against the glass.

Chapter 18

I am at my desk, studying to compensate for the guilt I feel after leaving dinner and driving back to school last night. Mom has called a few times. I should talk to her instead of texting. She did not deserve what I said, but the rest of them… They did.

Zane opens my bedroom door and sticks his head in. He has a jacket over his arm and sneakers—not flip-flops—on his feet. "I'm going to a Fielder with a bunch of people. You gonna man-up and step away from that desk?"

"A Fielder to you probably has a different meaning than the fraternity's." I rub my hand over my textbook. The disaster at home keeps rebooting in my head.

Zane leans on the desk. "It's the place your dad's precious MGD frat crowd goes. Bubba rents his farm out for their parties."

The smell of good weed floats by, even though he has not burned any. A longing comes over me, tempting, prodding, tormenting me deep in my bones. *Enough studying; enjoy your life* etches its way into my brain. "I will be ready in two minutes."

I scribble some notes in the margin of my notebook, using the blue pen to contrast the black ink so I can remember which parts I need to go over again. I pull on a pair of jeans and shoes, then dig around in my closet for my jacket. No way do I want to be out in a field in a T-shirt and shorts.

"How far is this place?" I ask, when the city lights fade and the road narrows to two lanes.

"Only about five more minutes. It's kind of remote, but it's a cool place to hang out." Zane turns his truck off the highway onto a dirt road. His headlights reveal the barn he posted a picture of online in the distance. The once-red paint is faded and peeling. Abandoned farm equipment sits scattered and rusting in a huge, unmown field. Not a car in sight.

I clear my throat, not masking my annoyance. "Nobody is here, Zane."

"They're in the barn." He nods to where a band of dull yellow light flickers from a broken window.

"You said this was a party."

"More people will show up."

"How many—two?"

Dread fills my veins while I glance around the vacant farm. Nothing is here except a creepy shed, which looks ready to fall, and the dilapidated barn. Why did I assume it would be something special? I should have stayed home.

"Hey, Bubba," Zane hollers, climbing out of the truck. "Bubba, this is my homie, Dave, I told you about."

"Took y'all long 'nough ta git here." Bubba, an old guy about thirty, balding with a beer gut, has a gas can and matches in one hand and is dragging a full cooler with the other. The plug for the spout at the bottom has broken off, dribbling a thin line of water while he drags.

"Where's Billy Beer?" Zane picks up the cooler. "Get that door, will ya, Dave?"

I tug on a rotting side door, which groans open, and am hit with the musty odor of decaying hay, dust, and a faint smell of something unsettling. "Billy Beer is his name?"

"That's what I call him." Bubba laughs. "He be cleanin' out the loft." The man nods to a ladder made with different sizes and types of wood leaning against what appears to be a small shelf near the top of the barn. "There's a bed up there." He winks.

"And Dave is gonna be the first one bangin' in it tonight." Zane laughs.

The sight of the rickety ladder makes my chest tighten. I never told Zane I am afraid of heights. Trying to do it in a tiny alcove thirty feet in the air would be terrifying.

"If I tried that, a girl would call for an Uber to get home."

"They won't drive this far out. That's why we crash here." The guy I am guessing is Billy pokes a head of greasy brown hair, pulled into a thin ponytail, out of the loft. His smile shows missing teeth.

The hairs on my arms stand. None of the usual gang has come. I made a mistake.

Zane drops his end of the cooler. "The ice is in the back of my truck."

"It's gittin' colder than a pig's ass in January out there." Bubba holds out the gas can. "Go git the fire goin', boy. The wood's wet. It needs more gas."

I shove my hands into my pockets. "I can take the cooler."

An ugly sneer covers Zane's face. "We've got the cooler covered. Go light the fire, dude."

My teeth lock together, and a muscle in my jaw pops. "I am *not* a fan of open-pit fires."

Bubba hauls out a huge doobie and lights it up. "Don't worry. It's not open. A couple years ago, we was so wasted we didn't notice it'd started a brush fire. Damn near burned down the barn."

Zane disappears in the night, and I follow him out to the truck. Long shadows distorted by cloudy, jagged window glass stretch past me into the dirt.

"This isn't my thing. I want to go back."

"What are ya, a pussy?"

"I thought our friends were going to be here. These guys look as old as my dad."

Zane tugs open the tailgate and lets it drop with a *thump*. "You're exaggerating. They're nice guys. Other people will show up. Watch."

"It's too cold to be out here." I try to make sure my voice is not pleading.

"That's why they have a fire."

"How about if I take your truck back and you get a ride with them?"

"Fuck that. You made a decision. Man-up and stick to it." Zane grabs two bags of ice, then shoves the tailgate closed with his shoulder.

I follow him back inside, not knowing what else to do. I am not walking twenty miles on the side of a two-lane road in the dark.

Zane drops the ice, grabs the joint from Bubba, and takes a hit. "You need some of this." He blows it in my face.

Though I find myself breathing in his spent smoke, I rack my brain on how to get out. I can have some of that at home, after I find a way back. "Not ready yet."

You already have rumbles into my brain. *You just breathed it in. It is done.*

I shake my head and dig my heels in the dirt strewn on the barn floor.

There's no getting out of here. You are stuck. May as well enjoy. Take the fatty.

I inhale deep. The smoke ebbs through me, releasing my anxiety and relieving the tension. Billy grins at me, and I feel like I am plummeting through the giant black hole in his teeth.

"I got an old oil drum set up outside to contain the fire." Bubba holds out the gas can with an expectant stare.

My fingers brush across the top of a bottle of vodka in the folds of my pocket, tangling my fear of fires in the memory of good times with Zane. "Where is it?"

"'Round back." Bubba's reckless laugh is followed by a swig from a bottle of Jack Daniel's.

Zane runs in, carrying two more bags of ice. "Should be wearing a damn parka. It's freezing out there."

"Okay, okay. I will get the fire lit."

I grab the gasoline and head out the door, into a night so dark I can barely see the gas can in my hand. The faint silhouette of a four-foot-tall cylinder stands in the distance, and I plod toward it. The stench of gasoline greets me six feet from a large steel drum with a rusted-out bottom. There is no way I am adding more.

I retreat and drop the gas can twenty feet away. Thirty-six inches is the farthest I figure I can toss a lit match before it goes out. I position myself sideways so I can run if the fire *poofs* at me. The cold penetrates my jacket and my jeans. I light the match, shivering.

A blaze of orange knocks me to the ground.

Pain sears my face, my head.

Fire.

Shrieking.

My hair. I bat the flames.

Shoulder burning.

Jacket on fire.

Roll.

I twist and turn in the dirt.

The world goes black.

Chapter 19

A white veil flutters with shadow. A man covered in bugs says he is the Bugmaster. He laughs and disappears.

I drift away.

Everything hurts. My eyes are stuck together. It is like I have a cotton ball wedged in my throat. The stench of rubbing alcohol and almonds stings my nose. I lift my hand to crack open my eye, and pain rips through my shoulder.

"Let me help you with that," a soft female voice says. A hand which smells like flowers wipes the crust from my left eye. "That's better."

My eye opens a tiny bit. A beautiful blond in blue.

Angel? Am I dead?

My mouth is all dried up, and it won't work right. I fish around for some spit. "You angel?"

"No, I'm Kelly, your nurse." She laughs. It sounds far away. She moves, and a blurry version of my mom comes into view.

Someone touches my left hand. It feels big, out of place.

"David, you're in the hospital. You got burned in an explosion." Mom's voice.

"I did?" My eyes slide closed. An orange ball of fire surrounds me. The heat is unbearable. I force my eyes open.

"You came in last night." She strokes my hand. "We got a call from the hospital and left right away."

My stomach twists. I wet my tongue. "I have burns?"

A machine by my head shrieks. The nurse clicks something to make it stop. Nobody speaks while I peer through the tiny, blurry slit.

The nurse rolls a stool over to sit beside me. "You have second- and third-degree burns on your head, right shoulder, arm, and ankle."

My breath catches. I remember my hair burning, batting, rolling to put it out. I try to swallow past the brick stuck in my throat.

"Face?"

Something crashes to the floor near Mom.

"Your face is burned on the right side." Kelly's voice is focused and level.

Air rushes from my lungs. I am history.

"We have your eye patched until the ophthalmologist can get here to evaluate it."

Mom squeezes my hand.

"I'm going to put some morphine in your IV," Kelly says, followed by more smells of rubbing alcohol.

Visions of charred black chicken skin flash through my head. I clamp down on Mom's hand. There is a coolness in my left arm, and I hear myself sigh. Induced sleep overtakes me.

My butt is sinking, and I am becoming upright. Coughing starts, like when I get up in the morning. My left eye has a sticky paste when I open it.

My parents are holding onto each other at the foot of the bed. The odor of rubbing alcohol with dried blood fills my nose, and I remember where I am.

"I'm Doctor Yew." A voice from my right side. "I'm here to check your eyes."

I turn toward him. A thin man with white-streaked hair and a light strapped to his head is the fuzzy image.

"David, there's a mesh over your burns, holding the dressings and the eye patch in place." Kelly's voice. "I'm going to take it off so Dr. Yew can examine your eye."

My heart thumps. "Will it hurt?"

"I have medication here if you need it." She places two gloved hands on the side of my face and lifts what looks like a fishnet over my nose, forehead, and ear.

Searing pain grips my head. I bite the inside of my cheek to hold back a scream. The patch on my eye falls to the floor, and Mom gasps. There's a *thud* in my chest. It must be bad.

"You have some swelling here, David, so I'm going to have to hold your eyes open."

I lift my face toward the doctor and bite harder.

His gloved fingers pry the lid apart with caution.

Fresh blood oozes into my mouth while he tugs. Light, color, and his hazy form come into view.

"I can see you." A wave of relief floats through me.

Mom starts to cry. She grabs my toes.

"Good." He opens my eye wider, then puts some drops in. They sting.

I grip the rail tighter.

"That's to dilate your pupil so I can get a better look." He lets the eyelid down, then puts a drop in the other eye. "We just have to wait a minute for it to work."

Dr. Yew shines a light in my good eye, then moves the lid around.

"Let's have a look, David… That one's in good shape."

While I grip the bedrails, he pulls my right eye open really slow. The brightness hurts.

"It looks like your right cornea has flattened from the explosion." The doctor adjusts his light.

I hold my breath.

My mother clutches my foot tighter.

He squirts some ointment into my eye. "We'll have to fit you with corrective lenses when your burns improve."

"Does that mean glasses or surgery?" a voice asks. My Dad.

The doctor slides the lid closed, then snaps his gloves off. "Glasses should do the trick. But we'll have to wait 'til that ear heals up."

Mom's exhale is guarded.

I choke back the blood in my mouth. My stomach lurches.

"Here's my card. Call for an appointment when he gets out of the hospital. I'll fit him in the office right away."

"Thank you," my parents say in unison.

Mom lets go of my foot. "We talked to Eric. He's driving up tonight."

I blink slowly a couple of times to stop the burning. "Tell him not to."

"He wants to see you before he goes back to school." Mom's voice pitches upward.

Who would want to see me now?

"Tell him I will call him." I turn my face away. "Morphine," I direct Kelly.

"We're going to clean your facial burns while this dressing is off. The timing is perfect for your next dose, David."

What is with this *we* bit? This nurse is way too cheery.

"We'll give you some morphine, and since you're more awake, we'll get you hooked up to a pump, where you can give it to yourself by pushing a button when you need it."

I open my eyes and stare at the nurse. "Really? As much as I want?"

She tows a rolling table near the bed and starts opening jars and packages. "It has a time limit. If you press the button too often, it shuts down until the set time is up."

I think about how I wanted to cut back on using anything. "What is this going to do to me? Maybe I can do without any."

"It's important not to let the pain get out of hand, David. If that happens, it can impede your healing. Go ahead and use the morphine button when it's set up. You're not going to become addicted." Kelly turns to my parents. "Sorry, but we stretched the visiting hours so you could talk to the doctor. It's time to go."

"Of course." Mom reaches for Dad.

He comes up beside me, his lip trembling while he whispers. "We'll be in the waiting room outside if you need us, David."

I watch them leave. Dad glances back. No criticism for being with Zane. No reaming me out for not studying. I must be in bad shape for him to be acting this way.

I steady my quivering hands on the side rails and take a deep breath. Kelly opens a package of wooden sticks.

"That for sore throats?"

"Similar. We use sterile ones to scrape away the white gooey stuff called Silvadene."

"You plan to scrape my burns? Mom?" I search for her beyond the closed glass door and inch away from the nurse. "What if it really hurts?"

Kelly moves the table aside and glides a stool over. "David, your burns need to be debrided to heal. That means the old dead skin needs to be removed so new skin can grow. In some places, more layers of the dermis are damaged, so we need to get down to new tissue."

My breath comes in short puffs. "Where is it the worst?"

"Your shoulder is the worst. You can get that done in the whirlpool, along with your arm and ankle, even your ear. It's the area around your mouth and eye that we're going to clean up now."

"We?"

Kelly laughs. "The healing process is a joint venture, David. We provide the environment, but you need to do the work. You ready?" She rolls the table over beside me and picks up a syringe. "I'm putting some morphine in your IV, then we'll start."

I nod and close my eyes, imagining distorted pictures of my face. How horrible do I look? Like some zombie from a video game?

Kelly snaps her gloves on. The wooden blade grazes my face. I grit my teeth. It feels like she is digging at my cheek with a snowplow.

"Stop." I push her hand away. "The medicine is not making me groggy. I need to be put to sleep for this."

"The morphine helps control the pain, but it may not make you sleepy right now." Kelly cups my jaw in her hand. "I'm going to wipe the rest of the cream off your face with some gauze. This may be uncomfortable."

Stabbing pain shoots through my jaw. Uncomfortable? The pain is *unbearable*. I pull my head back, but she holds her grip.

I dig my fingers into the sidebars and holler, "More medicine! Please!"

Kelly stops. "Sorry. That's all I can give you for now. You seem to have a low pain threshold. Do you take any drugs on a regular basis, for sports injuries or anything?"

Do beers and smoking count? They are not prescriptions or something like fentanyl. My bloated tongue blocks the truth, and I swallow it back down.

"No."

"Take deep breaths and focus on something else. Ready?" She grips my jaw again.

"Okay." I stare at a spot on the ceiling, and for some reason, I think of Maria.

We are on the beach. She laughs while waves swirl around our feet. Her fingers trace my face. She giggles and calls me a pirate before putting a patch over my eye. Maria runs into the surf, finds an old fisherman's net, wraps me in it, and tells me I look great.

"That's it. We're done." Kelly clears the table.

I let go and fall into a deep sleep.

***

Zane and I are at the apartment, wearing pajamas. I have no energy to dress or study. My breath and my words are foul. I brush my teeth, open my mouth, and look in the mirror. Maria walks in.

She tells me I have a rotten tooth, that it should be pulled.

I argue that I have no pain.

She takes a pair of pliers from her pocket and yanks out a molar.

Warm pus gushes over my tongue. I gag at the taste of pent-up infection.

Maria hands me a glass of peroxide.

I rinse my mouth, and the colors in the room brighten. My breath turns sweet.

***

A peculiar beeping wakes me into a haze of fluorescent light. The lack of windows and constant brightness makes it hard to stay oriented to night and day.

My parents sit up and plaster on some questionable smiles. Dad has dark circles under his eyes, and his hair is sticking out. They scramble to their feet and hurry to my side.

"What time is it?" As I say it, I notice my mouth is working better.

"Almost eight thirty." Dad gets there first and touches my arm.

I jerk away. "What day?"

"Sunday. Sunday night," Mom clarifies.

"We talked to Zane. He told us what happened. He wants us to stay at your place while he's at a friend's." Dad's gaze drifts past my left eye and sticks on the burns. "He said to say hello. He doesn't like hospitals, so he'll see you when you get home."

The only buddy I have and he does not even want to see me. "Great."

"Your friend Maria saw us coming out of the apartment," Dad continues. "She asked about you and said she heard about the explosion from some people in the complex."

Mom smooths a wrinkle in the bed sheet. "We talked for quite a while. She's a really nice girl."

"Who will never want to talk to an effing mutant." Her, Lucy, or any other girl.

I roll away, creating a tug on my catheter. Painful spasms tear at my groin.

"It'll turn out all right, David. The doctor said your burns aren't too bad," Dad says.

My face throbs when blood rushes into it. "Not bad? I look like a freaking monster."

"That was the wrong thing to say. I'm just glad it's not worse." Dad backs away.

"I am lying in a fucking hospital bed, my face seared off, with wires and tubes sticking out of my chest, my arms, and my dick. I will look like a damn alien for the rest of my life. How much worse can it get?"

His face pales, and he looks down, picking at a thumbnail. "I'm sorry."

"Visiting hours are now over," floats in from the PA system.

A nurse pokes her head in. "Time to go, family."

"Sleep well." Mom kisses the top of my head.

"Good night, David." Dad puts his hand over mine.

A lump forms in my throat. He has never done that. It must be really bad.

I close my eyes to hide the tears, then jam my finger into the morphine button.

"Hey." A soft voice accompanies a light touch on my arm.

I wake from a dreamless sleep, expecting the nurse, and jerk my arm away. The heart monitor screams.

Maria jumps back.

I fan my fingers in front of my face. "Maria, what are you doing here?"

A nurse zips in and scans me and the equipment.

"Everything okay?" Maria asks.

The monitor stops beeping.

"Yeah." I turn away to smudge the salt marks from the corners of my eyes. "Look the other direction."

"I don't care what you look like, David," Maria says.

My face flames hotter. I grope in my mind for ways to get her to leave. "Visiting hours are over."

"My sister went to school with one of the nurses here. She agreed it would be all right to sneak me in."

Great. Now she thinks she is Florence Nightingale.

"You should go."

"You're still the same. A few bandages don't bother

me." She grins and lays a gentle hand on my good arm, leaving it there longer than I expect.

Is she shitting me?

I lower my fingers an inch so I can read her better.

"I talked to your parents for a long time, so I knew what to expect." Maria drags a seat over.

"Have you seen Zane?" I ask.

"No. Rachel's the one who told me what happened. She says Zane feels terrible."

"Not bad enough to come see me."

"Some people are afraid of hospitals."

"You came, though."

"I also have an ulterior motive." Her eyes twinkle. "Don't worry. It's not bad."

The surface of my arms contract with an icy chill. Blotches of burnt hair rise against the dressing. I don't want to know. I want her to go away. My thumb squishes the knob for morphine without a thought.

She pulls her chair closer to the bed. "Tell me what happened the night you went to the beach house."

"Why?"

"Well, because you told me a little but not all of it."

"I should call the nurse to get you out of here," I grumble.

Maria laughs. "Except you won't talk to anyone else about this."

"Why do you care?"

"Things seem different since then. And, a long time ago, a friend helped me when no one else would. I appreciate that. I want to return the favor."

"If I tell you, will you leave?"

She laughs so hard I can see her stomach move. This girl is stubborn. I need to confess, or she will stay all night.

"I got stood up."

"What else happened?"

The painful emptiness from that night returns. "I was the only one in the house who slept alone." I swallow and hit my morphine button, even though I know it is too soon.

"Where were you?"

"Outside on a hammock." I picture myself on the porch, feeling the cold around me. "I saw a face in the bushes. It whispered to me. I invited it over. It was warming, like it was filling the emptiness inside. Then I went to sleep."

"It wasn't a person, but more like a spirit?"

"I guess. A few things have been weird since, but not as bad as being in a hospital."

Maria reaches into her bag. "I found this book. It's called *The Unquiet Dead* by a psychologist who helps her clients get rid of entities under hypnosis during their sessions."

Entities. That word again.

"Can you repeat that?"

"I was thinking about the face you told me you saw."

"I was tired. It was foggy out."

"This psychologist says addiction is a precursor to possession."

I want to yell at her, but I am glad she came. "Leave me alone, Maria."

"What else has seemed strange to you lately?" Her neck elongates toward me, her necklace swinging back and forth. It is a cross, which gets so close it almost hits me.

"Der'mo."

Maria jolts back. "Der'mo? That's slang in Russian. It means *shit*."

"I must have meant *damn*. It is probably the name of some bandage they put on me. Derm means skin. I heard them talking about the dermabrasions or cuts I got from falling."

Maria eyes me. "Anything else different? I mean, before you got here?"

My sight blurs. The face appears, carved into my memory. "I do not want to talk about this. You need to leave."

There is an awkward silence. Maria sits, waiting for my answer.

"I am really tired. I need rest so I can get out of here."

"Dave, I'm only trying to help you."

"Yeah, right. Go away."

We stare at each other as if we are fighting.

Maria slides the chair against the wall. "Let me go find your nurse."

The night nurse appears with a pill in a paper cup. "I got you a sleeping pill so you can get some rest."

Maria smiles, leans in, plants a kiss on my cheek, and disappears. Was that kiss for real or out of sympathy?

Chapter 20

A crowd of white coats surrounds my bed. When my good eye comes into focus, I look around the circle of faces barely older than I am and freeze at the last one—a beautiful blond staring at me.

"I'm Dr. Thompson, the burn specialist for this unit," says a short guy with straight dark hair. He brushes it back from his right eye, and I wonder if it is a reaction to seeing mine. "These people are interns. We're going to review your chart."

"Great. A freak show." The room feels hot with all these extra people in here. My morphine cord is missing from my hand. I feel around, frantic, find it, and hurry to jam my thumb on the button.

"Explosion injury, Friday night, mild concussion, six to eight percent first- and second-degree burns. Trace of third on the right shoulder. Neuro checks good. Did some third spacing, shifting back. Positive peristalsis, slightly febrile at ninety-nine, six." He looks from the chart to the monitor above my head. "BP looks okay. No arrhythmias, O2 sat is fine."

The morphine does not work. I push it again and shift around, wishing I could run.

The blond girl is still gaping. She thinks I am a monster.

I turn my burnt side away and stare at the wall.

"Anything else?" Dr. Thompson looks past me. He nods to the girl.

I brace myself for what she might say, keeping my head turned so they all see my good side.

"I recommend a regular, high-protein diet, starting whirlpool treatments, and getting him out of the burn unit," she says.

A rush of adrenaline surges through me. "I can go home?"

"No, that means you can get rid of most of the tubes and get transferred out of this unit," Thompson says.

"David, it's important to keep your hands away from your face to prevent an infection of your burn," the blond intern tells me. Her voice is soft and seductive.

I lower my hand from my mouth, a splinter of fingernail between my teeth. How embarrassing.

"Good observation." Thompson turns to me while they file out. "The nurse will get you set up for transfer."

Kelly steps from behind my shoulder. She is wearing blue scrubs like before and a jacket that has little stethoscopes on it.

"You were in here too?"

"I hang out in case they have any questions." Her ponytail swings while she disconnects the IV with morphine, then flushes a little plug in my arm.

I hope for a bonus dose but feel nothing.

"Kelly?" Dr. Thompson waves.

"See what I mean?"

The morphine wears off in no time. I hit the call button to get Kelly back and have to wait forever.

Kelly does not answer. She is not at the desk. I cannot see Kelly anywhere. My nerve endings ache with longing.

"Kelly, where are you?" I call out.

No one can hear me through the closed door. I bang the side rail and wave my arms. No luck. My nerves are going to jump out of my skin.

The morphine IV is in the corner. I have watched her run the machine enough to know how to get it going. Though I might get in trouble for doing it, I will never see these people again.

It feels like something is crawling up my shoulder onto my face. I cannot stand it anymore.

I lower the bed as close to the floor as it will go and find the latch for the side rail. My hands are shaking so badly I cannot loosen the bar.

An old man wearing a white shirt and pants comes in. He parks a wheelchair in front of me. "Hi, I'm Chester. I'll be taking you down to whirlpool."

"You think you know everything?" I bark at him in a strange tone. *That voice.*

"What am I supposed to know?" He sounds distant.

"You know the way of the world, the descent to Hell. You drive the bus." My lips chant. The irritation under my skin pulsates. "I want morphine."

Chester hurries out the door, leaving the wheelchair behind.

In a minute, he returns with Kelly in tow. She shakes her head and frowns.

"You are not the one lying here, shriveled and disgusting. Look at me. I am ruined." My voice bellows at the glass doors. I fidget with the wires. This is not me, but I cannot stop it.

As soon as Kelly reaches the door, I let loose.

"You left me here with nothing. The pain is killing me. I pressed the call button and hollered and waved, and everyone ignored me. What kind of place is this?"

"The light wasn't on that you called."

"I pushed this button, right here, ten fucking times."

She maneuvers her way behind the bed. "A leg from the morphine pump got snagged on the cord for the call button and wrenched it out of the wall. Sorry."

"Sorry will not cut it. I need something for this pain."

"I'm going to give you a shot. It will get you through your treatment." Kelly puts the head of my bed down flat. "Turn over, David. I'm going to put this in your backside."

My mouth goes dry. I stay on my back, butt down. "I want it in the IV, not a shot."

"You can take your pain medication in pill form once you get to your other room." Kelly holds the syringe in front of her, removes the plastic cover from a two-inch-long needle, and slowly presses the plunger. A tiny drop of morphine rolls down the needle, like the New Year's ball in Times Square.

"I need something now." My words are desperate.

She moves back and looks me over. "I'll give you a little of this in your IV."

Kelly reaches for the plastic hub that has become my lifeline. The familiar smell of rubbing alcohol... the cool sensation in my arm... The edginess disappears.

"You lucked out on the whirlpool treatment. Someone else had theirs canceled." She unhooks the wires from my chest. "You're going with Chester. Is that all right?"

"Fine." I look for him outside, but she has the curtain drawn. It flutters at me with malicious intent.

"He said you seemed unhappy." She hesitates. "And a little disoriented."

I need to make something up. "I am nervous about moving."

Kelly studies me, considers my words, and with doubt

in her eyes, rolls my butt up off the bed with her elbow. "Just a little pinch here."

Even though I resist, she refuses to ease up. While my ass is bare to the breeze, she jams the needle in.

"This stuff better work, fast."

"What day is it today, David?" Kelly takes the syringe to a red box on the wall beside a calendar.

Sweet move. "November twenty-sixth, at nine o'clock in the morning. I am getting busted out, and yes, I am all there."

She laughs. "Too bad 'cause now I have to remove the catheter from your bladder."

My compadre goes into retreat mode and tries to hide behind his two best friends. This is not the way I want her to see it. "Um… can I take that thing out myself?"

"Sorry, no," Kelly answers. "There's a balloon that's blown up inside your bladder, and I need to make sure that all the fluid is out of it. You wouldn't be happy if that balloon came out blown up."

I wince and feel a wave of nausea. "Can you put me to sleep to do that?"

She laughs again. "No."

I throw my good arm up over my eyes and pretend as if not looking will help me save face.

Kelly leans over my bed. "Take a deep breath."

I grunt when the feeling of a hot branding iron shoots through my groin and up to my stomach. It keeps on stinging, even with the catheter limp in her hand.

"That's it. You're done." Kelly leaves to finish flushing my dignity down the drain.

The orderly wheels me to the first bed in a semi-private room after an hour of sitting in a big vat, watching the flesh on my shoulder slough off. "This is your room. I brought your things from the burn unit."

"Thanks." I nod while I survey the bed, nightstand, big reclining chair, and white curtain drawn all the way around, to prevent me from seeing the person in the next bed. "Sorry I was nasty before." My cheeks heat up. "Being in the hospital is really weird."

"Don't worry about it." He points to a white box clipped to the far bed railing. "The call button is there if you need a nurse. Hope you get home soon."

"Me too."

When he leaves, a shadow hovers for a second and then disappears behind me.

My nerves turn to fiberglass, fraying, craving medicine to gather them back together. I snatch the call bell and push it.

After ripping into the plastic bag on the bed, I search for my boxers, finding only a plastic tub, a toothbrush, and Maria's damn book.

"Nothing."

A hazy memory of having my clothes cut off in the ER fills my mind. A flash of orange and a blast knocking me off my feet. Shrieking at seeing my clothes, my hair on fire. Zane screaming at Bubba. Terror in their eyes while they lift me onto a piece of plywood, then load me into the back of Zane's truck. The apologies from his lips on the bumpy road when my head bangs against lumber and my skin blisters, all mixed with intermittent blackness.

A salty taste fills my mouth. I swallow, run for the toilet, but stop.

A mirror.

I pivot toward the sink, fingers shaking. I grab the cold porcelain with both hands and slowly raise my face.

Chapter 21

Monster.

My stomach sours, and bile rises in my throat, unstoppable this time. I turn my head and vomit, a visceral attempt to purge the picture.

Monster.

I feel myself rising, gawking, like the scene of an accident when you do not want to look but cannot stop yourself. I stare at the reflection of… me.

No eyelashes or eyebrows. I swallow, trying to keep from gagging. My face looks like a dirty pink sponge full of mayonnaise. I wonder if this is a nightmare.

The pain in my skin tells me it is not.

I glance at my shoulder, which looks like a peeled grapefruit. Half my hair is gone, the rest singed. I hover over the toilet, retching emptiness.

"Are you okay, David?" Dad is in a pair of jeans and a collared Eagles shirt. He has to represent, even in the hospital.

"I've got no eyelashes," I blurt from behind the dirty toilet.

Mom's big purse drops to the floor with a *thud*. She pushes past him, sinking to her knees, and takes my hand. "Eyelashes grow back, David, just like your hair."

Her hand is cold, and she is wearing her zip-up lined jacket, like it is cold outside.

"Even the damn cowlick's gone." I brush barf from my chin.

Dad joins her on the floor. He touches my arm with a sweaty palm.

I wonder if it is to placate or pray.

My hands tremble out of control. "They told me in hydrotherapy that hair won't grow back if the follicles are damaged." I look away and fix my focus on the twisted pipes under the sink, where I feel like I am trapped by the things being dumped on me all the time. I wish I could get flushed away. "I need something to take the edge off. Where is the damn nurse?"

"She'll be here soon," Dad says.

Mom clears her throat. "Your hair is only burnt back a couple of inches, sweetie. You could wear it long to cover."

Her words ride my raw nerves, my raw skin, bringing out the monster. I stand up and shove them aside. "I am not a *girl*." I limp to the bed and yank the sheet over my head.

They race behind me. Dad offers Mom the beige vinyl armchair next to the bed. She refuses to sit, so he helps himself.

"I have been here forever and have not even seen a nurse. Do they not have any staff in this hellhole?"

Dad's chair leg drags on the floor. "Do you want me to go look for her?"

"Stay right there," I bark. I reach my hand out to find the call button and slam my thumb into the plastic.

They look at each other from behind the thin sheet. Dark silence hovers around the bed.

"My mouth tastes horrible. I have to rinse this puke out." After edging the covers from one side of my face, I reach for a pitcher of water on the table beside me. I miss and knock it to the floor. "Shit."

"I'll get more water." Dad dives for the pitcher and races out the door.

Mom finds a towel and mops it up. She puts the dripping towel in the bathroom. "Are you having trouble seeing, David?"

"Well, it looks that way, does it not?" I mock her voice.

Mom tugs a tissue out of her purse and grips it tightly in her hand. I strain to see if there are tears in her eyes. All I see are big bags underneath.

"Here's more water." Dad hurries in, pours me a glass, and retreats to the foot of the bed.

I swish my mouth and drink long. An awkwardness hangs in the room. Neither of them speak.

"This is your fault. You pressured me to come here. None of this would have happened if I had stayed at home," I yell at Dad.

He lowers his eyes and runs his hands across the footboard.

I toss the sheet back over my head. Through the thin cotton, I watch Mom place a shopping bag with the school logo at the foot of the bed.

"What is that?"

"We bought you some things. We found some Eagle pajama bottoms and slippers that won't touch your ankle." Mom puts the slippers on the bed.

"Half my face is missing, and you are worried about clothes? Was that *your* idea?" I snap at my father from under the top sheet.

His mouth opens, but no words come out.

"Actually, it was my idea, David," Mom says in a smooth tone. "You're right. Your burns are a priority. Let's talk about that."

"I do not want to talk about it," I say from behind the

sheet. "I know I am acting childish. I just want this to be over."

"It's a difficult time." Mom's tone switches to the same one she uses on patients.

No practicing psych shit on me. I need to change the subject.

"I am not wearing old fart slippers."

She gathers the slippers up. "I can take them back. Let's talk about how you feel."

"Do not bother." I sniff, trying to silence the drumming in my head.

"Okay…" She looks at Dad, who shrugs. Mom swallows. "We got you a robe too." She holds it up in front of her.

"That looks like something some tool from an old sitcom would wear."

Mom looks away. No one says anything for a minute. It is awkward.

I wish they would leave.

"We both took the week off, David, so we have plenty of time to take it back." She sits in the chair Dad left open when he got water.

"No need for you to be here. There is nothing to do."

Mom puts on a half-smile. "There will be when you get out. It won't be easy to take care of your burns and prepare meals, or even drive, with your vision blurry."

"I will be fine."

"Well, we're sticking around, just to make sure." Her jaw sets.

I know she means it.

"You can stay. He"—I scowl at my dad—"needs to go."

Dad turns gray. Mom's lips flatten.

"I have plenty to do at the office, if you're sure that's what you want." He looks out into the hallway, his eyes wet.

I do not care. Let *him* feel the rejection for a change.

"Here comes the nurse. You need to get out." I snort.

"You called?" A large, pear-shaped woman in blue scrubs, with shiny black hair tied up in a bun, waddles over and clicks a button on the wall behind me.

"Yeah, I need something for pain." I check the level of sympathy in her sharp blue eyes but cannot read her. "Please."

"Sure, honey. I need to get your vital signs first. Let me go get everything." She sashays out the door.

"She has to check me in. That means *you* need to go." I kick the sheet, flipping the stuff they brought off the bed.

Dad jumps like a startled kid, gathers the slippers and robe, and bolts out the door.

Mom pastes on a smile and pats my leg. "I'll help him pack up and come back later."

I sink into the bed and haul the covers back up over my head.

The nurse returns, rolling a computer screen on a stand in front of her. She tugs the sheet off my bare bean. "Whatcha doing under there? I can't check you in if you're hiding."

I spot a thermometer, not a medication cup, on the side table. Anger grows in my chest. Play it cool.

The nurse slides back the curtain, revealing a middle-aged black man in the other bed, with his face, chest, and arms burned. His fingers are wrapped in gauze, his hands in splints.

"How you doing there, Jackson?"

The man's head movement is slow, pained. "Well, if it isn't my favorite nurse. I'm doing just fine, thank you for asking."

She retrieves a Velcro-covered cuff and places it on my arm. The machine pumps up to take my blood pressure and pulse.

"All I need is pain medicine, not a whole physical," I say.

She puts a stethoscope on my back. "Take a deep breath."

I do.

"Again," she says. "Lean forward and breathe deep. I'll be right back."

"Do not forget the pain medicine," I call to her backside.

A voice inside taunts me. *What if she forgets to bring it?*

I want to go back to intensive care, where I had my own nurse. Panic rises in my chest. My sweaty hands wrap themselves around the sheet and hang on.

"Hi. I'm Jackson." The man beside me flashes a smile so big I can see it, even though he is flat on his back.

This man is way too cheery. I wish I could reach the curtain from here so I could shut it.

"David," is all I say. I look past him, out the window, to a parking lot below.

"What brings you here?" my skinny roommate asks.

"I got burned lighting a fire that some asshole dumped too much gasoline on."

Jackson winces. "That's nasty." He looks away and stares at the ceiling for a while.

I do not feel like talking, but the nurse is taking so long. It will keep me from losing it. I bring him into focus. His burns are noticeable against his brown skin.

"What happened to you?"

"Our house caught on fire when someone fell asleep with a lit cigarette." He lifts his shoulder to face me.

"Was it your wife?"

"No. My son lost his job and moved back in with us."

"Is he in the hospital too?"

"They both died in the fire." He lies back down. A tear trickles across his temple.

My heart catches in my throat. I watch my parents' car driving out of the parking lot.

"I'm so sorry."

Chapter 22

My eye opens to Maria, in my new hospital room. She is sitting behind her laptop, with a stack of papers strewn across the over-the-bed table. I wonder if I should pretend I am still sleeping. She probably would not leave, even if I did. I raise the head of the bed to see her.

"Why are you here?"

"I heard you were out of ICU. I figured you'd be happy to see a familiar face. Your roommate, Jackson, moved to another room while you were sleeping. He said to say goodbye."

"Oh." Was it because of me? "Maria, why do you keep coming? Do you not have other things to do?"

"I want to check on my buddy, to whom I owe a debt of gratitude."

"There is no debt."

"You said I knew enough about exorcism to do a paper on it, so I talked to my religion history professor. She agreed to take it in lieu of another assignment."

This is outrageous. She is like a mad scientist, and I am the ogre she wants to experiment on.

"I thought you had to be a priest to do an exorcism… until I asked my grandfather."

"Why would he know?"

"He was a shaman in the Amazon. The church talked

him into becoming a priest. He was preparing to go away, but he got my grandma pregnant, so he got married instead."

Wow, scandal, runs through my head, but I do not have the energy to ask about it. I watch while she scans an article. On the page she has highlighted, it reads, "Mathew 10:1, Jesus gave his twelve disciples power against unclean spirits to cast them out."

This girl is a religious freak, like Zane said. I need to call the nurse and boot her out.

Maria is highlighting away. "This is fascinating. A long time ago, people believed that mental illness was from lost souls, like those who died in accidents and wouldn't go to heaven 'cause they didn't believe they were dead. Others liked to drink so much they stayed after death to inhabit a drinker." She laughs. "They wanted an after-party."

My shoulders twitch in an effort to dismiss the idea. I look for my call bell. "I have heard enough."

Maria looks up from her book, her eyes dancing over her new discovery. "This stuff freaks you out, doesn't it?"

Maybe the bitch just likes to taunt me. "I do not know anybody who thinks about stuff like that. This talk about demons and souls creeps me out. I have plenty to deal with already."

Maria puts her hand on my arm.

It feels good. I do not pull away.

"I didn't mean to frighten you," she tells me with a sing-songy cadence.

"I am not scared," I sputter, straightening in the bed.

Maria laughs. "Don't you think it's interesting?"

"I think it is nuts."

"As nuts as your roommate?" Her brows arch, and her eyes lock on mine.

"More."

"I don't know… Zane has been acting weird lately. Jack says he's paranoid." She puts her paper down.

"Now you are *really* over the top. Zane is not afraid of anything."

Maria sits back, her gaze far away. "I guess I got used to hearing stories from my grandma. She used to say that things were different in the Russian countryside."

"Yeah, and you probably have werewolves in your family."

The corners of her mouth turn down. She slams her laptop shut. "What about the face you saw, Dave? You can't deny it. Don't you want to know what that was?"

"No." All her talk about spirits has me afraid to even *think* about it.

"Why not?"

"It was just medication. If you were hooked up to a morphine IV, you would see weird stuff too."

"You saw a face in the bushes *before* the morphine."

"Enough talking. What I want is pain medicine and for you to leave me alone."

Maria gathers up her stuff. "Okay, then. I'll go tell your nurse."

Glad that is over.

My nurse rushes in with pain shot in hand. "Your friend said you were grumpy and in pain."

Nice. I hate shots, but they make me feel much better than the pills. "Did I win the lottery? It is half an hour too soon."

She chuckles. "If you did, you can split it with me. It's shift change soon. I'll be busy, and so will the oncoming nurse. I figured I'd give you this a little early."

"That is great. Thanks."

"Bootie up, brother."

"I hate this part." I roll to my side, making sure to keep

things covered. The stuff stings going in. I try not to think about it. Soon, it will be working, and all will be well.

***

I am so bored I cannot stand it. There is nothing to do here except watch bad TV. I wish I had a phone. Even my roommate is not here to talk to. I click to see if there is something better than the same old crap in the news.

Maria walks in my door and drops her bag onto the chair. She peels off an ivory crocheted sweater she was not wearing before. "It's been an hour. Your pain medicine working?"

"How did you know?"

"When I told your nurse, she said to come back in an hour, so I went for dinner and made some phone calls."

"Why did you come back?"

"I want to talk about your experience with the face, the voice."

"Maria, can we not leave this alone? Everything in ICU was strange. You see and hear things constantly. I have seen faces covered in bugs and heard screaming from all over."

Maria's eyes get wide. "The same face you saw in the bushes at the beach?"

"Do not get all jacked up about it. The nurse said people often hallucinate in ICU from medication and sleep deprivation. They wake you up every hour to check your pupils and stuff. The lights are always on. The noise never stops. On top of that, my dyscalculia mixes things up in my head sometimes."

"Was it the same face you saw before?"

"Who knows?"

"Was it male or female?" Her eyes are intense. She is not giving up.

I may as well placate her. "Male."

"Was there a taste, a smell, a phrase it said?"

The smell of burnt corn registers in my nose. I wonder if it is my hair, but I did not smell it an hour ago. "Burnt corn."

"Oh," Maria mutters. "Indigenous people say entities can smell like burnt corn at times."

"*Der'mo.*" I gulp in a breath. "That saying again. I never said that before in my life. It is like something twists my tongue or something."

"What do you mean?"

"First, I started speaking without contractions, then this word…"

Maria gets up to close the door. "That word means *shit.* Did the thing respond to my burnt corn comment?" she says more to herself than me. "When did all this start?"

I try to think back through the fog. "Right after I went to Johnstown."

"Do you remember when I said that lost souls sometimes hang around with people?"

My chest stiffens. "Your little theory about Zane?"

Maria's face levels. Her lips squish together. "Not Zane." She puts her hand on my arm. Warmth radiates through her touch. "I'm talking about you."

Laughter from the face at the beach pierces my brain. My stomach drops. Visions of a horned, red-faced devil swirl in my mind, making me wonder if I am going to Hell.

"Could there be something inside of me?" I gawk at Maria, trying to blink away the picture in my head. "I have seen this… guy, heard him laugh at me. Am I losing my mind?"

"No, Dave, I don't think you're losing your mind," Maria says in her kindest voice. She strokes my arm. "He's not the devil. He's probably just… lost."

A blur of fire and jackal-like laughter engulf me. I drag the sheet from the edges of the bed, tugging it up under my chin.

She holds up the book—the damn book she left me.

Maybe I should read it.

"Dave, it's not like that at all. This says that something traumatic happened to him at or before the time of his death, and he didn't move on to Heaven."

I can't believe this is happening. "The nurses are right. I am hallucinating."

"Maybe you made yourself susceptible with your… um… habits." Maria's eyes are terrified but full of pity.

There is an emptiness in my chest. My finger finds the TV button and turns the volume up loud.

"There might be a way I can help you." She takes my hands—TV control, sheets, and all—and holds them between her trembling palms. While she lowers the volume, the cross on her neck swings back and forth, catching the light.

I follow the arc it makes, then tug at the twisted bed sheet. "What are you talking about?"

"I've been really studying this. Let me talk to the voice. Maybe he'll let you go."

I close my eye to block her out and tell myself it is just the medicine.

A deep, menacing chuckle resonates through the darkness.

My eye flies open. I squeeze her palm and pull it close, heart pounding.

Maria strokes the side of my face not covered in fishnet. "You'll be all right, David." She lets go of my hand and inches her seat closer. Her knuckles whiten while her fingers knot together in her lap. "I'd like to speak to anyone who isn't David Everest. What made you want to come to Dave?"

Bile burns the back of my throat. My voice comes out slow, gruff, like I am stoned.

"He asked me to."

Chapter 23

"It was nice of the optometrist to fit you for your glasses the same day you were discharged from the hospital. It's amazing he had a pair of rejected lenses that worked." Mom fumbles to get a key in the apartment door in the fading light. She flops heavily onto the couch, dropping my hospital stuff beside her.

The apartment is spotless and smells like bleach. There is not a stray glass or flip-flop anywhere. Mom even put the same V-type dents in the top of the couch pillows that she does at home.

"You okay? It almost looked like your legs gave out." I head to the fridge.

"I'm tired. I spent all day yesterday scrubbing down this apartment so you wouldn't get an infection from it. It stunk so bad that a vulture actually tried to fly in here the other day."

I stop. "What?"

"I opened the door, and the thing was flapping its wings right in front of the door. I had to shoo it away."

"Huh." I head for the window and check the courtyard but do not see the buzzard. The darn thing is out there somewhere. I wonder why it would try to get in.

"Why are you chewing your nails, David? I noticed it when you were home and in the hospital. You've never chewed your nails before."

I glance at my nail beds, reddened where they are gnawed

all the way down. "It started right after the Eagle-Pitbull game. The score was not high enough. *Haha*. Now, I catch myself doing it when I need another pain pill."

"Why don't you wash your hands and get all the hospital germs off? While you're there, look at the food I got for you. There's lunch meat, protein shakes, some electrolyte drinks… Even two kinds of ice cream. The instructions for being home stress the importance of good nutrition with a high-protein diet for healing."

"And no alcohol. I remember the nurse going over it. Thanks for getting the food, Mom."

She puts a plastic hospital bag onto her lap and hauls out some papers. "I need to change your dressing twice a day. If you take a pill now, it'll be working when I change the bandage." Mom fishes the container from her purse and blinks while she reads the label. "You can have one every four hours." She mashes down on the cap and twists it open. "There you go."

It is about time. I hold out my hand, like a baby for its medicine. Now she is my fucking pharmacist. This is not going to cut it.

"I am exhausted. I need a nap."

"David, wait. I bought towels to protect you from germs on this furniture. Your dad and I picked up an extra blanket and pillow before he left. I'll sleep on the sofa so you're away from the filth."

"Sleep in Zane's room. You said he offered it to you."

"No way." She opens my closet, grabs a stack of towels, spreads one on the bed, and heads to the living room to cover the sofa and chairs.

While she does her thing, I think of how to get my life back. The apartment looks like my great-grandmother's house, with everything covered in towels or plastic.

My phone beeps in a text. Thank God she got me a new

phone this morning before she picked me up. At least I can stay in touch with the real world now.

Where r u? from Zane.

Home.

On my way.

***

"Dude, whatcha doin' sleeping?" filters in my left ear.

I blink my way back to reality. Zane stands with a girl in the doorway to my bedroom.

The last rays of sun through the window cast an artificial halo around them. He had to bring a girl? Her teeth are nasty, like meth-mouth. Zane must owe her a favor because he would never have a girl like that.

He comes in closer, and I do a double take. Zane has some bizarre, flowy shirt on, and he has lost weight.

"They must have done a good job at that hospital. I don't see anything wrong."

Mom comes around the corner with a scowl on her face. "I'm making dinner, Zane." She stops. Her jaw unhinges while she examines the dark ink across the girl's back. Mom squares her shoulders and glares at Zane. "Do you want to join us?"

His brow scrunches. "What are you still doin' here?"

Mom smiles at me as if Zane is not even there. "It'll be done in five minutes, David." She hikes it back to the kitchen.

I swing my legs over the edge of the bed and let them crash down to help launch me upright.

Zane takes a step back.

"Eew," the girl screeches. Her gut contracts, blinding me with the reflection from her navel ring. "I'll be in your room, Zane." She hurries away on deathly spikes.

"Oh… *that's* what you're talking about. Does it hurt?" Zane sits at the desk and looks at me from the corner of his eye.

"Yeah, especially when my friend—the one who insisted I go to this Fielder—neglects to come see me."

"Hospitals really freak me out, you know?" Color etches his face. His voice is loud, the look fierce.

"Do you think *I* like them?"

Zane rubs the back of his neck. "At least you're out."

"Like, from jail?" My breath is hot.

He turns away and looks out the window. "They probably gave you some good drugs for it."

"They gave me Oxycontin."

"Greens are a good score, bro." Zane smiles while he picks at a thread on his shirt "I'll get you fentanyl lollipops if you'll lend me your car."

"What happened to your truck?"

"It's got a flat tire. I got the spare out, and it's flat too." Zane faces me head-on. "The lollipops will help you."

"No, thanks."

"Come on, bro. I'll have it back in the morning and bring you some Goodfella. I need to take the girl back where she came from. Did you see her teeth?"

Wonder if he got drunk and pulled his routine to get laid. I would want to drop her off somewhere too. "All right. Take the car."

A shit-eating grin breaks out, and he drums a victory tune on the desk. "Sweet."

"Mom?" I holler out. "Zane needs to borrow my car. Can you give him the keys?"

She shows up at my door with her hands on her hips. "No way."

"Mom, he's got a flat and no spare."

"I'm not doing it." Her lips clamp together.

"Mom, Zane has a date. He needs a set of wheels."

"David, you just got home. What if something happens and you need to go back to the hospital?"

"I have a burn, not a heart attack."

She shakes her head. "I pay the bills. No car."

"Wait, I bought the car myself, Mom." My statement seems to knock her off-balance.

She grabs the doorjamb and glares at me.

Zane exudes the innocence of a Boy Scout. "You can call me if you need it. I'm ten minutes away."

"Mom, it would take ten minutes to pack a bag to go back."

She looks at me, then squeezes the bridge of her nose so hard it looks like she has a unibrow. "David, I feel very strongly about this."

"We are not going anywhere. Please give him the car."

"This is very bad timing." She reaches into her pocket with an icy glare and slams the keys on the desk beside Zane.

Zane jumps up and snatches the keys.

Mom marches back to the stove.

"Thanks, bro." Zane bends close to my ear. "If you chew those pills, they'll work faster."

***

"Today, I am going off the pills." I tell myself when I climb out of the shower.

I survey my face in the mirror. The dead skin around the outside is pretty much gone, and new skin is starting to grow in. The shoulder is still raw. Hopefully, I can put a shirt on soon without it oozing everywhere. Last night, I saved the pill Mom gave me before bed, thinking I could sleep through, but

I had to get up in the middle of the night to take it when I rolled onto my shoulder.

"Did you take the morning pain pill I put in your room?" Mom's hair is sloppy, and she has a spot on her shirt. It is so unlike her to be unkempt. I guess sleeping on the couch is not great. She rolls up her sleeves, like she is ready for surgery, and opens the jar of the gooey stuff and a package of sterile tongue blades.

"I want to hold off." I plop down in front of her, checking the towel around my waist to make sure nothing is showing. This is embarrassing. I feel like a child. I wish she would leave. I feel like shit, and I want to avoid being nasty to her, but I am irritated all the time.

Mom peers at my shoulder and then my face. "You did a good job with your washcloth in the shower. They said I'm supposed to peel away any dead skin you missed with gauze, but I don't see any." She puts on her readers. "Wait, there's some behind your ear."

I grimace. "That spot is real sore."

"That's probably why you avoided it. Let's see if we can get this done fast." She opens a pack of gauze and wets it in a bowl of water.

"Easy for you to say. It will not hurt *you.*"

She slides her chair back. "Maybe you *should* take that pill. This can wait a little longer."

"Go ahead. I want it over with."

"Okay. I'm going to clean behind your ear first, then do the rest."

When she touches gauze to my skin, there is a loud knock on the door. We both jump. Her hand slips.

"Ow, damn!" I scream. "You trying to kill me?"

"I'm sorry, David. I didn't mean to. That scared me."

Another loud knock.

"Hang on!" Mom calls, laying down the gauze streaked with pieces of tissue and blood. She opens the door.

I grab my glasses and watch the muscles in the back of Mom's neck knot up. She swings the door wide. "Please come in, officer."

"Do you own a silver Honda Civic, license number R2M 0T1?" A male cop steps inside. He is bulked up under the black uniform. Other than his bleached-blond hair, he looks like The Hulk.

I leap from my chair. The towel slips. I grab it with both hands. "Did that asshole wreck my car?"

The cop's head hitches, but he keeps his stance. He gazes from my burnt hair to my shoulder, avoiding my face, then focuses on my mother.

Coward.

"The car was spotted near the scene of a drug raid last night," he says.

My throat dries, as if he shoved the gauze in it. I sink into the chair. "A drug bust?"

"As you can see, officer…" Mom cranes her neck in search of a name tag. "Evans. My son has suffered severe burns from an accident at a field party. He hasn't left this apartment since arriving home from the hospital yesterday."

"Mom, the fraternity term is *Fielder*," I say, hoping to show I am a student.

The cop thrusts his sunglasses onto his head. "Is it your car?" His angular features glare directly in my direction. "Your name is David Everest?"

"Yes, and that sounds like my car. I lent it to my roommate."

"You need to get rid of that roommate." Mom's lips head south, and she crosses her arms.

I refuse to tell her that Zane is my lifeline. "He said he

had a flat tire on his truck. He was with a girl. I assumed he had a date."

Mom crosses her arms. "A nasty-looking girl with a big tattoo across her back."

She wants to nail Zane to the wall. I shoot Mom a look.

"Where is he now?" The cop starts casing my living room without moving.

I spot the bloody gauze on the table and pick it up, hoping to distract him a bit. "I have no idea. How do you know my car had anything to do with it?"

"We don't know for sure, but a neighbor said your car was blocking her driveway right before the raid went down. She went into her house to call the precinct and report it, but the car drove away before we got there."

"I assure you, officer, that my son was *not* involved." Mom huffs.

The man's badge catches the light when he looks toward my bedroom. "You go to school?"

"Yes," I answer flatly.

"Where?"

"U of Mann."

"U of Mann, *sir*," my mother corrects, like I am a little kid. Heat starts building in my core.

"What's your roommate's name?"

"Zane Maddox," Mom spits out before I can avoid the question. Her crossed arms tighten.

The cop hauls out a pen and pad, then starts to write. "And the girl?"

A picture forms of her retreating to Zane's room. "I only saw her for a moment yesterday. Not long enough for an introduction."

Mom moves closer to the cop. "She had a navel ring and a big, diamond-shaped tattoo full of flowers on her back."

I wish she would knock it off.

The cop puts it in his notes. "When do you expect him back?"

I look at the skin I shed onto the gauze. Once again, I am pissed at Zane, but I don't want him to slough *me* off. "He said he was staying close by but not when he would be back."

Mom glares at me, lips tightening.

The cop keeps writing. "Do you have contact information for your roommate?"

"What do you mean?" I ask.

"Why don't you call him and see when he'll return your car? I'd like to talk to him."

My hand squeezes closed. Goop and blood squish through my fingers. I toss the gauze onto the table, where it hits the wooden tongue blade, knocking it to the floor with a clatter. Great.

"My cell phone got melted in the explosion." I grab some fresh gauze to clean my hand.

Mom bounces up and down on her toes, like she wants to run.

The cop stops writing and levels his gaze at me. "What kind of explosion?"

My blood pulses faster. I hope his thoughts avoid a meth explosion. "It was from a bonfire at a barn, where the fraternity goes."

"I have documentation of my son's hospitalization if you need to see it," Mom blurts out with a fake a smile.

The cop looks at the side of my face. "That won't be necessary." He hands me a business card. "Call me if your car doesn't come back."

"Thank you for coming, officer." Mom hurries to open the door.

He saunters out, still casing the living room through the window when he walks by.

"I am going to put some pants on." I run to my room before Mom gets the front door closed. After locking my door, I sink onto the other side of my bed, cell phone in hand, hoping she does not hear me.

Zane is not answering.

"Where the hell are you?" I hiss after the beep. "A cop just showed up here, asking about my car. I want it back, *now*." I hang up and text him. **WTF cops at the door about my car bring it back NOW.**

A shadow crosses the room. Is that the cop?

I check the window. The vulture is perched on the sill. It slips a little bit, flapping its dark wings to rebalance, then starts the *chkk-chkk-chkk* thing while staring inside my room.

Mom knocks at the door. "David, I need to talk to you." Her voice is tense.

"Be right out." I slide on a pair of jeans.

The vulture flaps, catching my attention. It is staring at the planning book on my dresser. Strange.

"David, open the door." Mom's tone is deeper.

My head hurts. The burns on my face are drying out so much my mouth is stretched in a grimace. I hurry to open the door and face Godzilla.

"What was that all about?" Her face is red, her eyes bulging.

"I do not know." A powerful, repugnant voice takes hold of mine.

"What do you mean, you do not know? And what's with the bizarre contraction avoidance?"

"Partially blocking a driveway for a few minutes is not a crime. It happens all the time around here, especially close to campus." I step around her. "There are a lot of old houses with single driveways or no driveway, and parking on the street is horrible."

"That kid is bad news, David. You need to get away from him."

"You need to stop correcting me like a six-year-old."

Her hands fly to her hips. "When a police officer comes to your home, asking about your car, you need to be as polite as possible, *especially* since you've already been arrested once."

"That is past history, and you are right. This is my home, not yours. You have no right to assume Zane is guilty of anything."

"How do you know? Have you talked to him?" She starts pacing behind the couch, sliding her hand along the back of it, changing hands when she turns back the other way—a strange move, even if she is nervous.

"I just called. No answer." I throw away the wooden stick and grab a new one, smearing the ointment on my face where it feels tight enough to crack.

"So, you don't know, then?"

"I know I am fine." I switch to my shoulder and lather it on thick. "I do not need your help. I can take care of this on my own."

I look out the window. Girls are stretched out by the pool in loungers, and guys are going into the workout room, all of them with the freedom to do as they please and not have their mother supervising their every move. Fury builds with a deep rumbling.

I stare at my mother, my mind racing. "I can take care of everything. I can shower and smear this stuff on, I can cook all the food you put in the fridge, and I can drive myself to the doctor." I wipe the last glob of cream on. "You do not need to be here."

She stops pacing. "David, you just got out of the hospital. You're in a lot of pain."

"The pain pills are working just fine." I grab her toiletry bag from the bathroom, toss it into her suitcase, and zip it up. "There, you are all set."

"I'm not leaving."

"Oh, yes, you are. I appreciate the groceries, but it is time to go."

"You know you don't like cooking, David." Her voice is quiet now. "They said you need to maintain a good diet for healing."

"I can do that. It is all there." I nod to the kitchen.

"What about your bad grades? I can call the LD coordinator to see if he knows tutors."

"We have a good relationship. I will talk to him."

Her color fades. "Come on, sweetie. You're being unreasonable."

"You are being ridiculous, thinking you can fit in here." I yank out the blanket and pillow neatly wedged between the sofa and end table. I take them both to my room, then shove them into the closet.

"David, I just want to make sure you're going to be all right." Her voice quivers.

"I am fine."

"I'm not leaving, David. Not until you're well."

You should decide what is best, not her pops into my head.

I roll her suitcase to the door and swing it open. "I am perfect. You can go back to your clients and take care of them."

"Come on, sweetie. I don't even have a car here. How am I going to get home?" Her eyes are pleading while she limps toward me.

"Take a bus," a menacing voice growls from down deep.

This is wrong, but it pours out anyway. I reach for her

handbag with my right arm. It hurts like hell, but there is no way I am going to show it.

"Out!" my voice snarls.

I shove the bag at her chest and keep pushing until she is out of the apartment. After slinging the suitcase behind her, I slam and lock the door.

"David, you can't do this. You've got to let me help you." She tries the doorknob and starts to cry.

I grab my headphones and lock myself in the bathroom.

Chapter 24

My shoulder and the guilt are killing me. I check the windows, half expecting for Mom to be leaning on them. The courtyard is barren except for the long shadows of twilight darkening lonely, vacant lounge chairs and tables. I am on my own, without a soul in sight. I wish I had ended it differently.

My heart has an ache as painful as the throb in my shoulder. Why do I have to do things like that? The bottle of pills on the counter draws me to it. I press my palm into the lid and hesitate. Though I want to hold off, the picture of me shoving Mom out the door keeps scrolling through my head. I swallow one down, hoping it will chase away the memory.

I open the fridge and spot a beer.

They said no alcohol.

I stare at the liquid in the bottle and think about how good it would taste. It *is* Miller Light, so it is half water, and they said to drink a lot of water.

I snag the bottle, then down a third of it. So good. They should serve beer in hospitals. A wild laugh breaks out, echoing in the recesses of my brain. Freaky. I think back to the hospital with Maria. *Could* something be inside of me?

A knock at the door. I duck below the counter. What if it is Mom?

Another knock, louder this time. Did she see me?

"Dave, it's Maria."

I unlock the door, then flop onto the couch, with my beer in the spot where Mom had put a towel. I miss her already, but I need to be my own man.

Maria is looking as plain as ever. She takes a seat across from me. "You got glasses."

"The explosion messed up the lens in my eye."

She maneuvers her head around to observe from a few angles. "They look good."

"You said that just to make me feel better." I snort.

"I saw your mother getting into a cab. She told me what happened. She looked really tired. She didn't look good, Dave."

I should have stayed on the glasses issue. The ice-cold brew on my tongue cools it off to keep me from saying something nasty. "I do not need her help."

"She's concerned about you. So am I."

"I can feed and smear Silvadene all by myself."

Maria scoots back in the chair so she is more upright. "That's not the part I'm worried about."

"What else?" I take another swig.

"Your personality has changed. You say and do things that aren't you."

"You would get grumpy too, if you had all this going on."

"I mean since the beginning of the semester." She gives me a flat smile.

"You are imagining things."

"No, I'm not. Other people have noticed too." Maria shifts in her seat and looks at me head-on. "Don't you feel like you're losing control?"

"If you mean the voice, I know what it is."

Maria lurches forward. "What?"

"Me when I am drunk or buzzed. Not some ghost."

"It may come out more then, but that's not you."

She is pissing me off, but the weird expressions are kind of bizarre.

"I want your permission to talk to the voice I spoke to in the hospital."

"I think you have this all wrong."

Maria uncrosses her legs and plants her feet on the floor. "I want to speak to the one who isn't David Everest."

The smell of burnt corn floats up my nose. Strange.

"What do you want?" comes out deep and menacing.

The beer in my hand slides between my knees. Is this really happening? Am I crazy? Could I be possessed? "Stop it, Maria. This is freaking me out," I say.

She puts a hand on my good arm. Her hand goes cold. "When did you come to Dave?" Her voice trembles.

"He was feeling sorry for himself at Johnstown Beach," spews from my mouth with a cavernous sound.

"What… do you want?" Maria tries to hold her tone steady.

"I have something to finish."

"What is it?" Maria's voice is close to a whisper.

"None of your business."

I try to make sense of this. My swollen eye struggles to open, locked on Maria. Her eyes are massive.

"Stop it. No more."

"Did you hear what it said?" Maria is sweating. She presses her shaking hands against the couch.

My heart is pounding hard. I wish I had the morphine button so it would go straight to my head and numb the memory of what just happened. I stare at the wall and listen to the echo of the horrifying voice.

"There *is* something inside me."

A pulsating mass of dread is forming in my chest. I down the rest of the beer. We need to get off this subject. "Everything hurts, and I cannot do a thing about it."

"That's why I came to help you," Maria says, eyeing my beer. "You're taking medication. Should you be drinking beer right now?"

"Why do you have to be so fucking self-righteous?"

"I'm thinking about you, not me."

"Bullshit. You want a new discovery that you can write about in your paper."

Maria's face clouds. "That's ridiculous."

"Get out of my house. Leave me alone." I throw the Miller at her, spraying beer across the table.

Maria catches the bottle in mid-air, eyes boring into my soul. "I want to say to whatever is in there… You're not going to get to me."

***

The phone beeps with a text. I rub the sleep from my eyes and reach for it.

How you doing? From Dad.

I check the time: 8:00 p.m.

It beeps again.

Mom got home okay.

Remorse seeps through my bones and into the hard plastic shell of the phone. She did not belong here.

I look for the pill bottle, pop one, and then wander back to my room.

Another beep.

Let us know if you need anything. Love you, Dad.

I sink down on the bed and text back: **Glad Mom is all right.**

How could I have shoved her around like that?

"What were you flipping out about on the phone?" Zane bangs through the door and throws my car keys on the kitchen counter. His hair is a mess, and his clothes are dirty. "I wasn't the one getting busted. Nothing happened to your car."

"I love to have the police show up, asking about my car in front of my mother."

"Oh yeah, her. Where is she?" Zane opens the fridge. He tosses in a case of Miller.

"I sent her home."

"About time." He laughs and looks at me. "You need to get out. You've been cooped up for too long."

"No fucking way am I going out like this."

"Whoa, Rager. At least have some fun, then." Zane cracks two beers and hands one to me.

"Stop calling me that," I snap.

"All right. You *have* loosened up since you first got here."

I pick up my keys and toss them into my room to keep them far from him. "What were you doing with my car anyway?"

"You want the good stuff. I went to Aaron's as soon as it got in. Good thing too. He woulda got nailed for even more."

"It better not be in my car. All I need is to get busted and go to jail like this."

"Quit whining. I got rid of it already. Traded half for some Xanax." He sinks into the big armchair on the other side of the room.

"What about the lollipop you promised?"

"Couldn't find any."

"Yeah, right. And since when do you like Xanax?"

"Why the hell do you care?" He plops his feet onto the coffee table. "It comes in handy when you're all cranked up and you're trying to sleep."

The answer knocks me back a bit. I take another hit of beer. "As in, meth-type crank?" A picture of the girl with bad teeth pops into my head. He is stooping low. "Where did you get that shit?"

"Bubba's got a setup in the back of the chicken coop. He's crankin' it out." A snicker bubbles up.

"Is that where you were? What about school?"

"That was my chemistry project." He laughs so hard his hair shakes. "Then I had to test out the final results. You gotta try the stuff, bro."

"I prefer to be chill."

"Why go down when you can go up? I found out why they call it crank. Makes you want to fly all night. Half the next one too. It's like inhaling lightning. That's why I need the Xanax, man, so I can get some sleep."

"Is that what you did for a whole week?"

"Sure as hell wasn't comin' back here to hang out with Susie Homemaker." He clicks the TV onto ESPN. "I slept for two days a couple of times."

"You are insane. You have not left any of that shit in my car, right?"

"You're so freakin' jumpy I can't stand it." He goes to his room, then comes back with his bong.

"Good thing that was put away when my parents arrived."

"Why? It's the healthiest method of smoking. Maybe they would have wanted to try it." Zane chuckles while he packs the bowl and inhales deep. "You need to relax, bro. This will help."

It smells magnificent. Should I do this with the Oxycontin and all?

The voice inside whispers, *It has been so long.*

I wonder if it will slow the healing of my burns.

It will calm you after the text from your dad.

Zane holds out the bong and nudges my arm.

I take it in. My lungs rejoice like a choir.

"I'm starved." Zane walks over to the fridge. He hauls out the lunchmeat Mom bought for me and piles half a pound onto a sub roll.

I want to say something, but I hold back.

He slathers the bread with mayo and stacks up the Swiss.

A wave of anger starts to build. My teeth clench together. I go to stand, when there is a sudden melding of my pain pill with the beer and the weed. Everything has slowed down. My legs are mush. My next thought melts away. I let it go. This is the first time since I got off the morphine that I feel good.

Zane is talking. His words bounce around in the clouds.

Finally, no pain. I tilt back on the couch and stare out the window at the gathering thunderheads.

***

A noise wakes me.

I roll to my side to see what it was, then jolt back in agony when my shoulder scrapes against a towel.

Someone pounds on the front door, yelling my name.

I drag myself over to find Ian standing there.

"Crikey." He jumps, scrambling to even his expression. "I heard you were home and wanted to say hello."

Rachael slips past him, wearing a Christmas sweater so bright it is hard to look at. "Love the 'do! You're getting into the spiky look a bit much, though, don't you think?" She pats me on the butt and charges through the doorway, with Jack behind her.

"You got glasses." Jack fixes on them at the bridge of my nose, as if he does not want to let his eyes slip to the left.

"Yeah. What time is it?" I go to the kitchen for a glass of water.

"Almost noon," Rachael chirps. "We wanted to see if you need anything before we go to the library."

While I chug down the water, my neck and shoulder start to throb. I have been waking up with more pain. I thought it was supposed to go the other way. "What day is it?"

Ian shoots Rachel a glance. "It's Sunday."

She lifts a big shopping bag. "I brought a bunch of Christmas decorations from home. Want some?"

"Since it is the most wonderful time of the year? No thanks."

Rachael perches on the arm of the sofa. She surveys the living room as if she were decorating.

Ian glares at Jack.

Jack rolls up the sleeves of his red flannel shirt, takes a step toward me, and stops. "Exams start Monday, so it's nice and quiet around here for you to get some rest." His words come out awkward. Forced.

"I need to email my professors."

Rachael sneaks a glance at my shoulder. "Your mother already called the school. I saw her outside one day when you were in the hospital."

They are all afraid to look at me. I reach for some more water, hand quivering.

"You saw her?"

Rachael tilts toward me. "You okay?"

Is she kidding? "Everything has kind of seized up," I sputter.

Jack is restless on his feet. "Can we get you anything else?"

"Not unless you got something that will keep me wide awake." I slide onto a barstool.

"You don't want to go there." Jack steps behind Rachael and clears his throat. He has fixed on my eyes again.

Ian slides a stool beside me. He nods at the pile of medical supplies on the table. "It looks like you've got a lot going on here already, mate. When I broke my leg a few years back, I slept a lot afterward. Don't let Zane tell you any different."

Rage starts to bubble inside. I jump up to shove my face at him. "Who are you to judge Zane?" My balled-up fists shake. It is all I can do to keep myself from grabbing his throat.

He darts his eyes between Rachael and Jack.

Rachael steps between us, then pats my good shoulder. "Just hang in there, Dave. You can go home and relax, and you'll be all fixed up by the beginning of next semester."

I think of going home and snort. When I started, I was a misfit with dyscalculia, and now I am freakish, inside and out. Pain is needling at me from all arenas, and they want to cut me off from Zane? I grab the pills and think. Lots of pain. Why not take two? I swallow them down.

"Need my medication."

Ian and Jack inch toward the exit. Rachael hurries there ahead of them.

"Let me know if you need anything."

Jack slips out without a word. Ian is right behind.

He pauses at the door. "Watch out for Zane's new friends."

My phone rings. I check the screen—Eric. I glance at the others while they walk away. They are so fucking self-righteous. They do not know what it feels like to have half your face burned off.

"I am not fucking talking to you!" I yell at the phone. "I do not care if I told you I would call when I got out."

It rings again. Then a third ring.

He is your brother, protests my brain.

I swing around and jam my thumb on the answer pad. "Hello?" I snap with a volume that surprises me.

"David?" Eric's voice rises. "Is that you?"

"Yeah, dumb shit. Who else would it be?"

"It doesn't sound like you. I thought that maybe you were sleeping and your roommate picked up the phone."

"The guy is not that type."

"Mom and Dad called yesterday to say you were out of the hospital."

"Yeah, and they probably said a lot more," I growl.

"Sorry I didn't call you then." Eric's voice stays cool. "I had my phone off to study and didn't see the message until today. How are you feeling?"

"Like a breath of fresh air," I mock in my grandmother's tone.

Nothing comes back through the phone, at all, for several seconds.

"Are you there?"

"I'm here."

Eric is such a suck-up. He will not even talk.

"Say something. There is nothing wrong with *your* mouth."

"I didn't know what to say."

"You could at least comment."

"On what? I can't see you. You didn't tell me how you feel, so I figured I'd just wait."

"What if I sat here for half an hour, then hung up the phone?"

"Well, at least I'd know you're alive."

"Geez, Eric, you are really fucked up."

He laughs.

I roll the golden pill container between my palms. "What do you want to know that Mom did not tell you?"

Eric's exhale is slow, deliberate. "Well, it's more what she didn't tell *you*."

"Like what?"

"It's her myasthenia."

My knees buckle. I fall into the couch. "No. She was fine when she was here."

"She said the symptoms started when you were in the hospital, but she didn't tell anybody." Eric's voice cracks. "She went to the doctor this morning, and he confirmed it. He's monitoring her closely, but she could be hospitalized next week."

The memory of Mom, with tubes sticking out of her in ICU, pops into my mind. My stomach knots. Shame trickles like lead into my bones.

"When will you be going home?" Eric's voice is expectant.

"I see the doctor tomorrow. When are *you* going home?" I hear myself throw into his face.

"Friday is my last exam. My flight leaves three hours later." He pauses. "Do you want me to change it? I could fly into Greenville and drive back with you."

I do not want him showing up here. My brain scrambles for an excuse. "Not sure what the doctor has planned for Monday. He may want me to stay another week or something. Just leave it the way it is."

I tap the plastic container against the edge of my desk. The pills dance back and forth inside it. I want to count them so I know how many I have left, but I need to quit this stuff so I can get home. When I hurl the bottle across the room, the cheap plastic cracks.

"I have to get in the shower and smear a new layer of slime on." My bark is fierce—*not* what I wanted.

A muffled sob filters through the speaker. A pause. "Sure."

When I hang up the phone, the horror of Mom lying in ICU on a respirator plays out like a movie in my head.

I snatch the bottle of pills, dump the remains into the toilet, and flush.

Chapter 25

Today is going to be a good day. I tell myself this when I climb into my car. It has been two whole days since I flushed the pills. Aspirin is getting me by. I am a little shaky this morning, but two cups of coffee does that. I have been taught to ask for help when I need it, and while I do not want to ask Maria, I see no other way.

At the first red light, I call her. "Maria? This is Dave. I am on my way to see the burn doctor."

"How are you doing?"

"It hurts to shift, but I can steer with my left hand." I inhale to steady my resolve. "Maria, I need to fix my grades. Will you help me?"

"Sure. While you're at the doctor's office, ask for a letter so you can get an incomplete or a medical withdrawal. I'm not sure which one applies, but we can look it up."

"That would be great, thanks."

"How's everything else going?"

I slow down when the green light ahead turns yellow, then to red. "What do you mean?"

"Well, with your… buddy."

A semi-trailer loaded with chemicals goes by. I grip the wheel tighter. "That is all finished. I dumped the pain pills down the toilet. My head is clear."

"I hope you're right."

"My mom's myasthenia is back. I am done with that stuff."

"Oh, Dave, I'm so sorry to hear that. Did you talk to her?"

"Eric called. I want to get home as soon as I can." The light turns green. I wince when I shift into gear.

"Good luck with the doctor."

"Thanks." I shut the phone off while I pull up to the medical arts building.

I wait for the elevator. A hot-looking nurse walks by. I turn away, tugging the hood of my jacket farther around my face.

"Elevator's not working," she calls before disappearing around the corner.

I ascend each step of the spiral staircase, planning how soon I can get home to Mom. In the doctor's office, dated pink chairs and a whiff of antiseptic greet me.

I tap on the frosted sliding window which hides everything from the people out here in the waiting room.

It opens slowly. An old bag with pink hair is on the other side. She is wearing a pink sweater, and her face is covered in dark pink moles. Enough of that damn color.

"Sign your name and the time on that sheet, honey," she croaks, pointing to a clipboard in front of me.

"I need to get a letter for the university about why I am not in class. Do you take care of that, or should I ask the doctor?"

No answer. I wonder if she heard me. Getting to her feet seems to take her five minutes. She hands me a stack of papers on another clipboard.

"Fill those out and give me your insurance card. Put your email address on there so I can send you a copy of the letter." She eases the glass curtain shut, leaving me alone.

Cramps start in my stomach. Something I ate? The food in the fridge is new.

I force myself to focus and press hard on the pen.

Half an hour later, the old crone cracks the door. "Come on, honey. The doctor will be with you in a minute." She puts my papers in a slot on the door and shuts me in the examining room.

I break into a sweat, pouring a corrosive mix which merges with the Silvadene into a toxic soup. I wonder why I feel so bad. Could I be hooked on the pain pills this fast?

Finally, the doctor comes in. "Hello there, David."

"Doc, before we get started, could you send a letter to U of Mann? My mom called the school, and they said they need something from you."

"No problem." Dr. Thompson hands me a bucket of warm, rolled-up washcloths.

"Wipe those burns clean for me, will you?" he says over his shoulder while he washes his hands.

I remove the layer of white goop with care. The nubs of the cloth feel like sandpaper against my raw flesh.

He checks my face, my shoulder, and sets a pair of thick magnifying lenses over his eyes. "Looking good. Your hair follicles are starting to sprout. These dermal layers are coming back nicely, except here." He grabs a cloth and rakes the skin behind my ear.

I scream and grip the edge of the seat.

"Sorry about that." He drops the cloth, gray and bloodied, onto a steel tray beside me.

I wipe my watering eyes. "That really hurt."

He looks closer. "Had to get rid of some old stuff there. How's your eye?"

"Getting used to wearing the glasses. They are painful, especially around that ear." The cramping in my stomach builds. I press my palms into my jeans to soak up the sweat.

The doctor hands me a mirror. "See this area over your cheekbone? You are going to have to be gentle with it to prevent scarring."

Charred hunks of flesh reflect the remains of what I used

to be. I turn the mirror away. The spot on my ear throbs. My mouth starts to water for the pills.

"That hurt my ear bad. I need something for pain."

"What were you taking?" He is looking at my shoulder now.

I swallow and shift my sweaty fingers to clutch the low side of my seat. "Oxycontin."

He removes the lenses and peers into my eyes. "How many do you have left?"

My head spins, trying to calculate how long they should have lasted. I draw a blank. "None." I hope he will not know.

"Hmm." The magnifiers go back on. "That shoulder burn is pretty deep. The good news is I don't think this will need grafting."

Sweat runs down my sides and soaks in at my belt. What if he will not give them to me?

"Let's take a look at your ankle." He rolls my leg inward. "Even better than I thought." Dr. Thompson takes the lenses off and looks at me again.

I wonder what to do if he does not give me the prescription. Can I get something through Zane?

"Keep cleaning your burns twice a day and apply the Silvadene liberally." He hands me two sheets of paper.

I look at the script. All the breath sucks out of me. It says Tylenol with codeine. I feel limp, telling myself it will work.

The rest of his words blend together. Something about my chart and no further prescriptions. I bolt down the spiral staircase and drive to the same pharmacy as last time. They know me here. I hold out the script at the drive-thru.

"You're David Everest?" the clerk asks.

"Yes, I am." I turn to the left to show the burns. "How long will it be? I am going to wait."

She looks at the pharmacist. "About twenty minutes."

"I know it does not take that long. Can you bump me up?"

"I'm sorry, sir."

"I have pain here." I point to my face. "You need to do something about it."

"There are other people ahead of you who don't feel well either."

"If I knew this pharmacy would suck this bad, I would have gone somewhere else. Hurry up." I pull away and park.

I close my eyes and try to silence the drumming in my head. But the drum bangs on. I scroll through my playlist. All the music is too hyped-up. I pound the buttons on the dash, rifling through for a radio station that will soothe my edginess.

There are none.

I get out of the car to look at the damage from the Professor Taft event. Seeing it pisses me off more. If that jackass had been in his office, this never would have happened. My grade would have been better, and my dad would not have been such a dick. Then I would have stayed home, and I would be fine right now.

My mother would be fine too. She would not have had to come here. Assholes.

I check the time. Ten more minutes. I search the surroundings outside for something to distract me, but I find nothing, and I cannot stand still. I decide to do a lap around the building.

On my way back, I notice a black Ford Mustang with tinted windows across the parking lot from my car. It was not there before. Its occupant is looking my way. Why is he staring at me?

He is still watching when I climb into my car. I start it, then drive around to the other side of the building.

My stomach is killing me. I feel like puking. I open the window to breathe in some fresh air and tell myself I can do this. I *need* to do this for Mom. I feel so bad I kicked her out. Why did I do that?

Five minutes. My hand goes to the ignition. I pull the car

up to the store window again and tug the edge of my seatbelt, hating the restraint.

"It'll be a few more minutes," the clerk says through a speaker.

"There is no one behind me. I will wait." I force a smile, wondering if my desperation is obvious.

A moment later, a car drives up behind me.

I go to lift my foot off the brake, but a voice in my head snarls, *Do not move!*

I sit, hands locked on the steering wheel, sweating ice.

"Sign here, Mr. Everest, and I'll need to see a photo ID."

I reach for the paper. My hands are shaking. I hope she cannot see when I send back the money and my license.

"Here you go." The steel drawer advances toward me and opens its cold jaw, delivering sweet salvation.

I jolt the car away and tear open the package. My sweaty hands struggle to get the cap off. After clamping it between my teeth, I twist the bottle open, then chew one down.

By the time I pull into our apartment parking lot, the pain is not any better. I need relief. I chew another pill, leaving panic in its wake… until I look up to see the black Mustang.

***

Sliding out of bed the next morning, I look for my pipe and hope a hit will take the edge off. It does some, but not enough. My last three pain pills got me to sleep, but now that is history. They went so fast. I asked Zane to get me some Oxy. But when I check his room, I find he is not there.

The apartment feels unbearable. I turn the fan on, then crank the air-conditioning lower. As I reach for the remote, my hand is so sweaty the remote slides through and crashes to the floor. Zane better show up soon.

After a shower, I call him. It goes to voicemail. I pace the floor while my heart races. I rack my brain for contacts.

Then… it hits me.

The shady guy at the frat.

I saw him dealing in the parking lot the year before, at the alum event. What was his name? I hate to go over there. Is there anybody else?

Zane has the apartment complex wrapped up. What was the name of the guy at the frat?

Og. They called him Og the Dog. He could sniff out whatever kind of stuff guys wanted.

What if he does not recognize me? What if he does, then refuses to talk to me? I feel so lousy, and I need to do something. My hands shake while I rush to put on a hoodie so I can hide the burns.

I wince when I put my car in gear. The pain makes me wonder if I should go, but Zane has not shown up or called. The agony inside is worse than outside. I have to suck it up and find Og.

After pulling up to the back door of the fraternity house, I shut off the car and stare at the cold red brick. The memory of getting walked out on Pledge Day races through my mind.

Ten minutes go by. My stomach is cramping, but I will not go in there. Should I ask someone else?

The argument volleys in my brain.

Og rides up on a scooter. He kicks the stand down and gets off. His thick hair is shorter than the last time I saw him.

Og grabs the doorknob. He may not be back for hours.

My pulse hammers. I cannot lose this chance.

I tug my hood tight over my bad side while I get out of the car. "Og, wait."

He stops with his hand on the doorknob, squinting in my direction. "Do I know you?"

I head toward him. "I was a pledge. I did not get in. I need your help."

"What for?" His eyes dart across the lawn to see if anyone else is around.

"You are the man who can get guys what they need."

"Sorry, I can't help you." He turns to go inside.

A resounding voice whispers, *Show him the burns. He will feel sorry for you.*

"Stop." I slam my arm against the door and throw my hood back.

The doorknob slides out of his hand.

"I know I am not a brother, but there was a fire. The doctor cut off my pain pills. You have got to help me."

His eyes jump from one side of my face to the other. "What's your name?"

"David Everest."

"I remember you." He looks away for a second. "I don't have anything."

My chest sags. Is he just saying that because I did not get in, or is it true?

My eyes search the barren ground for something, anything, to say.

Nothing comes. I turn away.

"I know someone who might, but he's not in the park."

"Which park?"

He does not answer, but hauls out a burner phone and makes a call. "Hey, I know a guy who got burned in a fire. He needs your help. Can I send him over?"

The guy on the phone says a couple of things and Og hangs up.

"He's in Malanola, at 24 Areca Drive. Tell him you're there for therapy."

Chapter 26

It should only take half an hour to get to Malanola, but it seems like I have been driving for hours. I grip the wheel while my body shakes and my stomach churns. My arms and legs ache so bad I wonder if I have the flu. I make sure to stay in my lane, keeping my eye on the little white lines going by.

This guy better have what I need. Tremendous stomach cramps seize my gut and hold on like a vise. Salty saliva pours into my mouth.

I jam on the brakes and clench the door handle—but not fast enough. Puke gushes across the panel.

Pulling off the road, I open the door to let the puke drip off. "I do not have time for this." I reach to the back seat, to grab a towel. The cramps start again, ripping, shredding, and eating away at my gut. I wipe my face and the door then drop the towel on the road.

I can make it. The car is almost to the exit. There will be one last mile.

On Areca Drive, the car bumps through giant potholes. Each one is like a hammer banging on my head. Finally. A black plastic mailbox marked "24."

I make my way down the gravel drive. Overhanging branches screech while they scrape the roof. My poor car. But I am not stopping.

A small house with blue peeling paint appears in a

clearing. The links in the fence around it remind me of a playground, but this is no game. A black pickup truck is parked on the side.

I pull up to a gate where two pitbulls snarl and jump, bashing into the fence. Great.

I stop the car and watch the dogs. This is dangerous. I should go back.

I put the car in reverse and wrench myself around to back up. A cramp rips through me, and I double over, slamming into the seatbelt. "Shiiiit." I jam the car into park, unbuckle, and crack the door, in case I puke again.

The smell of burnt corn runs up my nose.

If you just get in, you can feel better.

The dogs are terrifying, but I am being eaten alive anyway, so why worry?

I trudge to the gate. My focus flips from dogs to the door and back.

Someone parts the blind and peers out.

I turn my right side toward the glass, hoping he can see the burns.

A loud *clunk* comes from the back of the house. The dogs run toward it. I hope he put out food.

I open the gate, hesitate, listen for the dogs, and rush to the door and knock.

A deep growl at my heels makes my skin crawl.

I freeze. From the corner of my eye, I notice a brown and black pitbull, its face covered in scars, teeth bared.

Stay calm. Do not yell. "Call off your dog. I'm here for therapy."

The dog snarls.

My head throbs, and I count the steps to the nearest window ledge. Will I make it if the dog grabs me? It does not matter. *This* dog has me by the throat. I pound the door.

"Let me in, man. I am here for therapy, I swear."

The door opens to a tall guy with a big nose, holding a black pitbull by the collar.

It growls and rears up, tugging at the restraint.

The other dog lunges at me, and I brace myself.

It smashes into my leg, and when I grab the doorway, it slams past me into the house.

Damn. I exhale.

"Get out," the guy hollers.

The dog whimpers and slinks outside.

"Who sent you?"

"Og did. I got burned at a Fielder. My doctor gave me Oxy, then cut it off. It hurts, man. I need help."

"Come inside. Let me see your money."

I step across the threshold, digging into my pocket for my rolled-up twenties.

"Sit down. Stay," he snaps.

I am not sure if he means me or the dog.

The black pitbull sits but keeps its eyes on me. The room is dark. Blinds cover all the windows. Charcoal-colored walls, a black leather sectional, and a beat-up old wood floor—all give it an evil feel.

Brutal cramps grab my stomach, twisting it in two and doubling me over. I gasp and grab the door.

The guy fishes around in a drawer beside him. "Sixty bucks."

I hand it over, thinking this is the best deal around.

He holds out a closed fist. "Here's three."

"*Three*?" I count each one as they drop into my trembling hand. "Can you call me when you get more?"

***

Back home, I am watching TV, feeling chill after chewing down a couple of pills.

Maria waves when she breezes past the window. She does one of those girly song-type knocks on the door. "I was starving, so I ordered a whole sub." She has two little braids on either side of her head which tie together in the back. Maria waltzes to the kitchen, unwrapping the sandwich. "I won't be able to eat it all. It's turkey and Swiss. Here."

"Thanks. I was starting to get hungry." I take the sub and slide onto a stool at the counter.

"How's your burn doing?"

"All right."

She leans closer and peers at my face. "It looks really dry over there on the side."

"I need to put more goop on it." I avoid the truth—that it was accidentally wiped off with the towel after I puked in the car.

"Is it in the bathroom? I'll get it." She puts down her sandwich and hops off the barstool.

"On the dresser in the bedroom."

She disappears into my room.

"Look for a white jar, gauze, and a package of wooden sticks." I take a bite and spot the jagged scar on my wrist, the one from the bullies I had shoved away from Maria in grade school. The big one had pretended to leave but, instead, had grabbed a stick and swung. My wrist had taken the blow and bled like mad.

"The vulture is sitting on your windowsill."

"He has been staring in my room lately. It is starting to creep me out."

"Okay, bird. I don't know why you're here, but you may *not* bother us," I hear her say.

Flapping wings and *chkk-chkk-chkk* ensue.

Maria lays goop and gauze out on the counter. "It left. When did that start?"

"About a month ago, it started perching on the windowsill. Before that, it was hanging around in the courtyard."

She looks back at my room and runs a hand through her hair. "Before or after you went to the beach house?"

I open the jar and slop a fresh layer of white goo on. "I think it was after. *Definitely* before Thanksgiving."

"Hmm." Maria looks around, checking corners. "This apartment has always felt weird to me."

It feels better when she is here. Not saying that, though.

"Because you hate Zane."

"It was the same when I was dating him. It's, like, repressive or something."

"Seeing the way Zane operates, I am not commenting on that one."

"Shut up. It's not like that in any of the other apartments in the complex. It's the worst in your room."

"I have not made my bed, and the room is a mess."

"That's not it. Your room feels awful. It's restrictive, like there's something sitting on my chest."

I wonder if this has some weird sexual meaning. Not into it.

"Are you hitting on me?"

"No." She laughs. "I think your entity is hiding from you. Maybe the feeling is strongest in your room because you sleep there. I wonder if we should get someone in and have it cleansed."

"You have got to be kidding. Your crazy ideas are too much, Maria. I wish you would just leave me alone."

"But you're not the same as you used to be." She locks onto my eyes as if she is trying to see inside them.

The door bangs open, and Zane walks in. His chin is covered in stubble, and the side of his flip-flop has a rip in it.

"Get her out of here."

"What is up your ass?" I glare.

"I spent the night in jail for trying to get you your pills."

I jump to my feet. "What?"

Bubba saunters in behind him, dressed better than usual in a long-sleeved, striped shirt and new jeans. He slides onto the open barstool. "I just bailed him out."

"You got arrested?"

Zane closes the blinds on the living room window. "No shit. For trafficking." He looms over Maria. "I'm tired of looking at your face. You need to get outta here."

He shoves her so hard that she slams into the wall.

I grab the front of his shirt and stick my face in his. "Stop it."

"Get your hands off me." He slams me in the chest with both hands.

I push him back. "Cut it out."

"You ungrateful bastard." Zane lands a punch on my jaw.

Rage seeps into my bones. I ball my fists up and nail him in the stomach with a huge undercut.

He doubles over.

"Come on, Maria. I need to get you out of here." I usher her into the courtyard, rubbing my jaw. "Are you all right?"

"I'm fine. What about you?"

"You saved me." I laugh. "His punch slid on the goop, so it hardly connected."

Maria giggles. "Thanks for sticking up for me, goofball." She slides her arm through mine.

I grin at the silly name. "No problem, but you need to stop the voodoo shit."

"My family has talked like this my whole life. It's part of my upbringing. I told you how I saw a bad man around my cousin. My grandfather says it can happen. In my classes, I'm discovering it's not just my family. It's everywhere."

"Seeing things is a little far-fetched, Maria. I am sorry to hear your cousin died, but you had nothing to do with it."

"It feels like there's a bad man around you too, Dave, and I'm concerned." She fishes out her keys to open her door.

"Is this about Zane?"

"No. It's about you and whatever has a hold on you. Want to come in?"

This crap again. Anger builds in my chest. "You need to know that the only thing that has a hold of me is this damn burn, so knock it off and leave me alone." I slam the door shut.

Now I have her *and* Zane to deal with. I need more of those pills.

Zane is gone when I return. I go to my room and dig out the last pill. I can't believe the other two are gone already.

A voice inside tells me, *No big deal. You can stop before you go home.*

I chew it up, go back to the TV, and wait for the warm flood of relief.

Light flashes on the wall beside me. I look out at the pool, where it came from. It is deserted except for an old guy, about thirty, in jeans and a T-shirt, with a magazine in front of him. His dark aviators are pointed right at me.

It creeps me out. I check the lock on the front door and scan the living room. No sign of Zane's bong. In the kitchen, I tuck my last blunt away in a drawer.

The guy walks by and looks in the window.

I step out of his view, wondering who the hell he is.

I race to my bedroom window and look out at the parking lot, finding him getting into a black Ford Mustang.

***

A loud noise beside my head wakes me up. My phone. I must have changed the ring.

"Hello?"

"Hey, it's Eric. You sound like you were asleep."

"What time is it?" I sit up. My sheets are drenched in sweat.

"Noon."

I almost ask him what day it is but think better of it.

"I called to see how you're doing and give you an update on Mom."

"How is she?"

The vulture at my window is making the annoying *chkk-chkk-chkk* sound.

"Worse than I thought. You can't tell talking to her on the phone, but the weakness is getting pretty bad. She's holding on to the furniture when she walks."

My chest spasms. "Is there something new to stop it?"

"No. When are you coming home?"

Sweat is pouring from my hands. I need one more score to taper myself off before going home. "I have to get the burns checked out one more time," I lie.

"Mom really wants to see you. She's worried about you."

"Tell her the goop is doing its work. I will see you soon." I click off.

The phone shakes while I put it down. I should have asked Malanola Dude for his number or at least his name.

When I stand up, the cramps start. The stupid vulture is still *chkk-chkk-chkking*. I open the blind to shoo it away.

The bird cranes, stretching out the wrinkles on its ugly red neck to stare at the planner on my dresser.

"Leave me alone." I chuck the planner at the window.

The bird flies off.

"Zane, you home?" I holler.

Must be at Bubba's. He is hardly ever here anymore.

When there is no answer, I think about his stash. I shoot him a text but get no response. Good. Where would he hide something?

I check under the bed, lift the mattress and pillow, rifle through his closet, rummage through his backpack, and go through his desk. Nothing.

"This is bullshit."

I need relief. Where did I put that blunt last night? I hid it in a hurry. I search under the couch cushions and the chairs. The cramps get worse.

I rush to the bathroom, barely making it before I crap my drawers. If waking up is like this, I would rather stay asleep.

A few minutes later, searching the bathroom, I find nothing. I chew down four aspirin, hoping they help. Anything to avoid shitting myself again.

"Damn it."

I head to my dresser, grab a drawer, dump it onto the bed, and move to the next one and the next. There are none left. I wind up and kick the dresser, then kick it again. Something falls inside—a sealed manila envelope.

Hope surges. Did Zane stash something in my room, where he knew I would never look for it?

I grab the package and tear it open. Nothing but a bunch of old papers.

"You are an idiot." I chuck the package down the hall.

I pace the hall, racking my brain for sources. Alex must be getting his steroids somewhere else because Zane is hardly ever around anymore. I have no number for Alex, but Jake does. My thumbs fly across my phone screen with a text to Jake.

What am I doing? Alex is the guy who took Lucy. He made a fool of me.

A violent cramp rips my gut. I run for the bathroom.

Relief is just a text away.

I need to swallow my pride. Things cannot go on like this. I re-read my text to him. **You have a number for Alex?** My thumb hits send.

A phone number pops on my screen.

Bingo. I dial.

"Hey, Alex. This is Dave."

"Hey, Dave. I heard you were in the hospital. How you doing?"

"The burns hurt like hell. My doctor put me on Oxy, then cut me off. You know where I can get any?"

"You need to cool it, dude. Use different language. Let me make a call and see if I can get you into the concert. Hope you feel better, dude."

"Thanks, man." I yawn and click off, thinking I need to learn the code. I have been yawning a lot lately. I hope he does not think I was bored with him and not make the call.

Sweat pours out while I pace the floor. It has only been ten minutes, but it feels like forever.

Half an hour. Waiting is impossible. I start calling other people.

An hour drags by. I have called everybody I can think of. And I keep checking the time, hoping it will go faster, praying Alex will text.

My stomach is killing me. I smell of B.O., but I avoid showering because I want to leave the minute he calls.

The phone rumbles in my palm.

"Yes!" I holler, clicking it. "Hi. I was referred by my friend. I was—"

"He gave you a good reference," the guy interrupts. "The tickets are two hundred dollars. Meet me in the northwest corner of the CVS at 1226 Foxtail Lane."

"Great, thanks. Be right there." I click off and shoot a quick thank you to Alex.

I race to the parking lot. But when I climb into the car, I realize there was something familiar about that voice.

***

The traffic is light since most students have gone home. I weave quickly among the cars of people returning from work. A pitstop at the ATM makes me wonder what my dad will think. Right now, that does not matter. I need relief.

On Foxtail Lane, the cramps are worse. I race down the street, arms aching, and wipe the sweat from my hands. My eyes follow the numbers to 1226 and see it.

He had better be here. I do not want to wait.

When I slow down to turn in, I spot a silver SUV. It is the only vehicle in the lot. The license plate catches my eye: JRFTBL. Panic floods my body.

That is the youth league coach's football tag.

I keep driving.

Is it a setup? If I go there, will Coach call the judge and ban me from youth football? Will I be arrested?

Nausea sets in. I slow down and open the windows for fresh air. No, I never liked Alex, but would he do that to me?

Even though it is cool outside, my clothes are soaked. I need some water.

Water. Great idea.

I will tell Coach I am going to buy a case of water. Maybe it is not him. Maybe he sold the SUV to someone else. A horrible cramp kicks me in the stomach. I open my door and lean out to heave.

Nothing comes.

I need to feel better.

I park and peer in the windows of the SUV. Football gear fills the back. On the passenger seat is a copy of the team roster, with Coach's phone number at the top. It is not the number I called.

You are acting paranoid. It will be all right.

Then I see him, facing away from me. He stands under a huge oak tree. Spanish moss dangles in long trendles, masking his presence. I notice his signature black Adidas sweatpants and white sneakers.

Cramps grab my stomach. I lean on the truck and work hard not to heave.

Just do it, echoes inside my head.

I want to race toward my score, but I force my steps to slow. A string of excuses shoots through my brain.

"Hi, there."

"Hey, Dave." Coach gives me a quick grin. "I got a phone call from your mother that you were in the hospital. How are you?"

I stick my hands in my pockets so he will not see them shake. "Doing okay. I have a lot of pain."

A voice inside yells at me, *Go for it!*

"Do you know a guy named Alex?"

Coach stares at me, and his face turns fish-belly white.

Acid rises in my throat. I try to smile but wonder if I should bolt.

"I know Alex from the gym. I don't agree with his steroid use, but I've worked out with him and some other guys for a while."

I cannot believe what he is saying. Could this be a trick?

"Alex only told me your first name, so it didn't register." He fidgets with a twig sticking out of the side of the tree.

I am afraid to ask for anything or make the next move. There is an outline of a one-by-two-inch rectangle in his front pocket.

Coach peels the outer bark off the twig. It snaps and falls to the ground. He clears his throat. "You got money for the tickets?"

I freeze, aching for the packet tucked deep in his sweatpants. Can he tell that I am desperate?

"I only need a few more days' worth, until I leave for home." I give him the cash and watch my palm extend while he drops in my redemption.

Chapter 27

Zane flies through our front door and trips over a pizza box. "There you are, doin' nothin' in front of that TV again."

The TV and lights flicker. Did that happen for real, or was it me? Everything feels off, like looking through cellophane.

"TV good. Remote, you seen?"

"Frigging toasted with no energy. You're doin' the wrong shit, Rager." He jumps over the couch, then speeds into the kitchen. "Get your own remote."

I watch. Oxy slips in and out of my pores.

"Here." Zane hands me a beer. "Celebrate my decision."

"What?" Beer spills.

"Damn you." Zane grabs my hand and puts the beer on a table. "That's why your mother put a towel there. You need a fucking bib."

Eff. Zane on meth makes me dizzy. "Slow down." Drool on my chin. I wipe.

"You're so fuckin' slow you're drooling. I'm leaving this hellhole for a new start in Costa Rica," he mutters.

"You leaving?"

Vulture at window.

Zane waves at it. "Soon."

"Oh." Something wrong.

"How's your stash?"

"Low." The TV draws me.

"You owe me a few of those pills for all the herb I've given you."

No answer. I slip into a chasm of dreamless sleep.

***

"Hey, Dave. Wake up."

Maria's voice. It seems far away.

"David."

My arm is being shaken. I force my eyes open and prop myself up on the couch. "Hi."

"I saw Zane go flying out of here a while ago. I figured I'd come check on you."

I blink, try to focus. "I am fine."

"You don't look fine. Your hair is all mussed up, and there is stuff scattered all over your apartment. Are you okay?"

Maria slides her bookbag off her shoulder, then tugs off a nubby white jacket. That girl always has a book with her. She tries to pull out a bar stool at the kitchen counter. It is blocked by the manila envelope from the dresser. She picks it up.

"What's this?"

"It was in my room."

She searches through it. "Some guy named Ivan Cuervo must have lived here."

"Like Tequila." I laugh.

Maria smiles. "If he went to school, he was paying for it by working construction. He's got a bunch of pay stubs here for carpentry work. Here are some for Eradicator Pest Control. Guess he didn't like that job. There are a lot fewer than the construction ones."

"Mind your own business" barks from my lips.

I did not say that. The thing inside of me did. This is way too freaky.

The color leaves Maria's face. She lowers her head and looks at me funny. "I know that voice." Her hands shake while she puts down the newspaper. "Is your name Ivan?"

"Why would you care?" rolls from my tongue.

My hands are shaking now too. How do I stop this? "Maria?"

She holds up her hand, like a cop at a traffic light, and keeps talking. "You said before you had something to finish. What does that mean?"

My head hurts, with pressure in my ears. What is happening to me? I pull my knees to my chest.

Maria fishes a book from her bag. Her hands quiver while she turns a page and takes a deep breath. "Ivan, you can't stay with David. You're hurting him."

"I am not going anywhere" slides from my throat.

I gape at her.

"You have to," Maria's voice comes stronger. "It will be better for both of you."

"Go play with yourself." The sound is guttural.

Maria breathes in and crosses herself. "Go and join your loved ones. The ones who have moved on before you."

"You need to leave me and the monkey alone, bitch."

I pull my knees tighter.

Maria stiffens. "Ivan, you need to leave Dave."

A gruff voice in my head says, *She will make you insane. Get rid of her.*

My body flies off the couch, and I lunge at her.

"No more!"

Maria ducks behind the bar stool. Her book crashes to the floor. She grabs it, then runs for the door.

"Dave, I think you're in danger."

Chapter 28

I wake up on top of my bed in the dark. I must have fallen asleep again. In my hand is one of the paystubs from the envelope. Above my thumb is our address. *This* address, this apartment. Ivan lived here.

I rush to my laptop and type "Ivan Cuervo, Greenville" into a search. An article about him overdosing on heroin and someone unloading him at the hospital pops up. So does an obituary.

Ivan Cuervo died in a car accident… Leaves behind his mother, brother, and a pet bird.

"I wonder what happened?" I look for the envelope and dump out the rest.

There are two newspaper articles, each about someone dying on a construction site. One got electrocuted; another fell off a roof and broke his neck. A twinge hits the pit of my stomach. Did Ivan do it? Was Ivan a serial killer?

I read on. It says that Ivan's boss turned him in, but no foul play could be proven. I wonder if it was him or had the boss been trying to frame him?

A knock on the door jolts me.

The CVS I met Coach at is the same store where the guy with the Mustang was scoping me out. My heart races, and my head is etched with visions of jail. I wonder if it could be him. Is he after me?

I peer out the window but cannot see our front entryway. Instead, I inch over to my bedroom door and look for shadows on the living room carpet.

Another knock. Louder, heavier.

I hold my breath.

"Dave?" A woman's voice.

I sneak a glance out the living room window, see Maria, and exhale.

"Why are you here?" I open the door a foot, stand behind it, and check outside.

Beside Maria is a foot-long black feather. I search the courtyard and the sky for the varmint I know it came from. My eyes return to the feather, not knowing what is creepier— Ivan in my apartment or the Mustang.

"I'm worried about you." She frowns when she steps inside.

Do I tell her about the newspaper articles? It freaks me out, but if I show her, she might get some crazy idea that I should move.

"I am fine." A gust of wind catapults the feather toward me. I slam the door, then click the bolt home.

Maria parks herself next to the door. Her back is against the wall. "Um… your shoulder's not as bad as I thought." She gawks when I head to the kitchen.

It feels like she is not comfortable here, like she has to fish for something to say.

"Are you kidding?"

"No, really, Dave. It's looking better."

"Humph, you are not in my shoes." I grab a glass and fill it with water.

"Or your boxers." She laughs.

I look down. "Oh well."

While I open the fridge, Maria scans the inside. I wonder

why she came back here again, but I want her to go away so I can think this through.

"Everybody else has finals now. What about you?"

"I had a couple of papers due. I have a ninety-six in physics, so I don't have to take the final."

I think of my failing physics and my other bad grades and reach for the bottle of pills. Empty.

"That damn Zane stole my pills. He *stole* them. I *cannot* fucking believe it." I heave the empty canister against the wall.

Maria eyes the container. "I thought you were done with those?"

"I got a refill," I lie.

"Ibuprofen would be better. It might help with swelling too."

"How the hell do you know?"

Maria purses her lips. "I just know."

"Advil is weak. Burns are painful, Maria. I need the real deal."

"I'm sure they were painful. It's been a little bit more than two weeks since the explosion. A lot of those wounds are almost healed, except for your shoulder."

"You think this does not hurt? Look at it." I twist my shoulder, displaying the scab. "The damn burn wakes me up when I am sleeping."

"Couldn't you just cut back a bit?"

I slam my glass on the countertop. Water splashes over my hand. "I have." The fib jumps off my tongue before I can even think.

"That's great, Dave." Maria gives me a fake grin. "So, you've got everything under control."

"Right." But her voice echoes inside me. My life is a mess. I feel as if someone hooked me up to a car battery and is cranking the current on and off.

The front of the microwave reflects a husk of me—sunken eyes, skinny arms, sallow face. "I need to quit the stuff."

"You can make it through a couple of days. I'll help you." Her smile is like a fresh tide on the beach, cooling my blazing face, wiping everything clean. "When your mom was leaving, I told her I'd follow up with your paperwork for school. You want to pull up the registrar's page on your computer?"

"Sure. It's in my room."

Maria points to the dining table next to her. "Bring it out here. I'm not moving."

"Geez, you look jumpy." I go grab it and fire it up, but she stands an arm's length behind me. "The doctor's office said they would email me a letter, but it has not yet arrived."

"They may have to send it directly from their office to the school. That shouldn't matter, as long as the registrar gets it."

Her voice is far away. I blink and refocus. "Gets what?"

Maria positions a dining chair in front of her. "Gets the *letter*. David, you're acting weird."

"I just got out of the hospital. You think everything is normal?"

She shifts her weight. "Definitely not."

The scars around my throat tighten.

"What about the cravings?" Her pitch is higher. "You're wanting pain medicine and acting freaky, peeking around corners and locking the door behind you."

A low rumble starts at the base of my brain, the weight of something ancient and angry. "I saw the same guy watching me twice. I am not paranoid."

"If you really saw him, why did you open the door for me?"

"I knew it was you. I heard your voice."

She takes a deep breath. "What about the other voice you're hearing, Dave?"

"What do you want?" The gruff voice flows out of me.

Maria blanches and grabs onto the dining chair. "Can you talk to him? I think it's Ivan."

"You think you are some amateur shrink or something?" rumbles from my throat.

"Are you Ivan?" Maria leans forward, her gaze digging in, searching for something beneath the surface.

"We do not want any help. Fuck off."

"Ivan, you can't control David."

I shove my face at her.

"Watch me."

She jumps back, and the chair tips up on two legs. Maria's face reddens. She grips the chair with both hands. "Watch you what? Speak with that weird lilt that has no contractions?"

My teeth bang together, jolting all the muscles in my head.

"Get out, you cheap slut!"

I slam my fist on the desk.

She holds the chair tighter. "Dave, I'm worried about you."

I ball my fist up and aim for her face. The scent of her lemon shampoo wafts over, jostling a memory of us studying. I force my hand open. It grazes the side of her head.

"Get out of my way."

She shrieks and runs out the door, leaving it open to the damp night air.

The feather blows in before I can slam the door shut.

"Damn her."

Rage builds layer upon layer inside my chest, increasing with every breath. My hands fist, nails digging into my palms.

I open my mouth and release a primal roar, sending my fist through the wallboard.

A thousand needles stab my knuckles when they stop against the concrete block behind.

"Shiiit."

I rip the fragments of wallboard hanging from my shredded skin and throw them to the floor. The hole in the wall gawks at me. Paper brows shift, daring me to come closer, to do it again.

My fist clenches, and red dots rise to the surface around my raw knuckles. "I know just how to shut you up," I bark at the hole.

It smirks back at me.

I grab my physics book, seize a handful of pages, and rip them from their spine. "Take this!" I stuff the pages into the gaping hole. "A mouthful of stinking string theory."

I rinse my hand in the kitchen sink. Blood washes down the drain.

"You need to just chill," I mumble to the sound of the running water.

I snag a paper towel, dry my fingers, and slow my breathing. My last pre-rolled blunt is beneath a plate. I retrieve it. My hand and my head throb in unison.

That will calm you down. The flick of my lighter brings a smile. I draw in with a solid pull and trudge to my favorite spot on the couch, in anticipation of the *ahhh.*

No results.

I inhale deeper, holding on. Smoke swirls around my head.

"This is garbage." I throw the cigar onto the carpet and crush it with my heel. "That asshole took my pills and left me trash."

A kitchen stool looms before me. I hurl it out of my way.

It leaves a dark streak of paint—looks like old blood—on the wall. I stomp past it into my room.

My shadow searches for something in the closet. I try to regain command of my body.

The voice whispers, *Get out of here before the Mustang comes back. Before that girl comes back. You need something to protect yourself.*

I tug some clothes on and tuck my fishing knife in my belt. I snag my car keys and head out into the night.

***

Angry balls of light fire up on the street from either side. I slam the accelerator down and try to get away while flaming tongues reach out for me. One flares ahead on the back of a car that is trying to stop. I swerve, thrust the pedal down, then blast through the intersection.

Get off the main road.

Behind me, more red lights are coming. No flashing blue lights. Good.

I crank the wheel onto a side street, driving between rows of houses. I take a quick right to make sure no one can see me from the main street and stop the car.

If someone saw you pull in here, they will be combing the streets until they find you.

No blue lights flashing.

Just in case, I turn my headlights off and creep along the street until I come to its beginning, near the entrance of whatever subdivision I am in. I nose my car out to get a peek at the main street. Clear.

I sneak along, not slowing for the stop sign. I blast out, then flip my headlights on.

"That was close." I check the rearview mirror. Things seem less threatening.

Find someone who can replace the stash.

I keep driving. A few turns later, I realize I am on Elm Street—Aaron's street. Zane said Aaron is next to the pancake place.

"We cannot go there," I say to my car. "Police saw the car before Aaron got busted."

I take my foot off the gas and coast. My pulse quickens, and I slide down in the seat while driving by.

The place is dead. No lights, no cars.

"Shit." I sit back up and keep on driving. My limbs feel like lead, and my eyes start to sting. "I cannot fucking believe it. No shit around anywhere." I jam my foot down, leaving two long streaks of rubber in my wake.

The car swerves onto the next street and passes a house which seems familiar, but I cannot place it. I bear down on the pedal to speed past a white pickup truck in my way.

"Losers, losers—all of them."

I pull onto the main drag. The white pickup catches up and cuts me off.

"Fucking asshole." I brake hard, then race to bring the car up beside him. I roll down my window and holler, "You bastard!"

He flips me off.

Seething hatred sears in my chest.

Bide your time.

I grip the steering wheel and try to slow my breathing.

Fall back and trail him.

Half a mile later, the truck pulls into a gas station. PRECISION SHELL CONTRACTORS is written on the side.

It is him—the boss.

I follow and go around the corner, parking on the other side of the building before racing to the entrance. A tanned dude with a red flannel shirt and a huge belly climbs out of the truck. He looks so familiar.

I have no recollection of him, yet I know the *thud* of his booted footfalls, right heavier than left, the smell of sawdust. A deep inner hatred oozes from my chest.

I thrust my face in his. "You need to learn to fucking drive."

"You should slow down." He pushes me out of his way.

"Get the fuck outta here." I shove back.

"Some people are just assholes," he mutters and goes inside. *You deserve this, dick* echoes in my head.

I step into a shadow beside the door, unsnap the leather sheath at my waist, and inch the knife out. My sweat feels thick when I secure my grip.

I hold the tip down. My thumb is bridged along the handle for a good thrust. I place the blade alongside my thigh, invisible to the outside world, then coil to spring.

The door opens.

I raise my hand. Bright light glares in my eyes.

A car.

I drop the knife.

The guy rips open the door and runs back into the building. "Call the police. He's got a knife!"

I grab the fish filleting knife and sprint to my wheels.

"Hurry," I yell at myself, fumbling with the keys.

When I back out, I leave my lights off.

I round the corner. A vulture glides along next to my window.

I race toward the highway, watching the rearview mirror before turning my lights on. I was going to stab him…

Bile rises in my throat.

I check behind me. Okay, so far. I slow the car, shove open the door, and vomit on the road. Then I fly on to the interstate to head home.

The vulture was there.

This is bad. This is *really* bad.

Chapter 29

Daylight.

I sit up and scan the living room. Nothing is here but a stain on the couch from my shoulder. I raise my arm for a peek, then wince. Gross. The yellow crusty residue reminds me of my ugliness inside and outside.

I spot my fishing knife tucked between the cushions. Thoughts of the night before flood in. I was going to *kill* that guy. My burnt skin tightens while I think about how irrational the whole night was. I need to get rid of that knife.

I scramble to the kitchen, grabbing a wad of paper towels and a bag. I never want to see this thing again. While I am wiping my fingerprints from it, I hear a knock.

"Hey, Dave. You up? They were giving away pizza at school. I snagged you some," Maria calls.

I want to ignore her, but my empty stomach tells me otherwise. I duck into my room and drop the knife behind the open lid of my laptop.

Fresh air fills the room when Maria comes through the door. I breathe it in and drive away my horrific thoughts.

"You always manage to show up at the right time. This is awesome." I sink onto the barstool, steadying my elbows on the countertop.

Maria gawks at the tremor in my hand when I reach for some pizza.

"Low blood sugar," I lie. "Zane ate everything in the place." I should have stopped him, but I was a bit brain lagged.

Her face scrunches. "You look terrible, Dave. How are you holding up?"

"I am fine. Not much sleep last night." I take a bite to eat and chew fast.

"You look tired and… disheveled." Maria sits at the dining table, close to the door. "Dave, I was wondering if… Well." She steeples her fingers. "Maybe you should go see a priest."

My spine twitches. "Are you insane?"

"A shaman would be better, but I don't know any in this country."

"Fuck off."

"It's just that"—her hands grip together tighter—"you're not yourself. You seem to be having… problems."

I hold out my burnt arm. "No shit. Look at me. You expect everything to be normal after this? Every time I look in a mirror, I see some freak. It makes me want to vomit."

"Your burns are getting better. In a year, you won't even notice."

A shadow crosses the window. The vulture. Maybe it came to help me. Resentment toward Maria shoots through me and grabs a hold of my tongue.

"In a year, I could be dead."

Red creeps across her cheeks. "The church does Anointing of the Sick… I just thought it would be a good idea. I could make an appointment."

"Shut up. That is for people who are dying." I stare out the window, looking for a great bikini I can change my focus to.

"Maybe we should've done it when you were in the hospital," she murmurs, looking out the window as well.

"Not doing that."

"What if I cleanse your room with incense, like they do in church? It would improve the musty smell in here."

She's nauseating.

I push the pizza aside. "Guess my stomach shrunk when I was in the hospital."

"You *are* getting kind of thin. I'll put it in the fridge. Maybe you can try some later." She walks to the kitchen.

"Would you get my bottle of water from the desk while you're up?" I lean back and try to get the food to settle.

Maria grabs the water, then stops short. From my barstool, I watch her face blanch.

"You have no right snooping around my room" spits from my lips.

She hurries to the kitchen counter. "I wasn't snooping. I was getting the water you asked me for."

Her palms are wet when she hands me the bottle.

"Why do you have that huge knife on your desk?"

"That is my fucking fishing knife, if you have to know."

"It looks like something out of a horror movie."

From a corner of my eye, I notice the vulture land on a palm frond. It stretches its wings and flaps at me.

Get rid of her.

Rage bores in like a parasite infestation.

"You are full of shit. You were full of shit when you did not tell anyone you knew your cousin was going to overdose until it was too late."

Maria gasps. Her color drains. She grabs the countertop and holds on.

"Now you have some kind of mothering complex because of it, and you are saying all this shit so you can snoop. Get out of here before I dig up more of your little secrets."

Maria yanks open the door and runs.

"Nosy bitch."

I slam the door. The windows rattle their gritty little edges at me.

I grab the knife with a paper towel, shove it into a plastic bag, and hurry to the dumpster.

***

My hips jolt when I flop onto the couch. Must be because my ass is getting so bony. Who would have thought that sitting around could make me lose thirty pounds? I spot my blunt crushed on the floor and stoop to revive it.

That will help.

While I dig for the lighter, my mind goes back to the night before, with the guy from the white truck running his mouth, pissing me off. Sweet smoke fills the aching crevices of my lungs. But it does nothing to halt the irritating, sandpaper scraping at my nerve endings.

The picture of White Truck Dude burrows itself into my mind. Hatred fills me. A grin locks on my face.

That asshole needs to pay. I am going to find him.

Deep loathing bubbles up, spinning off plans, ideas.

At the computer, I search "Precision Shell Contractors + Greenville."

Nothing shows up.

It figures that loser has no website.

My sticky fingers bang at the keys. I click on "Florida Businesses," get sent to another website, then plug in the name. Unexpected joy brings a huge grin.

Here he is. Fucking bastard. Dwight Parsons. It even gives his address. Sweeeeet. You can watch him like one of those damn gargoyles.

A menacing chuckle spills out when I flip open my history notes to rip out a blank page.

You can follow him to work, make him fall off a scaffold. Have it look like an accident, the voice rumbles in my mind.

"I know nothing about scaffolds."

I close my eyes and rest my head in my hand. A picture of Dwight comes to my mind, walking around a construction site, yelling orders over the rhythmic bang of nail guns.

A nail gun will not do it.

I close my eyes again and concentrate.

A picture forms of an argument. Me—only, *not* me—spitting out truths he refuses to acknowledge. Dwight seething, pacing. A fight erupts. The police arrive. I go back to nailing down plywood at the jobsite. Dwight talks to the cop a long time in a low voice, checking sideways, narc-ing on me. Gooseflesh ripples across my arms, and an inferno of rage burns behind my eyes. I blink, and it disappears.

He always gets there half an hour before everybody.

I wonder how I know that. Did he say something at the gas station? I drum my fingers on the desk.

If he gets electrocuted, by the time somebody arrives at the job site, it will be too late.

I smile at the wit.

Fray the cord on his miter saw while he goes to measure. When he comes back to cut… Bam! rumbles through my mind.

Light from my window sparkles on my computer screen, drawing me in and telling me what an awesome idea it is. A cackle squeals from my lungs, and my heart hardens like a walnut.

I peruse the county records, trying to think of how to find where he might be working.

Search for permits he has pulled.

Bingo.

I scribble down the two most recent, then go back to search the location.

Here we are, only a few blocks apart.

I run and rerun the details of my plan again while I study the map. My hatred grows. I do not want to screw this up.

I hit print, grab the hard copy, and circle the addresses with a blood-red Sharpie.

***

It seems like forever since my last pill. I feel terrible. I need help.

A face full of bugs appears in the open jar of white goop. The mouth moves.

I need more.

Bugs start to nip at my legs.

I hit speed dial on my phone. "Ian, help me. You know where I can get something?"

"Sorry, Dave. It's exam time. I haven't seen anything around for a couple of weeks."

"You know anyone?"

"I used to get stuff from Zane. Everyone else has gone home now. How are you doing over there?"

"Bad." I click off and hit the button for Zane. It rings once and goes to voicemail. "Shit."

I hurl my phone at the floor. It bounces once, and the cover falls off.

The Bugmaster's face appears in its guts. The same face I saw in the hospital, laughing, mocking my efforts, making my skin bubble.

The bugs attack my feet. I stomp the floor. They jump on my legs and burrow in.

"They are not going to get me." I take off running.

You cannot stop it rumbles through my head.

I keep running, heading out of the complex and down the street, trying to stop the bugs.

Raucous laughter rings in my ears. My vision distorts.

I keep going, feet pounding, keeping me alive.

Nausea grips my stomach, twisting it with unbearable cramps. Vomit spews from my lips, splashing onto the sidewalk.

I stop. Eric's face smiles up at me, formed in undigested chunks.

The voice laughs.

"I am not my perfect brother. Leave me alone!" I holler.

Two old ladies walking out of a church jump. The taller one grabs her friend's hand and pulls her to their car, never taking her eyes off me.

I slow my breathing and try to clear my head.

Bugs chew on my feet.

I need relief. I start running.

Og mentioned a park. I saw one up this way, on the other side of the church.

My side cramps when I approach it. I slow my pace and spot a couple of dudes by a tree. My heart dances when I recognize the short guy with the brush cut who Og knows.

I dive through a knee-high hedge and sprint toward him. "Hey, I know you from Malanola."

The other guy takes off. Brushcut glances around, like he is not sure if he should bolt too.

"I came to your house. Og sent me."

He relaxes a bit when he recognizes me. His eyes scan the periphery while I approach.

"You only gave me three. I said to call me when you have more." I pant.

Brushcut adjusts his ball cap. "I don't have any."

"You have something. I saw you give it to him."

"That was smack, dude. I got plenty of that if you want."

My heart sinks. "Heroin? Forget it. I want the pills."

"Don't have them, man."

The guy who ran off is creeping back.

"He's cool," Brushcut says.

"I am *not* cool. I feel like shit. I need those pills."

"Look, dude… If you're in a bad way, this'll take care of you."

The other guy hauls a spoon out of his jacket.

His fist shakes when he hands it to Brushcut. The guy drops two white chunks that look like little mints in the spoon and digs a syringe out of his pocket. He takes the needle off, cracks open a bottle of water, and sticks the end in. After adding water to the spoon, he flicks a lighter underneath.

"Hold this." Brushcut hands me the hot spoon.

I juggle it back and forth between my hands. It smells vinegary.

Harmless appears in my head, like a flag flapping behind my eyes.

Brushcut drops a cotton ball into the spoon.

The guy puts his syringe in the cotton, sucks up some liquid, and puts the needle back on. He yanks out an alcohol swab.

The familiar smell hits me with a memory of morphine soothing pain, calming my nerves.

"Geez, just like the hospital."

"I don't take chances," the guy grunts. He hits his mark and leans against the tree with a satisfied grin.

Brushcut slips the rubber band off. "There's a little bit left in the spoon. I saved it for you."

"I said I want pills."

"It's only enough to make you feel better. It won't hurt you."

You need to feel better. You cannot go on feeling so bad.

The thought of the needle is freaking me out. "Not using a dirty needle."

He reaches into his ball cap and hauls out a brand-new syringe, still in the package. "I'll give you what's in the spoon, but the needle is five bucks."

You will feel so much better, the voice in my head whispers like a song.

"No," I tell the voice and Brushcut at the same time.

The bugs start again on my legs.

I stomp my foot, hoping to make the feeling go away.

Relief for five measly dollars rings between my ears.

Bugs climb to my back, picking at my flesh.

I twitch and moan. My hand goes to my pocket. I hand Brushcut a five and start rolling up my sleeve. Am I really doing this?

You need to feel better.

Brushcut puts the rubber band on my arm. "That's the spot." He rips open a new swab and swipes my skin.

A dark blue line on my wrist rises like a snake.

Brushcut opens the new syringe and draws up the leftovers. "You want to do it?"

"No way." I offer him my arm.

When he swipes with the alcohol, his sleeve moves, exposing track marks by his elbow.

My stomach knots. *What* am I doing?

I turn my head to think and spot a priest gazing at me from the side of the church. Did Maria call him? Did my mother?

Brushcut grips my hand and cranks my wrist down.

My mom's face flashes in front of me.

I jerk my arm from his grasp and run.

Chapter 30

Back at the apartment, I search for Maria's white Jetta in the parking lot. She is here, thank God. I spot the vulture in its favorite oak tree as well. The thing is almost starting to feel like my dog.

I keep running, past the vacant pool and loungers abandoned for exams, until I am at her door. I knock hard.

She opens it a crack but keeps the door chain on.

"I need your help."

"I've heard this before, Dave. You know your behavior is killing your mom."

Deep down, I have known for weeks. Time to admit it. "Yes, and I have to stop. I have to get rid of Ivan."

She rubs a strand of hair between her fingers. "Are you sure you're ready to do this?"

"Right *now*." I nod. "The sooner, the better."

Maria swallows and draws in a slow breath. "You can't take any more strong pills. Only ibuprofen.

"Fine. We need to get on with it."

"I'll check my notes on exorcism and call the priest I talked to."

Exorcism. The word makes my skin crawl. "I do not want you to talk to a priest."

"He's at the church by the park. It's close. I'll be over in a bit."

Bugs start to climb my legs. I am desperate for help. If she called the priest I saw, we have already sort of met.

"Hurry."

I run to my apartment. The rooms are dark, and Zane is gone. Bugs crawl across me. I rub my back against the wall. Nothing helps, damn it.

I race to the shower, run the water full-on hot, and holler when it hits the new tender skin.

The Bugmaster's face appears in the vapors of my scream. He laughs at my hideous body.

I shove open the shower door and reach under the sink for a scrub brush.

It is not there.

Ants keep crawling, more and more of them.

"Get off me." I rub my back against the shower door.

Not working.

I turn the water cold, spot a long-handled white brush in a white holder, and begin to scrub.

Scrub harder.

I smack my elbow on the shower wall and drop the brush.

It falls at my feet, the round, white end full of red and tan chunks.

I bend over to get it. Blood drips off my arm.

"Shit." I chuck the brush back at the toilet. "No more! Stop. Gotta stop." I sink to my knees and pound the floor. "Please, dear God, help me." I hug my legs.

Long sobs form in the back of my throat and echo off the walls.

The ants open their mouths and drink in the sound. Fire ants crawling, biting their way up my arms into my brain, gnawing through.

"Get off my face!" I slap at them.

Carpenter ants eating my bones, my insides. More swarm my back.

I run to my room and drop onto the bed to scrape them away.

It is not working.

I writhe, screaming into the empty apartment.

The hole in the wall from my fist opens and absorbs the sound. No one can hear me.

I curl into a ball and pray it will end.

A *thump*, as if the walls are contracting, squeezing out ants. I cover my ears.

A shadow crosses the room. More banging.

"Dave, are you all right?"

I roll over and see Maria, her face pressed against the glass.

"Let me in, Dave."

I scramble to the living room and rush to open the door.

"You're naked. Let's put a blanket around you." Maria stops at the entryway. "The priest can't come. He needs to fill in for someone who had surgery." She tugs my comforter off the bed but stops at my desk. "What's the map for?"

Do not tell her.

"Just stop the bugs. You have bug spray?" I moan, scratching at my legs.

"No, Dave." Maria wraps me in the warm blanket. Her hand touches my arm with such caring that my eyes tear up. "Precision Contracting was the company on the paystubs in that envelope."

"So what? Make it go away. Please." My knees give, and I drop, face down, onto the floor.

"Dave, what's happening?" Maria sinks beside me and lifts my chin to face her. Hope flutters somewhere deep inside. "What's he doing to you?"

"He is trying to mess me up good, sending ants to eat

me." A cold sensation clamps onto the back of my neck, a funnel of ants pouring into my spine.

"What? Who?"

"The Bugmaster. Can you not see them?" I claw at my arms. "Help me."

"Is Ivan the Bugmaster?"

"How the hell should I know?"

Maria rises off the floor and pivots to face me head-on. "I want to talk to Ivan!" she shouts.

"Fuck you," I growl, long and low. "Just stop the ants."

She jolts back, away from me. "There are no ants. It's from the medication."

I swat my face. "They are crawling all over me, Maria. Do something."

"I'm going to help you."

She picks up a stack of papers she brought in and glances through them. A tremor shakes her hand when she reaches inside her sweater and fishes out her cross.

"Dave, remember the swaying of the hammock at the beach house." She starts her necklace in motion.

My eyes slam shut.

"Not falling for this" comes out with a loud belch.

I steady myself and shove my eyes open, forcing them to watch the swinging arc. Time slows, and minutes meld.

"Dave," Maria says with a shaky voice. "I want you to go back to that weekend in your mind's eye and tell me what you see."

"Forget it. Who knows what you will do."

She lifts the pendant high and swings it more. "Listen to the sound of my voice, Dave. I want you to imagine, going deep inside yourself, the time when Ivan joined you. I want you to remember the word *imagine*. When you hear me say *imagine,* you will instantly connect with Ivan."

The room blurs when I picture the hammock. See myself stumble to the couch inside and feel the horrible headache.

"The beach house," I tell her.

"A damn good party," a harsh voice rasps. *"That sap, Dave, kept feeling lonely, so I moved right in."*

This is freaky.

"Ivan, why do you want to stay with Dave?"

My lips part.

"Dave likes to party, same as me. When he got the pills, it got even better."

"Dave, why have you allowed Ivan to hang with you this long?"

Fog clouds my eyes. My lips move without my thinking.

"I am nothing without him." A dark cackle rumbles out.

Maria sucks in a big breath. "I want to talk to the one who sent the bugs."

"Forget it. Not talking."

She stands there, ignoring the ants, as if I am making a joke. Fury ravages my mind. I slap at an ant.

"Kill the bugs." I swat harder.

Maria's forehead wrinkles into a trough which delivers more ants.

"Help me!" I scream.

She shies away, getting closer to the door. "There aren't any bugs, Dave. I want to talk to the one who is making you think there are." Maria's voice quivers.

"Help me, damn it." I grab for her shirt.

She gasps and runs behind the dining table.

I take a hold of the edge and shove it hard.

The table crashes at her feet.

She leaps over a chair and darts behind the couch, where she paces, breathing hard. The couch sits like an island between us.

"Dave, this isn't you," she says.

"That is what you think."

I lunge, trying to get her arm.

Maria jerks away and picks up a bar stool to hold between us. Her necklace swings at her throat.

A wild laugh pumps from my gut.

"Think you own me, bitch?"

I try to grab the cross.

She jumps back, raises the stool, and looks down at the pendant hanging from her neck. "You want it, don't you?" she taunts, moving the chain toward me like a pendulum.

My eyes follow, biding my time for the right moment.

I pounce.

She blocks me with the stool. "You can get it, Ivan. It's within your reach." The necklace continues to hover toward me.

I lunge again.

Maria dodges. The chain stays in motion. "Imagine that the bugs are going away now," she murmurs.

I stare at her while my skin becomes smooth.

The biting slows, stops.

"The couch is right behind you. Just bend your legs and sit."

I follow her instructions.

Maria stays behind the raised bar stool. "You can't stay with Dave, Ivan."

My blood slows like it is thickening, as if my cells are clinging together.

"I will" travels from my lips, dark and throaty. *"And you will run off like a scared little bitch, with that tail you think is so hot between your legs."*

"Don't listen," she mutters to herself, grabbing her papers.

"You are using me for an experiment." Ivan's voice

spews from my lips. *"You have been using me all along, like you used your cousin when you were little."*

"I did not."

"Yes, you did. She wants to use you, Dave. Do not listen to her. She is angry that you don't pay her enough attention. She wants to punish you."

The bar stool shakes. Maria's eyes dart side-to-side, like she is trying to read me. "I'm not trying to use you or hurt you, Ivan. All I know is that this isn't the David Everest I've been friends with since third grade."

"You are too busy with your nose in your books to notice anything."

I scowl at her.

"I know this isn't the real David Everest, and I want him back."

"Oh, so sweet."

I hurl a chair at her.

She jumps to the side. "You need to move on, Ivan. You're no longer wanted."

"David wants me. He just told me that he could not wait to get you out of here so he can make some phone calls."

"I did not," I say, as fast as I can.

"Sure, you did. The thought just crossed your mind. I watched it go by." A deep chuckle emerges. *"Ah, she is starting to sweat. Good."*

Maria's hair is damp around the edges. "I know Dave wants you to go, Ivan. He told me so." Maria straightens. The bar stool shakes harder. "I want you to leave. *Now.*"

"You need to leave!" the raspy voice barks at her.

A feral cackle fills the room, sending a wave of nausea through me.

My stomach revolts. I run to the bathroom and lean over the sink, but… it calms.

Got you covered rings between my ears.

I shake my head and make my way back to the couch. "Keep going, Maria."

Maria shivers. "It's not working, Dave."

A little voice screams from far inside me. It comes out slow, awkward. "I know you can do it. Please…"

Maria takes a step back, clutching the stool. She pores over her notes.

The room starts to spin.

"Get away!" I swat my leg. "No, not the bugs."

The laugh bounces between my ears.

I drop to my knees, roll onto my back, and shove myself across the floor, leaving bloody streaks in my wake. "Make them stop!" I writhe.

Maria bends down beside me. "Dave, it's okay."

My hands fly to her throat and squeeze.

She falls back, pulling me upright.

I hang on. My teeth gnash. "Swat the bugs."

With eyes wide, she hits my arm.

I press tighter on her neck. "Harder!"

Maria rips at my fingers, trying to drag them from her throat.

"Not enough."

I laugh when her eyes bulge.

Maria knits her hands together.

"A prayer. How cute."

She drops all her weight onto my elbows.

They bend, dragging her toward me, loosening my grip. She pulls my arms and lands a knee in my groin.

"Ughh." I let go and double over.

Maria bolts out the door, gasping for air.

Chapter 31

Fury builds in the spaces between my twitching muscles. I grab the back of the couch and toss it upside down.

"You bitch. Leave me alone."

I kick the couch until my foot throbs and shove it one more time. It topples on its back. There is a small, white dot wedged next to the arm.

I jam my hand into the layers of fabric. My heart soars while my fingers grope for the prize.

It feels like I found a hidden egg on Easter morning. I pop my winnings in and chew.

When I slide into my jeans and black hoodie, the bugs subside. Anger takes their place, pumping through my veins.

It is time to take care of business filters into my brain.

My life takes on new purpose. How did I not realize this before? I grab the map and head to my car.

Maria peeks through the blinds while I race by. Her deadbolt clicks into place.

Screw her. Find Dwight from Precision. The boss is going to die.

The sight of guys on the roof, laying sheets of plywood, at the first address on my list stokes me. My blood is fizzing. I approach, followed by a strange knowing that Dwight is not here.

I walk through the house anyway but find nothing.

"Shit." I kick over a bucket.

Water spills onto the concrete in the form of a face, laughing.

"Fuck you." I heave the bucket against a wall.

It bounces, rolls around, still laughing.

A loud grunt spills hatred from my lungs, and I run to my car.

Just get it over with whispers from inside me, soothing, enticing.

I *will* find that asshole.

The car roars when I slam my foot on the gas, leaving behind long streaks of hard rubber. I round a corner to the next site, where I see his white pickup truck. The company name is stuck to the door with a cheap magnetic pad.

Everything slows, and my focus sharpens. I scan the job site. The roofing plywood is finished. A big truck with a conveyor belt is backed up, with two guys offloading rolls of tar paper onto the roof. I cruise past a line of trucks, checking my GPS for the fastest way out.

The air chills. Rain clouds bang together. Daggers of lightning shoot through the air.

A guy on the roof stops to check the darkening sky.

"Speed up," another guy calls from below. He increases the pace of the conveyor.

I draw my hoodie up to mask my face and creep to a side window. Bare aluminum studs are lined up like silver corpses. No framers around, but I spot him, on his phone in the backyard, yakking into his earbuds.

He is doing nothing—as usual rings in my ear.

"Let's go," one of the roofers yells.

A door slams. The diesel engine fires up, spewing a cloud of black smoke at me. Perfect cover.

I hold my breath and move through the cloud to the edge of the house.

The cloud continues to the backyard, surrounding him. He starts to cough.

"Hold on a second," he hacks into the speaker, then heads right toward me.

I panic and retreat to the front of the house, where I press myself against the raw concrete block. My hands are shaking. I need to get out of here.

There is a stepladder around the corner.

I wonder how I know that. I spot a ladder beyond the gable at the front entry.

Take the ladder.

My heart hammers so hard my ears throb. I will *not* go up a ladder. If I run back to the car, he will see me and recognize me from the gas station. He will call the police.

He is still yakking through his earbuds. His every step encroaches on my lousy hideaway. Twenty feet, fifteen, ten feet.

The stepladder.

I rush to it.

Look at the wall.

I force myself to climb, but, staring at the rooftop, I freeze, gripping the ladder.

"Do not look down. Eyes on the roof," I tell myself, trying to control the convulsive shaking.

Dwight steps into the front yard just as a bolt of lightning surges across the sky.

I hold my breath and leap.

I splatter onto the roof. Thunder booms so loud that the house shudders.

I hinge my fingers around the edge of the roof and dig my toes into the plywood—and pray.

He is inside now. Go back down.

The thought makes me want to vomit. How can I ever let go?

Go after him.

The bugs start biting my arms, my legs.

A flash of lightning. Thunder roars.

I close my eyes to focus and will the bugs away.

Get Dwight.

I am not moving.

You will regret that courses through my ears.

I hear *chkk-chkk-chkk* coming in fast, and I force myself to look. The vulture is flying at me, jet-black wings spread more than twice the width of the chimney, feathers shimmering with excitement. The smell of rancid meat drifts up my nose.

The bird grabs my arm with its talons.

I shake it off.

Kill Dwight or it will destroy you.

The bird comes at me again, beak open, claws aimed at my eyes. I scramble closer to the chimney for shelter, throwing mad swings around my head.

The bird gets my thumb, its beak searing into my flesh. Its claws catch my forearm.

I push and tug, but it will not let go.

I throw myself toward the chimney, slamming against the brick.

The bird releases its grip, then flaps upward.

My arm is covered in blood, but at least my thumb is still there. I cling to the chimney while the vulture closes in from above.

I spot a two-by-four left by the roofing guys and inch forward.

The *chkk-chkk-chkk* grows to a whine.

The whine sharpens to a hiss.

Feathers scrape my face, and the buzzard grabs my arm.

I dive for the board.

My fingers connect.

I roll over and knock the bird away.

It falls to the roof, but it grabs my leg with its talons, then spins, dragging me toward the roof's edge.

I dig my nails into the board, hauling it with me. We thump down the roof. I get one foot in front of me, creating traction, slowing the slide.

I stretch and get a grip on the board, then swing with all my might.

I make contact.

The vulture's claws extend and contract.

The bird goes still.

A cold shiver grips my spine. I have never killed anything before.

***

I inch back to the chimney, feeling the wind pick up. It is not as terrifying here as it was by the edge. Guilt engulfs me while I gape at the vulture's limp wings splayed across the plywood. How I could have killed such a magnificent creature? My fingers creep over to stroke the pristine feathers, and I feel an unusual sadness.

I listen to Dwight moving around in the house. He must not have heard anything, or he would have come outside. What a dumb-ass.

Cramps start in my leg. The bugs are tunneling into my calves.

Anger builds within me. The asshole is *still* on the phone. Does the dude ever shut up?

"Ivan?" blasts from his lips, then he bursts into laughter.

Overwhelming hatred grabs my bones. I pivot to a stack of rolled-up tar paper and listen for his voice.

In the back of the house, he is standing just beyond the drip edge of the roof.

"You will never laugh at me again" growls from my lips.

I slide a black log to the brink of the summit and smile.

"Fifty pounds of dead weight on your head will shut you up forever."

A low chuckle rumbles inside. My heart pounds, my breath coming faster. I jack myself onto my knees, readying my muscles for the final shove.

"Got a present for you, boss, you son of a bitch" comes through with a riot of laughter.

"Dave."

I freeze. Maria is at the top of the ladder, her jaw set with determination, shoulders broad in a thick, winter jacket.

This is what we have been waiting for, hisses the voice.

I grip the tar paper harder, fingernails embedded.

"Dave, *stop!*"

Do it.

I gawk at my hands, which are poised to shove a heavy black log onto someone. "What is going on?"

"Help! The ladder's tipping!" she screams.

Maria is inching to the point of no return. Time morphs like a slow-motion film. All her attempts to help me gel. The only person who knows what has happened to me is about to plummet to earth.

"I can't get a grip!" her fingers claw at raw plywood.

Finish it snarls in my ear.

I shove the roll against the stack, then dive toward her.

Our hands connect.

"Gotcha!" With a vise-like grip, I drag the ladder straight and get Maria up the last two rungs.

She collapses onto the plywood.

"Are you okay?"

She stays down flat, panting, not moving. "Yes, but you… you could have killed that man."

I look at the roll of tar paper and the scene replays. My stomach drops into a cavern of terror. "Maria, this is freaky. You have got to help me."

"I didn't sign up for this."

"I need to get rid of Ivan. He is the one doing all this."

"You have to want it, Dave. No one can do it for you." She turns her face the other way.

I understand her fear, so I try to think of what to do next.

Dwight wanders out to his truck, still on the phone, earbuds in place, oblivious. He drives off.

Something flickers in the distance—the face I saw from the hammock.

My insides turn cold as ice. I will not let him get a hold. "You need to get out of here, Ivan."

"That's it, Dave." Maria draws her legs up into a sitting position on the roof. She leans back, balancing on her palms.

"Your body died, Ivan. You need to go."

I see a wisp of dark hair. White layers of gauze float around me.

My skin bristles. "Leave, Ivan!" I roar.

"Never," comes a growl, electricity crackling in the air.

Rage builds behind my eyes, making them burn with hatred.

If you are useless to me, you are dead.

My foot goes out from under me, as if it was hit by a bowling ball. "No!" I topple over, fingernails digging, grasping, and skid down the roof.

"Hang on, Dave!" Maria scrambles toward me.

"Maria." I scream when my feet go over and throw my arms at the edge, trying to catch hold—I go over.

Situations in my life speed through my head like a ticker tape. My Dad, Eric, the frat, Lucy… Rejection.

The ground comes closer.

Rejection. *That's* why I stayed with Zane… and Ivan. I am afraid of rejection.

I line my feet up underneath me. When I hit, I throw myself to the side to roll, but my legs buckle, and I land in the dirt.

Pain, pain, pain.

But I am alive.

Pain, pain, pain.

I straighten my arms and then my legs. My ankles, my knees, my hips, all scream with pain. Maria is running toward me.

"Dave. Oh my God, David." She drops to her knees beside me. "Is anything broken?" she asks, running her hands along my arms with a light pressure.

"My ankles are killing me." I hold my leg up in the air, do a circle with my ankle, and try the other. "They both seem to work."

"We need to leave before that guy comes back."

"I am not going anywhere, Maria. Get your necklace out."

"My necklace? Are you all right?"

"Ivan caused all of this. He wanted to have me kill that guy. I will not wait another minute to get rid of him."

"Dave, you're hurt. Maybe this isn't the best time."

"Forget that. Get the necklace. I am over this crap."

Maria's forehead creases. "You sure you want to do this now?"

"Yes." I concentrate. "Ivan, you are outta here!" I snap.

You cannot get rid of me, you stupid monkey.

My vision clouds. Rage builds like hot lava inside.

She is in our way. End it.

My muscles coil beneath me, hands fisting with dirt. My chest flares like a cobra's hood. I chuck the dirt in her face and strike out with my fist.

"Dave! No!" Maria whimpers.

Her hand flies up to block the blow.

Our arms collide.

My fingers grope the air for flesh.

She twists to the side, just as my weight is about to hit, and… I find myself falling.

Maria grabs my good arm, follows the arc of my dive to the ground, and lands with a knee in my back.

Little round globes spark in my eyes. My legs writhe in the dirt.

"Get off of me!" I scream, splayed face down, with my arm wrenched so far up I can touch my hair.

"No way!" She grabs my arm with both hands, keeping her knee between my shoulder blades.

"Let go!" the voice hollers with everything inside my body.

"Ivan, you need to leave." Maria pants.

"Take your sorry dry cunt to some other loser."

I try to roll but cannot get her off.

She shoves my elbow half an inch higher. "I'm not letting up."

"My shoulder is going to dislocate. Please, just a bit."

"Dave, I can't trust him." Maria holds tight.

"I am with you. Get out your cross."

"Please, God, protect me. Keep me safe," she mumbles. Maria steadies her knee against my cranked-up elbow.

The chain swings in front of me.

"Dave, watch the cross."

"Forget it, bitch" erupts from my lips.

My eyes jam shut, but I pry them open and watch the pendant move back-and-forth.

"Dave, imagine you are free of Ivan," Maria coaches.

I force the pain from my thoughts, slow my breathing, let my eyes blur, and surrender. "Time to go, Ivan." I swallow my fear and set trust in its place. I know she can do it. "Get out of me, you vulture-loving scum."

"Imagine you see him in your mind's eye," Maria prompts in my ear.

"Ivan, I will not help you. I will not feed your addictions. Go home to your mama. Get out."

"That's it, Dave."

Wispy white clouds surround me. The clouds start to spin.

"My brain is in somersaults," I cry. "Pressure… In… My… Head. Worse than the beach house."

"Hang in there, Dave."

"My eyes feel like they're being pushed out of my skull."

The hair rises on the back of my neck. Something tugs the top of my head, cresting, pulling. I hold my breath and push through my crown, like pushing a baby out the top of my head.

"Come on, Dave. Imagine you can do it."

"Ughhh," I grunt, holding my breath. I strain against the crushing pressure. My eyes bulge from their sockets.

"Go, Ivan!" shouts Maria.

My chin scrunches down to my chest. The back of my neck lifts, stretching and tugging down to my tailbone. The pressure in my head is insane. I suck in a breath, hold it, then bear down hard.

Clouds whirl like a tornado around the bones of my skull.

I hold my breath and push again. "Go!"

Air leaves my chest. Blood vessels in my head pulsate to bursting. Flashes of heat surge through me. A violent shudder rocks my body, as if I am being torn apart. My brain jolts like I swallowed lightning.

"Ivan, cross over!" Maria screams.

A calm wave rises like water, filling in the holes, chasing away the heat.

My head drops to the ground. I lie, panting, in the dirt.

"I knew you could do it," she whispers. Maria lets go of her hold and climbs to her feet.

I want to wrap myself around her, but I'm too worn out to move.

"How do you feel?" She holds her hand on my forehead, cooling, soothing.

My head is spinning. I stay there, stunned, not sure what to process. "Tired."

"That's it?"

I take in a breath, taste the sweetness in the air, slow the thumping in my chest, and do a quick body scan. "Okay. Exhausted. And lighter somehow, as if I just came up from a deep scuba dive and there's less pressure on the bones in my head."

My shaking stops. The drug cravings ebb. An outgoing tide rolling farther away from me. In its place, contentment settles in.

"The bugs are gone."

Chapter 32

Maria has me tucked in on my couch, with my feet up and icebags on my ankles. The cuts on my thumb and arms have been cleaned and bandaged. A cup of herbal tea steams beside me.

"What's in this stuff? It smells like licorice rolled in dirt."

"It's a mixture of things that support your nervous system and your liver. My dad sent me the recipe after calling my grandfather."

I take a sip. "It's only been a couple of hours since we got home. Even though I don't feel great, I'm not having stomach cramps and wanting to climb the walls. The dirt must be working."

Maria laughs. "I know you don't want to, but I agree with your mother that you should be somewhere where they can monitor your bloodwork and be there to help you until everything normalizes."

I think about the conversation with Mom, how hard it had been to explain how bizarre the situation had gotten and that I'm sane. Thank goodness Maria was on the call to help me.

"Mom was very understanding. I'm lucky she knows how to handle an issue like this."

"She jumped into action. I'm amazed that she got a flight home and a facility set up for you within an hour."

"Dad and Eric can come up here to pack up my things and bring the car."

Maria checks the ice on my ankle. "My car has the check engine light on. It happened yesterday."

"You drove with the light on? Not a good thing, Maria," I say.

Her brow rises. "If I hadn't, you wouldn't be here talking to me."

The scene on the rooftop flashes through my mind. The crawly sensation, the overwhelming urges… I gulp down my tea, then pour more.

"Thank you for not giving up on me."

"That's what friends do. Anyway, when I called the car shop, they said it could be a week. You'd be doing me a favor if you let me take your car south for you."

"That would be great," I tell her.

"My mom said my cousin from Atlanta is coming for Christmas. She can drop me off on her way back."

The thought of other people knowing how bad I screwed up makes me squirm.

"You told your mom about this?"

"Well, yeah. I *did* almost get killed." Maria smirks.

My stomach catches. "Sorry. Things got out of hand fast."

"At least it's over." She gives me a warm smile.

"It's hard to believe that really happened."

Maria pours more tea. "I can't imagine the torment of having something in you."

"It's like I was in a bad dream and I couldn't get away. I thought Ivan was a joke at first, like a character in a videogame. I thought I could get rid of him. I'm glad you came along. There's a lot about the world that I don't understand."

"You needed someone on the outside to help."

I gawk at my bandaged hand. "Thank you for everything you've done. For hanging in when I was such a jerk."

"Thank goodness that's done. I knew that wasn't you, but I was trying to not be terrified."

"I did some bad things under his influence. I'm going to make sure that never happens again."

She glances at her phone. "We need to leave for the airport in an hour. What do you want to take on the plane?"

"I'm only going to bring my laptop and a couple of things. I have enough clothes left at home that I can use."

"Let me pack it up for you."

"Don't do that, Maria. You've done enough. I can get it."

"I want you staying off those ankles. Should I put your laptop in the backpack?" She zips into my room.

"Yes, please, and the yellow pocket folder with school info in it, along with my jacket on the hook on the back of the bedroom door."

"Gotcha." The door closes.

***

Zane bursts into the apartment. He's clean-shaven, with his blond curls trimmed, a fresh T-shirt, and board shorts. He doesn't look high. Things are improving.

"What are you doing? Why are you here?" he demands.

"My ankles are sore. I fell off a roof."

"What about the bird?"

That's a strange question. "Since when do you care about the bird?"

He rushes to the window to scan the courtyard "It's usually sitting out front, waiting."

"The vulture is dead," I say.

Zane spins toward me, mouth downturned. "What? That thing was my pet."

"Since when? I never saw you with it."

"I fed it critters Bubba shot at the farm."

"That's disgusting."

Zane ignores me. His cheeks redden with every word. "The vulture did whatever I wanted. Do you think it decided to pull off a girl's bikini top all by itself?" His face is crimson. His fists are balled as if he wants to lunge at me.

The bedroom door bangs shut after Maria rushes into the room. "You did *what*?"

Zane twists to face her. "You're not the only one who can see or sense things and talk to them."

"That's why you went out with me." Maria's voice is dripping with sarcasm.

"No shit. I wanted to find out more. I discovered you're only a wanna-be."

I'm not sure what Zane means, but I hate them arguing. I'm not getting into it.

Maria crosses her arms. "You're such a liar."

Zane opens his mouth to reply, but then his eyes widen, and he snags the envelope on the counter. "Where did you get this?"

"It fell out of my dresser." I wonder why he cares.

His expression softens, like someone flipped a switch. He spreads out the contents of the envelope. "Ivan was my brother."

I drop my feet to the floor, then sit up. "Oh, come on. You don't have the same last name, and you don't speak Russian or Spanish. What is up with you today?"

"Half-brother. His dad took off, and my mom married my dad. Ivan spent summers with his grandparents, who were from Cuba." Zane fondles a ticket stub to a concert. "I knew something was wrong. I didn't get here soon enough." He stares at the ticket. "This was my first concert. Ivan took me."

Maria's hands fly to her hips. "None of this is making sense."

Zane places the ticket back into the envelope. He sifts through the paystubs before squaring off to us.

"Ivan dropped out of school but stayed in this apartment. I moved in right after he died, when I graduated. I could feel him hanging around me, buffeting my legs, probing my heart, my head. I guess he missed being here. It was hard to keep him out until you showed up. Then all I had to do was make you more vulnerable."

"What do you mean?"

"He talked to me through the vulture somehow. He told me to get you kicked into orbit party mode so he could be near me through you. That was Ivan; he liked to party. He could gather a crowd together like nobody else. I miss him."

A face peers through the window.

Zane high tails it to his room.

A loud rap on the door makes me jump.

"Do you want me to answer it?" Maria asks.

"May as well. Whoever it is knows we're in here."

Bubba and the guy with the aviators plow past Maria and rush down the hall.

"Where are you, you little scum bag?" Aviators yells.

We hear grumbling, furniture scraping, then a *thud*.

I push myself to my feet. "What's going on?"

Maria scurries to my side when I hobble down the hallway. "I'm going with you."

"He's gone!" Bubba yells while Aviator Guy rifles through the closet.

"He can't be," I say. "There's only one way out, unless he climbed out the window."

"The windows are locked from the inside, and there is

no attic access. He's not under the bed, in the closet, or in the bathroom. He's gone," Aviator dude cries.

The ache in my ankles is worsening with every step. I sink to the bed. "What do you want him for?"

"He owes me six thousand dollars."

My guess is for a drug deal, possibly the one that got busted. I don't want to know, though. "You're the guy with the Mustang. What were you doing following me?"

"Zane took your car more than once for short runs. He bragged about it," Bubba says.

My throat dries. "What happened?"

"I saw him, that's what happened. He took off, and I couldn't catch him. I spotted you in the car the day you went to the pharmacy, so I followed. When I got a good look, I knew you were the wrong dude."

Aviators crouches to look under the bed.

Bubba leans against a wall. "You may as well quit. Zane is gone. Ivan told me Zane could do that."

"You knew Ivan?" I sputter. "Ivan the man or Ivan the thing that was inside me?"

"I was friends with Ivan when he was alive. Fun guy. He did all kinds of crazy stuff. He even trained a vulture by feeding it with critters he'd trapped doing pest control."

My head is spinning, trying to sort out what he's saying. "You knew about the vulture?"

"Hell yeah. When Ivan died, I'd give Zane critters from around the farm. One day, I got a rabbit. The bird went nuts. And Zane said it was hilarious when you bought a planner with a rabbit on the front and the vulture perched on the window, staring at your book."

I look at Maria, not sure what to say next.

Maria eyes Bubba, in his dirty jeans and messy hair. "Were Ivan and Zane brothers?"

"Yeah, they could both do weird shit, but Zane is better at it. Ivan taught him how to use the vulture over a couple of weekends, when Zane came to visit." Bubba examines Aviators, who is back to looking through the closet. "Don't worry, man. He'll turn up. He did this disappearing thing once before."

"Shapeshifter," Maria mutters.

This conversation is getting stranger by the minute. "What's that?" I ask.

Maria sits on the bed beside me. "It's said some people have the ability to change form. They take on the energy of something else, like, maybe an ant, and crawl out the window."

"Yeah right," the Aviator guy snaps.

"I'm tellin' ya," Bubba says. "He did it before. I thought it was some magic trick, where he'd be back in a couple of minutes, but he was g-o-n-e. Didn't show up for a week."

I need to get out of here. This is too much for one day. "Okay, so he's not here. Take one more look, then go home. Bubba says he'll show up, so we're just gonna have to wait for that."

I have a feeling he won't, but I don't care. I have a plane to catch.

***

I'm sitting by the Christmas tree, reading, with my feet up and Touchdown curled up, with his head on my lap. More than a week after the holiday, the scent of fresh pine is still in the house. Mom picked me up at the airport and took me straight to a rehab place. They let me out after two weeks—on Christmas Day. It feels good to be here.

Mom emerges from her office, looking smart in a navy dress and heels. No work-from-home sweatpants for her.

"Did you say Maria was coming over?"

I smile at how well she's walking. "She'll be here in a few minutes. You look perky today."

"Cutting back to half-days and working from here has helped a lot."

I'm sure having me home, where she can watch how I'm doing, and knowing I'm seeing one of her professional peers is helping also.

"Glad I'm home to keep an eye on you, Mom."

A loud belly laugh bursts from her lips. "Me too." She grabs a bottle of water. "Looks like Maria's here." Mom continues to chuckle all the way back to the office. She closes the solid door Dad installed to soundproof her client talks.

I head for the front door.

"You look amazing." I fold Maria into a giant hug and feel her warmth against me while she hugs back.

I have so much respect for this woman. I adore every inch of her. I want to tell her that, but I don't want to move too fast. Before, I was stupid and immature. It's time to grow up. I pull away awkwardly.

Her oversized brown leather satchel has a book about nursing sticking out.

"Are you changing majors?"

"Maybe. Just checking it out. How are you doing?"

"Much better. The rehab people were amazed at how quickly I improved—bloodwork and all. I think it was from the tea you dropped off. Thanks for doing that."

"I'm surprised they let you keep it."

"They analyzed it to make sure there was nothing intoxicating inside." I laugh. "I begged for mercy. Mom looked up your recipe and found some documentation that it works."

"I'm glad." She grins, leaning closer. "Those burns have healed well."

"My hair is a little wonky, but I'm happy it's growing

back. I need to keep the other spots out of the sun for a year, to keep the scarring down."

We make our way to the living room, and Maria looks down at my feet. "I noticed a limp in your walk."

"My ankles are getting better. The doctor said soft tissue damage can take a while to heal. I'm swimming in the pool every day, which helps. My homework now includes lots of reading, talk therapy, and a daily workout." I laugh.

Maria giggles along with me. "Did you get the medical withdrawal?"

"Yes. Professor Taft has been particularly kind. He messaged me on Eaglechat to see how I am and said he wants me in his class again."

"What's your plan?"

I take a deep breath. What do you say to a woman who has helped you do the impossible? I want to tell her I'll be back to start winter semester in a couple of weeks and move to another apartment with her, far away from the bad memories, but… I can't.

"I need to take some time to learn about myself, to figure myself out before I venture back."

Maria smiles, as if she knew it was coming, but her eyes are sad. "That's a good idea."

I want to kick myself for sounding so weak. Zane would say I need to work it and project confidence. I wrap my arms around her and kiss her, relishing her soft lips, the sweet taste of her tongue.

Maria slips her arms around my back, rising onto her toes.

Eventually, we come up for air.

I grab her hand, and we sink to the couch. "I can take a couple of preliminary classes here that will transfer," I babble, searching for the words I want to say. "Will you wait for me?"

She bursts out laughing. "You're not going off to war, you big goofball."

"You got me through a tough battle, though."

"Are you calling me a battle axe?"

I laugh. "No, you're stronger than one. You've given me the hope I never had."

The End

I hope you enjoyed *Campus of Shadows*. I'd be grateful if you would write a review on Amazon, Goodreads, or Bookbub. I would love to hear what you think. If you would like news about my upcoming books or a free short story, you can sign up at JoLoveday.com.

PLAYLIST FOR CAMPUS OF SHADOWS –
Listen to the official playlist.

Spotify: http://bit.ly/44oeP6M

Bad Guy—Opening party in the courtyard
We're Going to be Friends—Meeting Maria after many years
Mama Told Me—Shunned by frat and lost at home with Zane
Lonesome Town—Zane leaves Dave for football game
Light Year—Zane's partying is moving fast for Dave
Ho Hey—The Lumineers—Dave is adrift
Run Devil Run—Maria's attitude toward the vulture
El Bueno Y El Malo—Dave is trying to keep up
Sticky Treez—Zane is dealing, and Dave starts buying
Earned It—Alex's seduction of Lucy
One Toke Over the Line—At the Beach House
Only the Lonely—Dave's loneliness at the Beach House
Lose Your Soul—Dave meets Ivan
Seven Devils—Ivan takes hold
I Love Doing Drugs—Dave on Ecstasy
A Horse With No Name—Dave losing himself
Psycho—Dave's insanity
Demons—Dave vs Ivan
I found—Dave and Maria

ACKNOWLEDGEMENTS

I'd like to thank you, dear reader, for taking a chance on this book. I fretted a long time over how to convey my *what if* question about lost souls and mental illness so that it would make sense in a story.

It took me years to write this book, and so many people helped me, I'm afraid I'll forget a name. Thank you to every soul who offered an idea, a suggestion, a laugh, or comfort.

Thank you to my wonderful husband who listens intently to my wins, losses, and struggles while always helping me move forward. Your belief in me helps me believe in myself.

Thank you to my children who offer technical, legal, and literary advice whenever I call, desperate for help. Your advice on your college experiences, which were much richer than mine, have been a huge help.

The Tuesday Writers—Cathi Castelli, Faran Fagan, Melody Maysonet, Stacie Ramie, Jonathan Rosen, along with others who came and went as we progressed. This critique group has disbanded, but I miss you, and I owe you a huge debt of gratitude. You always offered help and suggestions to make my writing better. You endured years of bad plotting and prose on top of listening to me read out loud as I stumbled over words—a common problem for people with dyscalculia when reading aloud. Special thanks to our writing coach, Joyce Sweeney, for lending your expertise and for your amazing dedication to our group.

To my critique groups in Avon Park, Florida, as well as Blue Ridge, Georgia, and online via Sisters in Crime. Thank you for your support and encouragement.

Thank you to my beta readers—Melody Maysonet, Jeff Shaw, Peg Christie, Mima Mendoza, Karen Gelveles, Dr.

A.M. Schreuder from dyscalculiaservices.com and Dr. Edith Fiore for sharing your knowledge and expertise in your fields.

Thanks to Jonathan Hayes for your musical expertise in creating a playlist.

Thanks to Martha Baker, RN for your advice on patient burns in a burn unit.

Mr. Yung, I am so grateful for the patience and dedication you showed to your Glenlawn Collegiate students. Without your help, I would not have succeeded in my math classes.

Thank you to the Alachua County Sheriff's department for a tour of their jail and for walking me through the booking process.

To Sisters in Crime, especially the Citrus Crime Writers, MWA Florida, SWMWA, and The Canadian Authors Association. Thank you for your constant flow of information and support for writers.

Indie bookstores are the best! Thanks to all of you who carry my books. Indie bookstores will not only remember your favorite genres, but they'll also recommend books and new authors for you.

Thanks to author Kris Monty of PJ Parrish for telling me I had a theme, but no plot at the beginning. Thank you, Debra Sharp for brainstorming the buildup to the climactic scene with me.

The Dyscalculia Network is a great place to learn more about dyscalculia. Thank you Cat Edie and Rob Jennings for sharing your wealth of knowledge. Please visit dyscalculianetwork.com for info. For help in the USA: discovering dyscalculia.com or dyscalculiaservices.com.

Thanks to all you wonderful readers who take a minute to tell your friends about a book or to write a review.

QUESTIONS FOR DISCUSSION

1. Zane creates a lot of trouble for Dave. Why do you think Dave stays rather than moving when his mom offers to pay for a new apartment?

2. Have you been in a situation where you wanted approval and did something that was against your normal values?

3. Do you think Dave's dyscalculia contributed to his addiction? Do you think it contributed to his recovery?

4. Do you think if Dave had gotten into the fraternity that the outcome would have gone differently?

5. Which of Dave's choices did you disagree with the most?

6. Do you think Maria was interested in Dave at first, or because of their shared experience in the climactic scene?

7. Did Dave do the right thing with how he defended himself against the vulture? What would you have done differently?

8. What do you think would have happened to Dave if Maria hadn't seen the map & followed him to the construction site?

9. The novel poses a *What If* question about lost souls stuck on earth. Do you think it's possible? Do you know someone with addiction or mental illness who becomes another person?

10. Do you think Zane really was able to communicate with the vulture? How?

11. The final scene in the apartment ends with a twist. Did you see it coming? If you didn't, what did you think was about to happen?

12. Do you think Dave should return to the same school in a semester or attend one close to home?

ABOUT THE AUTHOR

Jo Loveday is the award-winning author of the thriller, *Terminal Lucidity*. With years of experience as a registered nurse, she brings uncanny insight into the human condition—both its fragility and its resilience. A dual citizen of Canada and the U.S., Jo splits her time between Florida, Georgia, and frequent pilgrimages to Winnipeg.

Visit her online at JoLoveday.com

instagram.com/jolovedayb

facebook.com/jolovedaybooks

youtube.com/jolovedayb

x.com/JoLoveday

goodreads.com/author/JoLoveday

amazon.com/stores/Jo-Loveday/author

bookbub.com/authors/jo-loveday